WHAT, REMO WO

Remo wasn't worried when his parachute was slow in opening. He only began to worry when he realized that there were five hundred airmen freefalling in nine lines two miles above the desert floor, and he wasn't seeing *any* parachutes, including his own.

Remo pulled on his emergency chute. It turned into a white bell, as perfect as a big silk flower. Then he realized that while the parachute was floating gracefully above him, he kept droppng like a stone.

Remo looked down and saw a gentle puff of sand. It looked like smoke. Another puff followed it. And another, as the first bodies reached the ground.

And Remo realized that he was witnessing cold-blooded wholesale murder where he was simply the last to die. . . .

The Destroyer

#79

SHOOTING SCHEDULE

Created by

WARREN MURPHY & RICHARD SAPIR

A SIGNET BOOK

NEW AMERICAN LIBRARY

A DIVISION OF PENGUIN BOOKS USA INC.

PUBLISHER'S NOTE

This book is a work of fiction. Names, characters, places, and incidents either are the product of the author's imagination or are used fictitiously, and any resemblance to actual persons, living or dead, events, or locales is entirely coincidental.

Copyright © 1989 by Warren Murphy

SIGNET TRADEMARK REG. U.S. PAT. OFF. AND FOREIGN COUNTRIES
REGISTERED TRADEMARK—MARCA REGISTRADA
HECHO EN DRESDEN, TN, U.S.A.

SIGNET, SIGNET CLASSIC, MENTOR, ONYX, PLUME, MERIDIAN and NAL BOOKS are published by New American Library, a division of Penguin Books USA Inc., 1633 Broadway, New York, New York 10019

First Printing, January, 1990

1 2 3 4 5 6 7 8 9

PRINTED IN THE UNITED STATES OF AMERICA

For my friend Nick Carr

And for my favorite Cold Warrior,
MSG James P. Kinnon, Jr. (U.S. Army, ret.)

And for the Glorious House of
Sinanju, P.O. Box 2505, Quincy, MA 02269.

Prologue

Nemuro Nishitsu knew that the emperor would one day die.

Many Japanese refused to think about it. Almost no one believed in Emperor Hirohito's immortality anymore. That he was immortal was no more logical than the belief that the emperor's father had been immortal or his grandfather before him and on back to the fabled Jimmo Tennu, the first of his line to sit on the Chrysanthemum Throne. And the first Japanese emperor to die.

That the emperor was divine was without question. Nemuro Nishitsu believed it on the day he left for Burma on a troop transport in 1942. He believed it all through the monsoon rains that beat on his helmet and his resolve through the endless days fighting the British and Americans.

He believed it in 1944, when Merrill's Marauders captured General Tanaka's Eighteenth Army. Then-Sergeant Nemuro Nishitsu managed to escape. He took his faith in his emperor into the jungles, where he would fight on, even if he was the last Japanese to hold out. He would never surrender.

Nemuro Nishitsu learned to eat from the monkeys. What they ate, he knew was safe. What they avoided, he assumed was poison. He learned to subsist on bamboo shoots and stolen yams, and to use the jungle maggots to clean out the pus from the ulcers that infected his legs. Sometimes he would eat the maggots after they had done their duty to the emperor.

He killed anyone wearing an unfriendly uniform. Months passed and the uniforms became fewer and fewer. But Nemuro Nishitsu fought on.

They found him in a ditch during monsoon season.

The water cascading around his body was an unhealthy diarrhea yellow. Nishitsu had malaria.

British soldiers took him to an interment camp, where he recovered well enough to enter the general POW population.

It was in this camp that Nemuro Nishitsu first heard the whispers among his unit—the traitorous suggestion that Japan had surrendered to the Americans after some mighty military blow.

Nemuro Nishitsu had scoffed at such a thing. No blow could bring the emperor to surrender. It was not possible. The emperor was divine.

Then they were told they were going home. Not as the victors, but as the vanquished.

Japan was no longer Japan, Nemuro Nishitsu discovered, to his horror. The emperor had renounced his birthright. Japan had surrendered. It was unthinkable. Americans ran the country under the mandate of an American Constitution that prohibited the mere existence of a Japanese army. Tokyo was a sea of rubble. And his home town, Nagasaki, was a desolation of shame.

What astonished Nemuro Nishitsu more than anything else was the meekness of his formerly proud countrymen.

He discovered this the day in late 1950, the twenty-fifth year of the emperor's reign, when a drunken SCAP bureaucrat nearly ran him over while Nishitsu was crossing the ruined Ginza to the little stall where he sold sandals in order to eat.

Nishitsu was not hurt. A Japanese policeman came upon the accident scene, and instead of berating the obviously drunken American, asked him if he wanted to press charges against Nishitsu. Or would he settle for restitution?

The drunken American settled for Nishitsu's sandal stock and every yen on his person.

On that day, Nemuro Nishitsu tasted the bitterness Japan had spread throughout Asia, and it galled him.

"Where is your rage?" he would ask his friends. "They have humbled us."

"That is the past," his friends would say in furtive whispers. "We have no time for that. We must rebuild."

"And after you have rebuilt, will you find your anger then?"

"After we rebuild, we must build upon our accomplishments. We must catch up to the Americans. They are better than us."

"They have conquered us," Nishitsu had retorted hotly. "That doesn't make them superior, only fortunate."

"You were not here when the bombs fell. You do not understand."

"I understand that I fought for my nation and my emperor and I have returned to find my people have lost their manhood," he spat contemptuously.

Nemuro Nishitsu was disgusted by all he saw. Shame blanketed Japan like the smog that came as the industries were rebuilt and revitalized. When he awoke in the morning, he could smell it in the air. It etched the faces of the young men, and the fine women. No Japanese could escape it. Yet they all tried. And their faith was not Bushido, not Shinto, but American. Everyone wanted to be like the Americans, who were so mighty that they had humbled the once-invincible Japanese.

Nemuro Nishitsu knew that he never wanted to be like the Americans. He also understood that the destiny of Japan lay not in the past, but in the future. He joined his countrymen in building that future until even he gradually lost his bitterness and hatred in the great rebuilding frenzy.

It took years. The great *Zaitbatsu* companies had been dismembered by the Occupation government. Work was hard to come by. But opportunities awaited the bold. Slowly Nishitsu started a radio business to fill the manufacturing void. It grew, thanks to American transistors. It prospered, thanks to American markets. It diversified, thanks to American microchips—until Nemuro Nishitsu's bitterness faded as he was hailed as one of the rebuilders of Japan's postwar economy, friend of the emperor, and winner of Japan's highest honor, the Grand Cordon of the Order of the Sacred Treasure. He became an *oyaji*, an "old man with power." And he was content.

The bitterness all came back when the emperor died.

Nemuro Nishitsu was in his Tokyo office, with its view of the Akihabara area, the electronics district he had helped turn into one of the most expensive stretches of real estate in the world, when his secretary came in and bowed twice before informing him of the emperor's death. He was surprised to see the tears in her eyes, for she was of the younger generation who never knew a time when the emperor was universally believed divine.

Nemuro Nishitsu took the news in silence. He waited until the secretary had left the room before succumbing to weeping.

He wept until he had no tears left.

The invitation to attend the funeral was not unexpected. He turned it down. He preferred, instead, to watch the funeral procession from the street, with the multitudes. As the one-ton cedar coffin rolled by, carried by black-gowned pallbearers, he let the rain fall on his face. And in his heart, he felt that it had wiped away the years since he had gone off to war in his emperor's name.

It was not too late to redeem his faith, Nemuro Nishitsu decided as tears of release mixed with the softly falling rain.

He spent the next week going through the employment records of the Nishitsu Group. He spoke with his office managers and vice-presidents in quiet, forceful tones. Those who gave the correct answers to his artfully crafted questions were asked to find others who thought as they did.

Months went by. The wisteria blooms of spring gave way to the heat of the summer. By fall, he had culled the most trustworthy employees of the Nishitsu group, from the highest officers to the lowliest salarymen.

They were called to a meeting. Some came from the halls of the Nishitsu Group world headquarters in Tokyo, on the island of Honshu. Others came from Shikoku or Kyushu. Some came from abroad, even as far away as America, where they managed Nishitsu car factories. They had many names, as many faces, and skills in plenty, for the Nishitsu Group was the largest conglomerate in the world, and it hired only the best.

The chosen ones sat on the floor in their identical white shirts and black ties. Their faces were impassive as Nemuro Nishitsu stepped up to the bare floor at the head of the room. The room was the conference assembly hall of the Nishitsu Group, where every morning the workers joined in morning calisthenics.

"I have called you here," Nemuro Nishitsu said in his throaty but subdued voice, "because you are all right thinkers."

Heads bowed in acknowledgment.

"I am of the generation that restored Japan to the economic state that it enjoyed in the world. I remember the old days. I do not cling to them. But neither will I forget them.

"You are the generation that made Japan strong again. I salute your industriousness. For my generation was the generation that allowed itself to be humbled by American military power. Your generation is the generation that will humble America economically."

Nemuro Nishitsu paused, his head quivering with age.

"In two months," he continued, "it will be the first anniversary of the emperor's passing. What a gift to his spirit it would be if we were to erase forever the shame of our military defeat. I have devised a way to do this. It will summon no retaliation on our shores, for like you, I would do nothing to bring the terrible nuclear fist down on our people again.

"Give me your faith, as I gave my emperor my faith when I was as young as you men. Give me your trust, and I will hand America a military defeat so shameful they will dare not admit it to the world."

Nemuro Nishitsu looked upon the sea of faces before him. They were set, resolute. There was neither joy nor fear evident in their features. But he knew from their eyes that they were with him. He also knew that they had doubts, though they were unwilling to voice them.

"I have given much thought to my plan. I have selected a man who will assist us in implementing it. You know his name. You will recognize his face. Some of you have met him, for he has worked as a Nishitsu spokesman in the past."

Nemuro Nishitsu pointed his cane at a wiry young man standing off to one side of a massive projection screen.

"Jiro," he said.

The Japanese addressed as Jiro quickly hit a switch. The lights dimmed. In the rear a slide projector blinked on, throwing a dusty beam over the heads of the squatting assemblage.

And over the head of Nemuro Nishitsu appeared a still image of a bare-chested muscular man with flowing black hair held in place by a headband. He cradled a portable Nuclear missile in his arms. Above his head, in English, was a legend in red block letters:

BRONZINI IS GRUNDY

The stony faces of the Japanese reacted instantly. They broke into smiles of recognition. Some clapped, a few whistled.

And through the crowd raced a name. It was repeated over and over again until it became a chant.

"Grundy! Grundy! Grundy!" they shouted.

And Nemuro Nishitsu smiled. All around the world, in palaces and jungle huts, people universally reacted that way. The Americans would be no different.

1

When it was all over, after all the bodies had been buried and the last foreign soldiers had been driven from what was, for three days in December, Occupied Arizona, world public opinion was in agreement on only one thing.

Bartholomew Bronzini was not to blame.

The United States Senate passed a formal resolution

declaring Bronzini's innocence. The President of the United States awarded Bronzini a posthumous Congressional Medal of Honor, as well as burial in Arlington National Cemetery. This despite the fact that Bronzini had never served in any branch of the United States Armed Services, nor had ever held public office.

Various groups protested the Arlington burial offer, but the President hung tough. He knew the controversy would blow over. Unless someone recovered Bronzini's remains, which no one ever did.

On the day that began the last week of his life, Bartholomew Bronzini sent his Harley Davidson blasting through the gates of Dwarf-Star Studios with the wind tearing at his long black ponytail and a plastic-covered script tucked into his black leather jacket.

He was not stopped at the gate. The guard knew his face. Everyone knew his face. At one time or another, it had been on every supermarket tabloid cover, magazine, and billboard in the world.

Everyone knew Bartholomew Bronzini. Yet no one did.

The receptionist asked for his autograph at the front desk. Bronzini grunted amiably when she slid a mustard-stained paper napkin across the desk.

"Got anything white?" he asked in his flat, slightly nasal voice.

The receptionist jumped up from her chair and slid out of her panties.

"White enough for you, Mr. Bronzini?" she asked brightly.

"They'll do," he said, signing his name on the warm cloth.

"Make it out to Karen."

Bronzini paused. "That you?"

"No, my girlfriend. Really."

Bronzini automatically added a "For Karen" above his signature. He passed the underpants back to the receptionist with a shy smile but absolutely no readable emotion in his brown eyes.

"I hope your girlfriend has a sense of humor," he said as the receptionist read the inscription with dazzled gray eyes.

"What girlfriend?" she asked dazedly.

"Never mind," Bronzini sighed. They never admitted it was for them. Only kids did that. Sometimes Bartholomew Bronzini thought that his only true fans were children. Especially these days.

"Mind telling Bernie I'm here?" he prompted. He had to snap his fingers to get her attention again.

"Yes, yes, of course, Mr. Bronzini," she said, coming out of her trance. She picked up the phone and hit a button. "He's here, Mr. Kornflake."

The receptionist looked up. "Go right in, Mr. Bronzini. They're ready for you now."

Bartholomew Bronzini pulled the script from his jacket as he walked down the fern-decorated corridor. The ferns were festooned with expensive Christmas ornaments. Despite being handcrafted of silver and gold, they looked tacky, Bronzini thought. And there was nothing tackier than Christmas in Southern California.

He was, Bronzini thought for not the first time in his long career, a long way from Philadelphia. Back home, the snow didn't scratch your skin.

Bronzini didn't knock before he entered the sumptuous Dwarf-Star Studios conference room. No one ever expected Bartholomew Bronzini to knock. Or to speak fluent French, or to know his salad fork from a shellfish fork, or do anything a civilized person would do. His image had been indelibly burned into the consciousness of the world, and nothing he could say or do would ever change that image. If he could have cured cancer, they would have whispered that Bronzini had hired someone to cure cancer just to hog the credit. Yet if he started swinging from the chandelier, no one would have batted an eye.

Every head came up when he entered the room. Every eye was on him as he paused at the open door. Bartholomew Bronzini was nervous, but no one would guess that. Their preconceived ideas would reinterpret everything he said or did to fit their image of him.

"Hi," he said quietly. That was all. The men in the room would read a world of meaning into that one word.

"Bart, baby," one of them said, rushing to his feet to guide Bronzini to the only empty chair, as if he was too stupid to sit down without assistance. "Glad you could make it. Take a seat."

"Thanks." Bronzini took his time walking to one end of the conference table. Every eye followed him.

"I think you know everyone," the man at the opposite end of the table said in a too-bright voice. He was Bernie Kornflake, the new president of Dwarf-Star Studios. He looked about nineteen years old. Bronzini swept the faces at the table with his sullen, heavy-lidded eyes. A birth accident had damaged his facial nerves so that only yearly plastic surgery kept them from closing completely. Women found them fascinating, and men, threatening.

Bronzini noticed that every one of the executives was under twenty-five. Their faces were as unlined and devoid of character as Play-Doh fresh from the can. Their hair was moussed into a variety of rock-garden shapes, and red suspenders showed from under their unbuttoned Armani coats. The business had come to this. Fetuses in expensive silk suits.

"So, what can we do for you, Bart?" Kornflake asked in a voice as smooth and colorless as vegetable oil.

"I have this script," Bronizi said slowly, flopping it on the immaculate tabletop. It slowly uncurled like a Venus's flytrap. Every eye went to the script as if Bartholomew Bronzini had laid down a soiled diaper instead of four agonizing months of writing.

"That's great, Bart. Isn't it great?"

Everyone agreed that it was great that Bartholomew Bronzini had brought them a script. The phoniness in their voices made Bronzini want to puke. Fifteen years ago every one of these pansies had cheered him on in one of his now-classic roles, each one of them burning with a single desire: to make movies.

"But, Bart, baby, before we get to your perfectly wonderful script, it just so happens we have this idea we think would, really, really fit your current profile," Bernie Kornflake said.

"This script is different," Bronzini said slowly, an edge creeping into his voice.

"So's our idea. You know, we're about to turn the corner into the nineties. It'll be a whole new ball game in the nineties."

"Movies are movies," Bronzini said flatly. "They haven't changed in one hundred years. Sound came in and title cards went out. Color replaced black and white. But the principle is still the same. You tell a solid story and people will pack the theaters. Movies will be the same in the nineties as they were in the eighties. Take my word for it."

"Wow! That's profound, Bart. Isn't that profound?"

Everyone agreed that it was profound.

"But we're not here to talk to you about movies, Bart, baby. Movies are out. We figure by 1995, 1997 tops, movies are going to be passé."

"That means old," a grinning blond man on Bronzini's right said helpfully. Bronzini thanked him for the clarification.

"TV is the next big thing." Bernie Kornflake beamed.

"TV is old," Bronzini countered. His face, flat-cheeked and sad, grew stony. What kind of a game were they trying to run on him?

"You're thinking of old TV," Kornflake said pleasantly. "The new technology coming in means every home will have wide-screen high-definition television. Why go to a sticky-floored movie house when you have the next-best thing in the privacy of your own home? This is the new trend, staying home. It's called cocooning. That's why Dwarf-Star is opening a new home-video operation. And we want you to be our first big star."

"I'd like to talk about the script first."

"Okay, let's. Give me the concept."

"There's no concept," Bronzini said, sliding the script across the table. "It's a Christmas movie. An old-fashioned—"

Kornflake's hands came up like pale flags. "Whoa! Old is out. We can't have old. It's too retro."

"This is classic old. This is quality. That means good,"

Bronzini added to the blond man. The blond man thanked him through perfectly set teeth.

Dwarf-Star president Bernie Kornflake leafed through the script. Bronzini could tell by his glazed eyes that he was simply checking to see that there were words on the pages. His eyes had that shine that comes from pulling white powder into the brain through the nostrils.

"Keep talking, Bart," Kornflake said. "This script looks good. I mean, check out all these words. A lot of scripts we see these days, they're mostly white space."

"It's about this autistic boy," Bronzini said intently. "He lives in a world of his own, but one Christmas he wanders out into the snow. He gets lost."

"Hold up, I'm getting lost. This sounds complicated, not to mention heavy. Think you could give this to me in six or seven words?"

"Seven words?"

"Five would be better. Just give me the high concept. That's what it's all about now. You know, like Nun on a Skateboard. I Was a Teenage Dumpster Diver. Housewife Hookers in Vietnam. Like that."

"This isn't a concept film. It's a story. About Christmas. It's got feeling and emotion and characterization."

"Does it have tits?" someone asked.

"Tits?" Bronzini said in an offended tone.

"Yeah, tits. Boobs. Knockers. You know, if there's enough boom-cheechee in this thing we can maybe get around the fact that the audience has to sit through a story. You know, kinda take their mind off it. We expect escapism to be very major in the nineties."

"What do you think I built my career on?" Bronzini snarled. "Ballet? And I don't want them to take their minds off the story. The story is what they're paying to see. That's what movie making is about!" Bartholomew Bronzini's voice rose like a thermometer in August.

Every man in the room got very, very still. A few edged their chairs away from the table in order to give them leg room so they could bolt if, as some of them imagined, Bartholomew Bronzini pulled an Uzi from under his black leather jacket and started spraying the room. They knew he was capable of such atrocities because they had seen him mow down entire armies in his Grundy films. It could not have been acting. Everyone knew what a terrible actor Bronzini was. Why else was he the top-grossing actor of all time, but had never won a best-actor Oscar?

"All right, all right," Bronzini told them, throwing up his hands. A few people ducked, thinking he had tossed a grenade.

When no one exploded, the room relaxed. Bernie Kornflake extracted a plastic nasal-spray bottle from his coat pocket and took a couple of hits. His blue eyes were sixty candlepower shinier after he put it away. Bronzini knew that it was not filled with a commercial antihistamine.

"I want to make this movie," Bronzini told them seriously.

"Of course you do, Bart," Kornflake said soothingly. "That's what we're all here for. That's what life is about, making movies."

Bartholomew Bronzini could have told them making movies was not what life was about. But they wouldn't have understood. Every man in the room believed that making movies was what life was about. Every one of them was in the movie-making business, as was Bartholomew Bronzini. There was just one difference. Every man at the table had the drive and ambition and connections to make movies. None of them had the talent. They had to steal their ideas, or option books and change them so much that the authors no longer recognized them.

Bartholomew Bronzini, on the other hand, knew how to make movies. He could write screenplays. He could direct them. He could star. He could also produce—not that that was even a skill, never mind a talent.

None of the men in the room could do any of those things. Except produce, which in their case was the same as unskilled labor. And each of them hated Bartholomew Bronzini because he could.

"I have an idea!" Kornflake cried. "Why don't we cut a deal? Bart, come in with us on this TV thing, and during the summer hiatus we can knock out this little Easter film of yours."

"Christmas. And I'm not some frigging TV actor."

"Bart, baby, sweetheart, listen to me. If Milton Berle had said that, he'd never have become Uncle Miltie. Think of it."

"I don't want to be the next Berle," Bronzini said.

"Then you can be the next Lucille Ball!" someone shouted with the enthusiasm usually reserved for scientific breakthroughs.

Bronzini fixed the man with his sad eyes.

"I don't want to be the next anyone," he said firmly. "I'm Bartholomew Bronzini. I'm a superstar. I've made over thirty films. And every one of them made millions."

"Uh-uh, Bart, baby. Don't kid us. You forgot *Gemstone*."

"That one only broke even. So shoot me. But *Ringo* grossed over fifty million bucks at a time when nobody went to prizefight films. *Ringo II* topped that. Even *Ringo V* outgrossed nine out of any ten films you could name."

"That's if you include foreign markets," Kornflake pointed out. "Domestically speaking, it was a dud."

"Half the world's population saw it, or will."

"That's wonderful, Bart. But the Filipinos don't give Oscars. Americans do."

"I don't pick my fans. And I don't care who they are or where they live."

"You know, Bart," Kornflake said solicitously, "I think you made a mistake killing off that boxer of yours in that last *Ringo*. You could have ridden him another five sequels. Extended your film career a little."

"You make me sound dead," Bronzini challenged.

"You've peaked. *Variety* said so last week."

"I'm sick of Ringo," Bronzini retorted. "And Grundy and Viper and all these other action-film characters. I spent fifteen years doing action films. Now I want to do something different. I want to do a Christmas film. I want to do the next *It's a Wonderful Life*."

"I never heard of that one," Kornflake said doubtfully. "Did it hit?"

"It was filmed back in the forties," Bronzini told him. "It's a classic. They show it every Christmas week. You could turn on your TV right now, and somewhere, on some channel, they're showing it."

"Back in the forties?" one of the others asked. "Did they have movies then?"

"Yeah. But they were no good. All in black and white."

"That's not true," a third man said. "I saw a film like that once. *Copablanca*, or something. It had some gray in it. A couple of different shades of it, too."

"Gray isn't a color. It's a . . . What is gray, anyway. A tone?"

"Never mind," Kornflake snapped. "Look Bart, tell you what. I have a better idea. We can do your Christmas story here. What's it called?" He flipped to the cover. It was blank. "No title?" he asked.

"You have it upside down," Bronzini told him.

Kornflake flipped it over. "Oh, so I did. Let's see . . . *Johnny's Christmas Spirit*. Stunning title."

Bronzini leaped forward. "It's about a little autistic kid. He gets lost in a blizzard. He can't speak or tell anyone where he lives. The whole town is looking for him, but because it's Christmas Eve, they give up too soon. But the Spirit of Christmas saves him."

"The Spirit of Christmas?"

"Santa Claus."

Kornflake turned to his secretary. "Find out who owns the rights to Santa Claus, Fred. There may be something in this."

Bronzini exploded. "What's the matter with you people? Nobody owns Santa Claus. He's public domain."

"Somebody probably got fired for letting that property go public domain, huh?" a sandy-haired executive co-producer said.

"Santa Claus is universal. Nobody created him."

"I think that's true, Bernie," a co-executive producer said. "Right now, back east there's a guy running around in a Santa suit chopping off the heads of little kids with an ax. It's on all the talk shows. I think it's in Providence. Yeah, Providence, Massachusetts."

"Providence is in Rhode Island," Bronzini said.

"No, no, Bart," the co-executive producer said. "I beg to differ. This is happening in an American city, not some nothing foreign island. I read it in *People*."

Bartholomew Bronzini said nothing. These were the very people who laughed at him behind his back at cocktail parties. The ones who dismissed him as a lucky musclehead. Five best-picture Oscars and they were still calling him lucky. . . .

"I read about it too," Bernie Kornflake said. "You know, maybe we could bring that in. What do you say, Bart? Do you think you could change your script a little? Make this Christmas Spirit an evil demon. He kills the kid. No, better, he kills and eats a bunch of kids. It could be the next major trend. Maniacs killing teenagers is getting stale. But preteens, even infants . . . When was the last time anybody did a movie where babies were being devoured?"

Everyone took a minute out to think. One man reached for a leather-bound book containing the synopses of every movie plot ever filmed, cross-referenced to theme and plot. He looked in the index under "Babies, devoured."

"Hey, Bart may have something here, Bernie. There isn't even a listing."

At that, everyone sat up straight.

"No listing?" Kornflake blurted. "How about reversing it? Any killer-baby movies?"

"No, there's nothing under 'Babies, Killer.' "

"How about 'Babies, Cannibal'?"

There were no cannibal babies listed in the index.

Every man was out of his chair at that point. They crowded around the book, their eyes feverish.

"You mean we got something entirely new here?" Kornflake demanded. His eyes were as wide as if he'd found a tarantula on his shell-pink lapel.

"It's not based on anything I can find."

Twelve heads turned with a single silent motion. Twelve pairs of eyes looked at Bartholomew Bronzini with a mixture of newfound respect and even awe.

"Bart, baby," Bernie Kornflake croaked. "This idea of

yours, this killer-baby thing. I'm sorry, babe, but we can't do it. It's too new. We can't do something this original. How would we market it? 'In the tradition of nothing anybody's ever seen before'? Never hit in a million years."

"That's not my idea," Bronzini grated. "It's yours. I want to do a fucking Christmas movie. A simple, warm story with no guns and a happy fucking ending."

"But, Bart, baby," Kornflake protested, noticing that Bronzini's street upbringing was creeping into his manner, "we can't take a chance. Look at your track record lately."

"Thirty films. Thirty box-office successes. Three of those are among the top money-makers of all fucking time. I'm a superstar. I'm Bartholomew Bronzini. I was making movies while you assholes were counting the first hairs in your crotches and wondering if you'd seen too many werewolf flicks!"

Kornflake's voice became stern. "Bart, *Grundy III* bombed. Domestically. You should never have used that Iran-Iraq story line. The war was over by the time you got into the theaters. It was yesterday's news. Who needed it?"

"It still made eighty million worldwide. They can't keep it in the video stores!"

"Tell you what," Kornflake said, sliding the script back across the polished table. "Put Grundy or Ringo into this script and we'll read it. If, after we kick it around, we don't think it will fly theatrically, we'll talk about turning it into a sitcom. We're going to need a gang of sitcoms for our new TV venture. Normally we only offer a thirteen-week guarantee, but for you, Bart, because we love you, we'll commit to a full season."

"Listen to me. I can act. I can write. I can direct. I've made millions for this industry. All I am asking is to do one lousy Christmas movie, and the best you can offer me is a sitcom!"

"Don't sneer at sitcoms. Do you know that *Gilligan's Island* has grossed over a billion dollars in syndication? A billion. That's a million with a B. None of your films ever did that, did they?"

"I'm not in Bob Denver's league. So sue me. You're talking to a superstar, not some comedy reject. My films kept this industry afloat during the seventies."

"And we're about to turn the corner into the nineties," Kornflake said flatly. "The parade is marching on. You gotta get on the train or walk the tracks."

Bronzini jumped onto the table. "Look at these muscles!" he shouted, tearing off his jacket and shirt to expose the lean tigerish muscles that had sold fifty million posters. "Nobody has muscles like these! Nobody!"

The men in the room looked at Bartholomew Bronzini's physique, then at one another.

"Think about redoing the script, Bart," Bernie Kornflake said, flashing a good-riddance smile.

"Go piss down your leg and drink from your sneaker," Bronzini snarled, scooping up his script.

As he stormed down the corridor, Bartholomew Bronzini heard Kornflake call after him. He half-turned, his dark eyes smoldering.

Kornflake approached Bronzini fawningly and flashed him a capped-tooth smile. "Before you go, Bart, baby, could I get your autograph? It's for my mother."

When Bartholomew Bronzini kicked the stand down on his Harley again, he was in his ten-car Malibu garage. He walked into his living room. It looked like an art-deco church. One entire wall was covered with custom-made hunting knives. Three of them he had used as props in the Grundy movies. The others were for display. The opposite wall was covered in authentic Chagalls and Magrittes, purchased as tax shelters.

Nobody believed that Bartholomew Bronzini had selected them because he appreciated them too, but he did. Today, he didn't even notice them.

Bronzini sank into his Spanish leather couch, feeling like a man at the end of his rope. Movies were his life. And now the public laughed at the much-larger-than-life roles that a decade ago they had applauded him in. And when he did a comedy, no one laughed. And everyone wondered why this street-kid-turned-millionaire-actor was so unhappy.

Woodenly he noticed that his message-machine light was on. He flipped a switch. His agent's voice boomed out.

"Bart, baby, it's Shawn. I've been trying to get you all afternoon. I may have something for you. Call me soonest. Remember, you're loved."

"I'm fucking half your income, too," Bronzini growled.

Bartholomew Bronzini came to life. He lunged for the phone and hit the speed-dial button marked "Agent."

"Yo! Got your message. What's the deal?"

"Someone wants to film your Christmas movie, Bart."

"Who?"

"Nishitsu."

"Nishitsu?"

"Yeah. They're Japanese."

"Hey, I may be having a bad streak, but I haven't sunk to doing cheap foreign films. Yet. You know better than that."

"These guys aren't cheap. They're big. The biggest."

"Never heard of them."

"Nishitsu is the biggest Japanese conglomerate in the entire world. They're into VCR's, home computers, cameras. They're the ones who landed the contract to produce the Japanese version of the F-16."

"The F-16!"

"That's what their representative told me. I think it's a camera."

"It's a fighter jet. Top-of-the-line Air Force combat model."

"Wow! They *are* big."

"Damn straight," Bartholomew Bronzini said, noticing for the first time that his message machine had the word NISHITSU on the front.

"They have money to burn and they want to go into films. Yours will be the first. They want to take a meeting with you soonest."

"Set it up."

"It's already set up. You're on the red-eye to Tokyo."

"I am not going to Tokyo. Let them come to me."

"That's not how it's done over there. You know that. You did those ham commercials for Japanese TV."

"Don't remind me," Bronzini said, wincing. When his film career had started to slip, he accepted a deal to do food commercials for the Japanese market, on the understanding that they never appear on U.S. TV. The *National Enquirer* broke the story as "Bartholomew Bronzini Goes to Work in Slaughterhouse."

"Well, that ham company is a Nishitsu subsidiary. They've got their hands in everything."

Bronzini hesitated. "They want to do my script, huh?"

"That's not the best part. They're offering you one hundred million to star. Can you believe it?"

"How many bucks equals one hundred million yen?"

"That's the beauty of it. They're paying in dollars. Are these Japs crazy, or what?"

Bartholomew Bronzini's first reaction was, "Nobody pays that much to any actor." His second was, "What about points?"

"They're offering points."

"Against net or gross?" Bronzini asked suspiciously.

"Gross. I know it sounds insane."

"It is insane and you know it. I'm not going near this."

"But it gets better, Bart, baby. They lined up Kurosawa to direct."

"*Akira* Kurosawa? He's a fucking master. I'd kill to work with him. This can't be real."

"There are a few strings," Shawn admitted. "They want to make a few script changes. Tiny ones. I know you usually get complete creative control, but I gotta tell you, Bart, there may be a lot of fish out there, but this is the only one biting."

"Tell me about it. I just came back from Dwarf-Star."

"How'd it go?"

"It was a bad scene."

"You didn't tear off your shirt again, did you?"

"I lost my head. It happens."

"How many times do I gotta tell you, that won't work anymore. Muscles are eighties. But okay, done is done. So are you on that plane or what? And before you answer, I gotta tell you it's gonna be either this, or you'd better start thinking seriously about *Ringo VI: Back from the Dead*."

"Anything but that," Bronzini said with a rueful laugh. "I've fought more rounds than Ali. Okay, I guess beggars can't be choosers."

"Great. I'll set it up. *Ciao*. You're loved."

Bartholomew Bronzini hung up the phone. He noticed that although the phone said MANGA on it, the corporate symbol matched that of the Nishitsu symbol on his message machine.

He went to his personal computer and began typing in instructions to his flock of servants. He noticed the keyboard carried the Nishitsu brand name too.

Bartholomew Bronzini grunted an explosive laugh.

"Good thing we won the war," he said, not realizing the irony of his own words.

2

His name was Remo, and he was going to kill Santa Claus if it was the last thing he ever did.

There was snow falling on College Hill, overlooking Providence, Rhode Island. Big puffy flakes of it. They fell with a faint hiss that only one possessing Remo's acute hearing could detect. The snow had just started, but already it formed a pristine blanket under his feet.

It remained pristine after Remo walked over it. His Italian loafers made no imprint. He walked deserted Benefit Street, as quietly and stealthily as a jungle cat. His T-shirt was so white that only his skinny arms with their unusually thick wrists showed against the falling flakes. Remo's chinos were gray. Snow clung to them in patches so that they too were predominantly white. The camouflage effect made Remo almost invisible.

Camouflage had nothing to do with not leaving footprints, however.

Remo paused in mid-stride and ran his eyes along the silent rows of well-preserved Colonial-style homes with their distinctive glass fanlights. There were no cars on

Benefit Street. It was after eleven P.M. Providence goes to bed early. But this week, the week before Christmas, it was not the ordinary sleeping habits of this insular city that made its inhabitants retire early. It was fear—fear of Santa Claus.

Remo started off again. In the spot where he had stood there were two shallow but well-defined footprints. But none leading away. Had Remo looked back to observe this phenomenon, his high-cheekboned face might have registered surprise. Not at the two inexplicable footsteps themselves, for he took it for granted that when he walked, leaves did not crinkle under his tread, nor sand displace. But for what they represented— the fact that, officially, he no longer existed.

Once, many Christmases ago, Remo had been a New Jersey cop. A pusher's murder was blamed on him, and Remo got the chair. And a second chance. The chance effectively erased his previous existence and brought forth a new, improved Remo.

For Remo became a Master of Sinanju. Trained as an assassin, he worked for a secret arm of the United States government known only as CURE. His job was to locate and eliminate the nation's enemies.

Tonight his assignment was to kill Santa Claus.

Remo had nothing against Saint Nick. In fact, he had not believed in Santa in a long time. Saint Nick was a jolly elf who symbolized childhood, a childhood that Remo had never really experienced to the full. He had been raised in an orphanage.

But while Remo had been denied a normal childhood, he did not resent it. Much. Maybe a little. Usually around this time of the year, actually, when he realized that the universal celebration of childhood, Christmas, was something he would never truly know.

This was why Remo had to kill Santa Claus. The bastard was ruining it for other children—children who had fathers and mothers and brothers and sisters. Innocent children with warm homes and Christmas trees they decorated with family instead of orphanage nuns. Remo would never see a Christmas like theirs. But he'd

be damned if another little boy or girl would be denied
Christmas by a fat slob in a red suit carring a fire ax.

Remo finished his sweep of Benefit Street. This was
the old section of Providence, where time seemed to
have stood still. The streetlamps might have been standing a century ago. The houses belonged to another era.
Most of the low stone steps boasted wrought-iron foot
scrapers, which in the days of horse-drawn cars saw
constant use. Now they were merely quaint relics.

Santa Claus didn't trouble Benefit Street tonight. No
corpulent figure haunted the rooftops. No bearded face
pressed to windows, tapping gently, enticingly.

Remo walked to Prospect Park. Set on an embankment,
it gave a commanding view of Benefit Street and the city
of Providence. Remo sat on the parapet beside the statue
of Roger Williams cut from granite. He stood with one
broken-fingered hand lifted helplessly as if to ask, "Why
my city?"

Remo wondered that as well, as his deep-set dark
eyes picked through the snow. His face, the skin tight
over high cheekbones, was tense. He rotated his thick
wrists unconsciously.

Usually Remo did not concern himself with the why.
Not on the small hits like this. He never asked the
crack dealers whose necks he broke why they sold
cocaine. The Mafia hoods never tried to explain themselves before he fractured their skulls like eggs. Remo
wouldn't have listened. After twenty years in this game,
it had come down to the same tired old story: new
people committing old crimes. That was all.

But Santa owed him an explanaton. And just this
once, Remo was going to ask why.

The moon was a fuzzy snowball as seen through the
swirling snow. It shone down on the golden dome of
the State House. It was a beautiful city, Remo realized.
He could easily imagine himself back in the nineteenth
century. He wondered what his ancestors did then. He
wondered who they were. He had no idea. But he
could recite from memory exactly what the emissaries
of a certain Korean fishing village were doing at any

time in the last century. They were, like him, Masters of Sinanju. But they were his spiritual ancestors.

The unusual quiet made it possible for his highly sensitive ears to pick out conversations emanating from the picturesque homes huddled below. He turned his head from side to side like some human radar dish. Instead of trying to listen, he let the snatches of conversation drift to him.

". . . Molly, come quick! The lost episode of *Murphy's Law* is on! . . ."

". . . Ward! Ward Phillips! If you don't answer me right now . . ."

". . . Santa! You're early." It was a little boy's voice. Instantly, another voice joined it. A pouty girlish voice.

"What is it, Tommy? You woke me up. Bad boy."

"It's Santa. He's at the window."

Tiny feet scampered. "Oh, let me see. Let me see!"

Remo forced himself to relax. Tensing up would constrict the blood flow to his brain and lower his sensitivity. His head made decreasingly smaller turns as he narrowed his focus.

He got a fix on the sound of a window being raised and a thick blubbery voice saying, "Ho ho ho!"

The sound made Remo's blood run cold. He had read the newspaper reports that Upstairs had supplied him. They had made him sick, then angry, and then burning with a rage that was as hot as the sun.

It was a thirty-foot drop from the parapet down to the tangle of underbrush that was clotted with leprous snow. It was the most direct way to the house.

Remo stood up. The snow fell around him like white spiders slipping down invisible webs. His breathing keyed down to its most minimal efficiency. He felt the falling snow, its rhythms, its inexorability. And when he was at one with the snowfall, he jumped into it.

Remo felt the flakes gravitate toward him. He felt each one individually. Not as a puffy bit of emphemeral frozen water, but as strong, structurally sound ice crystals. He sensed their inner strength, their uniqueness. They clung to him like brothers, not melting when they touched his face or bare arms. His skin was as cold as

they were. Remo thought like a snowflake, and like a
snowflake he became.

Remo floated to the ground at the exact speed of the
falling snow. He was covered in snow when his feet
touched the ground. This time he made footprints. Just
two. He floated down the embankment without leaving
any further sign.

Remo's eyes were on a brown house with a single
lighted window. Then an oblate shape fell across the
light like an evil eclipse.

Cursing under his breath, Remo moved for it.

Tommy Atwells had to climb onto his windowsill to
reach the latch. He stood there in his pumpkin-orange
Dr. Denton pajamas. His little knees trembled.

"Hurry, Tommy," his sister said. "Santa's cold."

"I'm trying." And on the other side of the snow-
sprinkled glass the wide smiling face grew eager.

Tommy used both hands to push the latch clear. It
sprang with a sharp sound.

"Okay, that's it," Tommy said, climbing down.

The window squeaked as it rolled up. Tommy stepped
back into a corner, near the toy box, where his sister
stood with wide eyes. He had heard about Santa Claus
for years. But he had never seen him with his own
eyes. He was very big.

After Santa has squeezed himself through the window, a question occurred to Tommy.

"How come . . . how come you're early? Mommy
says Christmas isn't till next week."

"Ho ho ho," was all Santa would say. He unslung his
big sack and let it slump to the floor, a long red handle
sticking out of it like a shard of ribbon candy. And then
he was clumping toward the shivering children, his
hands outstretched, his eyes very, very bright. His vast
shadow covered Tommy and his sister.

The window was already closed when Remo reached
it. It was a first-floor window. The glass was held in
place by dry wood putty. Remo tested the pane with
the flat of his hand. It gave slightly. He pushed harder,

instinctively reading the points of maximum weakness in the putty. Repositioning his hand, Remo smacked the glass, firmly but with restraint. The putty gave like stale bread. Remo caught the glass in both hands and flung it back into a growing snowbank. He went in.

Remo found himself in a children's bedroom. Both beds were rumpled but empty. The room smelled of peppermint. A half-eaten candy cane lay on a toy box.

Remo glided to the open door, every sense alert.

"Oooh, presents," a girl's voice was saying.

"Can we . . . can we open them now, Santa?" A boy's voice this time.

"Ho ho ho," Santa said. His laugh was very quiet, and the sound of tearing and crinkling wrapping paper overtook its echoes.

Remo eased into the hallway. His shoes made no sound on the varnished floor. Weak light spilled from a room at the end of the hall. Fresh pine scent wafted from it, carried by hot air from a floor register.

Remo came up on the door. He peered around it.

At first he saw only two children. A boy he took to be five and a girl who might have been a year younger. They were on their knees at the foot of a popcorn-and-tinsel-decorated Christmas tree. They were opening presents eagerly, the way Remo never had. He always got new clothes. Never toys.

Remo brushed the wistful thought from his mind. For on the far wall, next to the shadow of the bedecked tree, was another shadow. Short, round, it was a blot of darkness that any child in America would have recognized from its shape.

Except for the upraised ax in its hands.

Remo flung himself into the room as the ax came back.

The children didn't see Santa, for Santa stood behind them, his too-avid eyes fixed on the backs of their fresh-scrubbed necks.

"No!" Remo shouted, for once forgetting everything he had been taught about silent attack.

Santa started. The children's heads came about. They saw Remo. Their eyes widened in surprise. They didn't see the ax descending for their skulls.

They never saw the ax. Remo's hands intercepted the chipped blade as it came down. He pulled the weapon from Santa's two-handed grip.

"Run," Remo called to them.

"Mommy, Daddy, Mommy . . ." Tommy yelled as he scampered from the room. "Some strange man is trying to hurt Santa."

Remo broke the ax in two, flung both pieces away. He took Santa Claus by his rabbit-fur collar and yanked his bearded face into his own.

"Why, you bastard? I want to know why!" he said fiercely.

"Mommy, Daddy!"

Santa opened his mouth to speak. Instead, as he looked past Remo's shoulder, his thick wet lips broke into a foolish grin, showing yellow teeth like old dice.

A new voice broke the stillness.

"Stand where you are! I have a gun!"

"Don't shoot! Daddy, please don't shoot Santa."

Still holding on to the rabbit-fur collar, Remo whirled in place. Santa's black boots left the floor. When they touched down, Remo and the fat man had changed places. Remo now faced the hallway. Over Santa's red-velvet shoulder he saw a man in a terry-cloth bathrobe. He had a .45 automatic pointed in Remo's direction. The little boy clung to his leg. But the girl was still behind Remo, in the line of fire.

"Get away from my daughter," the man shouted. "Cathy, call the police."

"What is it?" a woman's twisted voice demanded. "Where's Susie?"

"Put the gun down, pal," Remo said. "This is between Santa and me. Isn't that right, Santa?" Remo shook the fat man angrily.

Santa only smiled slackly. It was a horrible, unbalanced smile.

"Susie, come here," the father prompted. "Walk around the men, honey."

"Do as he says, Susie," Remo said tightly, looking into Santa's eyes.

Susie stood unmoving, her thumb in her mouth.

"The police are coming, George," the mother's voice said. She appeared in the doorway, saw Remo and Santa Claus in a clutch, and let out a stricken scream.

"Cathy! Will you get back!"

"George, for God's sake, put away that gun. You'll hit Susie!"

"Listen to her," Remo said. "I have this under control." To prove it, he lifted Santa Claus off his feet and bounced him up and down on his boots.

"See?" Remo said.

From his wide black belt, Santa pulled a switchblade.

Remo sensed the knife coming up. It didn't concern him. He saw the father draw a shaky two-handed bead on the broad red back of the Santa suit and exert pressure on the trigger.

Remo pushed Santa aside. He ducked under the first wild shot. One open hand swept in and batted the muzzle up. A single shot pocked the ceiling.

Remo tripped the father. He went down. The gun ended up in Remo's hand. He yanked out the magazine and disarmed the weapon by pulling back the hammer with one strong thumb. The hammer broke off like a gingerbread man's leg.

Remo turned his attention back to Santa Claus. Santa was halfway out the door.

Remo started for the door, but felt a drag on his leg. He looked down. Little Tommy was clinging to his ankle, banging on it, hot tears streaming down his cheeks.

"Oh, you're bad. You made Santa go away."

Gently Remo bent down and pried Tommy's fingers from his pants fabric. He took the boy by his tiny shoulders and looked him in the eye.

"Take it easy," he said. "That wasn't Santa. That was the Boogey Man."

"There's no such thing as the Boogey Man. And you hit my daddy. I'll kill you! I will!"

The vehemence of the little boy's words shocked Remo. But he had no time to think about that. Outside, a car started up.

Remo released the boy. He went through the door like a cannonball. The sturdy panels flew apart.

Out on the pavement, a little foreign car spurted from the curb. Its tires slipped on the slick snow. The car was Christmas-ornament red.

The car turned the corner at high speed. Remo cut through a backyard to intercept it, but the car had already slid into the maze of College Hill when he reached the sidewalk.

Remo spotted it again at the top of Vertical Jenckes Street, so called because it was as steep as a San Francisco avenue.

The car went down slowly, brakes on. To release them would have invited disaster.

At the top of the hill, Remo put his feet together and pushed off.

Knees bent, arms at his sides, Remo went down Vertical Jenckes as if skiing from a steep slope. He caught up with the car and grabbed the bumper.

Hunched low so that he wouldn't be visible through the driver's rearview mirror, Remo locked every muscle and joint, and allowed himself to be towed. It brought back memories of his childhood in Newark, when he used to skip-hop the length of Broad Street. Back then, cars had big chrome bumpers that were easy to hold on to. The modern composition bumper afforded Remo no real purchase. So Remo's fingers dug into the plastic like claws and made his own. When he let go, there would be permanent holes.

The car weaved through College Hill with Remo attached it like a hunched-over human trailer. Snow collected at the tips of his shoes. When it got too thick, it fell away, only to start collecting all over again. Remo watched his shoes with interest. He had no idea where Santa Claus was taking him, but when the car came to a stop, the expression on Father Christmas' face was certain to be priceless. For the few seconds it would take before Remo started peeling the flesh from his skull.

Then Remo would get his answers. He might have to tear an arm off as well. Maybe he would rip off every limb and dump the bastard in a remote snowbank somewhere, where he could scream to his heart's content as he bled to death. It was a method that the man who had trained him to kill would frown upon, but this was a special case. This was the Christmas season.

The car took Route 95 North, heading for the Massachusetts border. Remo recognized this only after the car drove past a pesticide company which displayed a huge papier-mâché termite as an advertising gimmick. Remo had overheard this bug jokingly referred to as the Rhode Island state bird. He had laughed when he heard it. Now, hours later, with the snow falling like a shroud and a homicidal maniac towing him to an unknown destination, nothing seemed funny anymore.

The car turned off the highway in Taunton, Massachusetts. Remo didn't know that this was Taunton, and had he known, he would not have cared. His thoughts were red. Not Christmas-ornament red, but blood red.

The red car pulled into a blacktopped carport beside a row of snow-burdened evergreens.

Remo kept low. The car door clicked open and slammed shut. Clopping boots carried Santa Claus to the side door of a Cape Cod-style house. Remo heard a key tickle a door lock. The tumblers clicked so loudly that he heard them twenty feet away. A glass storm door clanged. Then there was only the hiss of the falling snow.

Remo got to his feet. He eased up to the door and received a shock. Staring back from the reflective glass of the storm door was an eerie sight.

It looked like a snowman. Not a jolly rotund snowman, but a lean sculptured one. There was no carrot nose, but it did have what looked like coal eyes. Remo peered closer. They were not coals, but the deathlike hollows of his own eye sockets.

Remo lifted his arms. They looked as if they had been rolled in powdered sugar. The snowman was himself. He realized that he had lowered his temperature so much that instead of melting, the snow clung to him.

The reflection in the glass gave Remo an idea.

He knocked on the storm door. His knuckles left leprous patches on the glass.

A wide-eyed man's face appeared at the window. It was a round face, simple and without guile. Not the kind of face Remo expected. Not the face of a man who had chopped off the heads of seven children in the middle of the night and left their headless corpses under the trees for their parents to find.

"Who . . . who are you?" the guileless face asked. His voice had a weirdly distorted quality.

"Frosty the Snowman," Remo said seriously.

"Really?"

Remo nodded. "Really. I'm canvassing the neighborhood on Santa's behalf. Here to find out if you've been naughty or nice."

The face broke into a frown.

"Santa Claus isn't real. Vincent told me so."

Remo blinked. "But Frosty is?"

The moon face puckered like a dried orange. "Vincent didn't say *you* weren't real. And you're here. But maybe I should ask him before I let you in. I'm not supposed to let strangers in the house, you know."

"Look, friend, I have eighty-seven thousand homes to get to by Sunday night. If you won't cooperate I'll just have to mark this house down as 'Naughty.' Thanks for your time." Remo turned to go.

The doors suddenly banged open and the moon-faced man lumbered out. He wasn't wearing a Santa suit. He looked twenty-eight. Going on twelve.

"No, no, wait!" he pleaded. "Come in. Please. I'll talk to you. I will."

Remo shrugged. "Okay." He followed the man in. Remo decided that he tipped the scales at nearly three hundred pounds. Almost none of it muscle. The guy's stomach flopped over his rope belt like a glob of marshmallow fluff. He had enough chins to distribute among the Jackson family and still have one left for himself.

And as Remo followed him into a cheerful if unkempt living room, he noticed that the guy's upper thighs rubbed together. He was wearing corduroy, and the sound was loud enough to frighten mice.

"Please sit down," the fat man said. "My name is Henry. Are you thirsty? Would you like hot chocolate?" His voice was pathetically eager to please.

"No, thanks," Remo said distractedly, looking around the room. "I'd only melt."

The living room lacked the usual Christmas decorations of the season. There was no tree. No stockings hung above the sullen fireplace logs. But in one corner stood a three-foot-tall plastic reindeer. It was plugged into a wall socket. It glowed faintly. The nose burned a cherry red. It belonged on a lawn.

"Rudolph?" Remo asked.

"Don't you recognize him?" Henry asked in an injured voice.

"Just checking," Remo said. "Now, let's get down to business. I have a report that someone in this house has been naughty."

"It wasn't me!" Henry shrieked.

A querulous voice called from another room.

"Go to bed, Henry."

"I will, Mother. When I'm done talking with Frosty."

"Go to bed now!" a male voice bellowed.

"Yes, sir. . . . I gotta go to bed. Vincent says."

"This will only take a minute," Remo said. He noticed that his arms were melting. He felt cold watery fingers crawling down inside his T-shirt. Remo figured he had five minutes to get the answers he wanted. The rest would be easy.

"Okay," Henry said, quietly closing the door.

Remo put his hand on Henry's trembling shoulder.

"Henry, is it true?" he asked.

Henry looked away. His eyes sought the plastic reindeer. "Is what true?" he asked evasively.

"Don't beat around the Christmas tree," Remo growled. He was staring into Henry's twisting face. The mouth belonged to Santa Claus. There was no mistaking that. So did the personal scent, an equal mixture of Ivory soap and underarm deodorant. It was hard to match Henry's whining voice to the sinister "Ho ho ho," Remo had heard, but there could be no mistake. "We know you're the one," Remo said flatly. "The one who's been killing little kids."

"I . . . I had to," Henry said miserably.

Remo grabbed him by the shoulders. "Why, for God's sake?" he demanded angrily. "They were only kids."

"He told me to," Henry blubbered.

Remo looked. Henry pointed to the plastic Rudolph. Its flat white-and-black eyes stared back innocently. The nose flickered.

"Rudolph?" Remo asked.

"He made me do it."

"Rudolph the Red-Nosed Reindeer made you cut off the heads of seven little children. Why?"

"So they wouldn't be sad. Like me."

"Sad?"

"Vincent said there was no Santa Claus. I didn't believe him at first, but Mommy said it was so."

"Who's Vincent?"

"My stepfather. My real father ran away. Vincent said it was because I was a retard, but Mommy hit Vincent when he said it, so I guess it's not true."

"Why did this happen?" Remo felt all his anger drain out of him. The big oaf was retarded.

"After Thanksgiving. I asked him how come we didn't have a tree. Vincent said we didn't need one."

"Keep talking. I still want to know why."

"Well, I didn't want any little kids to be hurt," Henry said, twisting his sausagelike fingers. "And Rudolph said that if a little kid died before he found out there wasn't any Santa, he would always be happy and go to heaven. But if he grew up, then he would go to hell when he died and burn forever. Like bacon."

"You killed them so they wouldn't find out there wasn't any Santa Claus?" Remo asked incredulously.

"Yes, sir, Mr. Frosty. Did Vincent lie?"

Remo sucked in a hot breath. It was a long moment before he answered.

"Yes, Henry," Remo said quietly. "Vincent lied."

"I'm the one who's going to burn in hell, aren't I?"

Remo answered the question without hesitating.

"No, Henry. You're going to heaven. Are you ready?"

"Can I say good-bye to Rudolph?"

"No, there's no time. Just close your eyes."

"Okay." Henry obediently closed his eyes. His face squinched up and his knees knocked together. He looked so pitiful that Remo almost changed his mind. But then he remembered the news clippings of the headless children under the trees and the pathetically regretful quotes of the parents who had found them. And he remembered his own empty childhood.

Remo stepped up to Henry and with a two-fingered blow struck the padded spot over his heart.

Henry fell backward like a refrigerator. The house shook. The querulous, sexless voice called again.

"Henry, go to sleep!"

It was joined by a male bellow. Vincent. "You control that idiot of yours or I'm going back to Sandra."

Remo looked down at the fat man's face. It was peaceful. There was a hint of a smile at the corners of his mouth. The smile only made Remo angry. He had wanted to kill the guy slowly and painfully. He wanted him to suffer for all the suffering he had caused. He felt cheated. The Santa Claus killer was dead, and he felt no sense of accomplishment or victory. He felt nothing. Just as he felt every Christmas of his life.

He wondered if maybe he should do Vincent.

Then the sexless voice was shouting again.

"Henry, if I don't hear your snoring in five seconds, I'll turn you in to the police for driving without a license. I'll put you in jail. Do you hear me? Jail!"

Remo decided that Vincent would suffer a lot more if he let him live. He walked out of the house and hot-wired the Christmas-red car. He drove north to Boston and Logan Airport.

Just when the snow looked like it would fall forever, like salt onto a raw wound, it stopped.

"Sometimes I hate this job," Remo muttered into the night. "Especially this time of year."

On the flight back to New York, he hoped someone would try to hijack the plane. But no one did. Maybe when he got back, Upstairs would have a decent assignment for a change. Something big, worthy of his talents. And bloody.

He was going to get his wish.

3

Bartholomew Bronzini was doing wrist curls in his private gym when the gym telephone whirred. Bronzini did another few reps with his left arm before he answered it. He took pride in his daily regimen of exercise. And he always gave his left side more exercise because he knew that right-handed persons developed larger muscles on the right side. Bronzini had worked out a compensating regimen so that he had nearly perfect muscular symmetry.

Bronzini scooped up the phone as he toweled off his pecs. They gleamed as if greased.

"Yo!" he said briskly.

"Bart, baby, *que pasa?*" It was Shawn. His agent.

"What's the word?"

"Our Japanese compadres just Fedexed me the script. It looks great."

"Did they change much?"

"How do I know? I haven't read it."

"You just said it looked great."

"It does. You should see this binder. Looks like Spanish leather or something. And the pages are—get this—hand-lettered. Looks like—what do they call it?—calligraphy."

Bronzini sighed. He should have known better than to ask. Nobody in Hollywood read scripts if they could help it. They made deals and hoped for the best.

"Okay, messenger it to me. I'll look it over."

"No, Bart, sweetheart. There's a Nishitsu corporate jet waiting for you at Burbank Airport. That producer you met in Tokyo, what's his name? Sounds like a Greek sandwich shop."

"Jiro something."

"That's him. He wants you in Yuma by noon."

"Yuma! Tell him no way. I spent three days in Japan

with those Nishitsu guys. They gave me the creeps, always bowing and scraping and asking me where I bought my shoes and if they were for sale. They were so polite I wanted to punch them."

"Yuma isn't in Japan. It's in Arizona."

"Why do they want me there?"

"That's where you're filming. They've been scouting locations since you got back."

"This is a freaking Christmas movie. It's set in Chicago."

"I guess this is one of the changes they made."

"They can't film *Johnny's Christmas Spirit* in Arizona."

"Why not?" Shawn said in a reasonable tone. "They filmed *Star Wars* in Southern California. Looked like outer space to me."

"It doesn't snow in Arizona," Bronzini said acidly. "They don't have evergreens. They have cacti. What are they gonna do? Decorate the cacti?"

"Don't cacti have needles too?"

"Don't you fucking start, Shawn!"

"Okay, okay. Look, talk to them. Straighten it out. But they need you to smooth things over. They're having trouble with the Yuma Chamber of Commerce or something. It's about film permits and work rules."

"What am I, head of the local? Have them take it up with the union."

"Uh, they don't want to do that, for some reason."

"What do they mean? I'm the star, not the shop steward. This *is* a union movie, isn't it?"

"Of course it is, Bart," Shawn said placatingly. "These are major, major people. They're looking for a piece of the U.S. film industry. No way they're not union."

"Good, because if this isn't a union production, I'd back out right now."

"Can't."

"Why not?"

"They got your name on the contract. Remember?"

"So let them sue."

"That's the problem. They will. And they'd win, because they'll try it in a Japanese court. They're big, a mega-corporation. They could clean you out. No more

polo ponies, no more Renoirs. They'd probably bag you
for your comic-book collection if they find out about it."

Bartholomew Bronzini was silent for a long time.
Before he could speak, his agent spoke up.

"You know what they'd do if you backed out. They'd
turn around and give the part to Schwarzenegger."

"No chance!" Bronzini exploded. "That side of beef
couldn't cut it in my Christmas movie. He's the only
actor in the world who steps on his own lines."

"No argument there. But let's not let it get to that.
Okay? Burbank Airport. The jet's waiting."

Bartholomew Bronzini hung up the phone with so
much force that Donald Duck's beak fell off.

The Nishitsu jet was waiting for him when Bronzini
pulled up on his Harley Davidson. A white-coated Japanese steward stood meekly by the door. He pulled it
open from the top, exposing a flight of plush steps.

The steward bowed quickly when Bronzini dismounted.

"*Konnichi wa*, Bronzini san," he said with a tight
smile.

The smile fell off when Bronzini began pushing his
motorcycle up the plush steps. "No, Bronzini san."

"Where I go, my bike goes," growled Bronzini. He
pushed the bike up as easily as if it were a ten-speed
and not a monster Harley.

The steward followed him up, and as Bronzini leaned
the bike against a bulkhead, he pulled up the staircase
door. The engines immediately began warming up.

When the Nishitsu jet landed at Yuma International
Airport slightly more than sixty minutes later, the Japanese steward lowered the ramp stairs manually and
jumped out of the way while the maniac American actor
piloted his bouncing motorcycle down it at full speed.

Bartholomew Bronzini hit the tarmac with a bump,
nearly wiping out. He recovered, dismounted, and
walked the bike up to the Nishitsu corporate van, gun-
ning the engine impatiently while the unhappy face
which he recognized as Jiro Isuzu peered out of the
side window with horrified eyes.

Finally Isuzu slid open the door and stepped out.

"Bronzini san. Good of you to come."

"Save the soap," Bronzini said. "And it's plain Bronzini. So what's the problem?"

"Shooting start in two day. We have much to do."

"Two days!"

"Production on tight shooting schedule. Must hurry. Wirr you come now. Prease?"

"Lead the way," Bronzini said, kicking the bike stand up. "This is bogus."

A brief flash of anger showed in Jiro Isuzu's eyes. For a moment the Japanese looked as if he were going to say something, but he only bobbed his head repeatedly and slid the van's side door closed.

Bronzini followed the van into the city. His initial impression of Yuma was that it was flat. The highway leading into town was dotted with fast-food restaurants and discount stores. He saw very few cacti.

But when they turned into a residential area, several stubby cholla cacti decorated front yards. Most homes had Christmas decorations up. But to Bronzini, the warm desert air and lack of snow made it seem not like Christmas at all.

"How the hell are they going to film a Christmas movie in this godforsaken place?" he muttered as he passed a Pueblo-style home with the inevitable flagstone patio. There was a cow skull by the front door. It wore a Santa Claus cap.

Bronzini was still turning the question over in his mind when the van pulled up to Yuma City Hall.

"What are we doing here?" he demanded of Jiro when the latter emerged from the van.

"We have appointment with mayor. I told him you would come. Now, forrow, prease."

"The mayor?" Bronzini muttered. "I hope this isn't another key-to-the-city deal. I already got enough to open up a store."

Basil Cloves had been mayor of Yuma for nearly six years. He was very proud of his city, which was one of the fastest-growing desert communities in the West.

He was proud of its three TV stations, its important military bases, and its crystal pure air.

He would never knowingly surrender it to a foreign aggressor.

But when his press secretary ushered in representatives of the Nishitsu Film Corporation, who were accompanied by the world's number-one film superstar, Bartholomew Bronzini, he broke into a baby-kissing smile.

"Mr. Bronzini!" he gushed, taking Bronzini's hand in both of his. "Wonderful of you to come. I've seen every one of your movies."

"Great. Thank you," Bronzini said quietly. Everyone in the room interpreted his comment as bored disinterest. The truth was that Bronzini was embarrassed by the sunglasses-and-autographs side of his business.

"I loved you in *Conan the Mendicant*. You were so . . . so . . . muscular!"

"Nice of you to say so," Bronzini said. He decided not to mention that that was Schwarzenegger. He hated when people confused him with that Austrian water buffalo.

"Well, Mr. Bronzini," the mayor of Yuma said as he gestured everyone into seats. "Mr. Isuzu tells me that you want to film a movie in my beautiful city."

"Yes, sir," Bronzini said, and everyone in the room assumed he was being condescending when he used the word "sir." He was not.

"You can understand that when folks I don't know, no offense, gentlemen"—he indicated the representatives from Nishitsu, who sat with straight backs and stiff necks—"come to my city and apply for permits and things of that sort, I have to secure certain assurances. We don't see many flicks made in Yuma. So I told these fine gentlemen that if they could offer proof of their sincerity and good intentions, I would do what I could to get it past the city council."

Here it comes, Bronzini thought. As an occasional producer, he had gotten used to being strong-armed. You contacted the local government for permission to film on public streets and they never thought about the revenue that would be brought into the local economy, the local people who would be employed. They only wondered what was in it for them. If it wasn't the politicians, it was the teamsters or the Mafia.

"So when Mr. Isuzu told me that you'd be willing to come here and allay our fears," Mayor Cloves went on, "I said, well, that might just do it."

At that moment the press secretary put his head in the door. "They're here, Mr. Mayor."

"Wonderful," said Mayor Cloves. "Come, let's go meet them."

Bronzini caught Isuzu's arm on the way out.

"What is this?" he hissed.

"Quiet. This wirr be over soon."

"Oh," said Bronzini when he saw the news crews setting up their video cameras. Newspaper reporters stood with pencils poised over notepads.

"Thank you for coming, ladies and gentlemen of the press," the mayor said in a booming voice. "As you can see, the illustrious Bartholomew Bronzini, star of such modern classics as *Conan the Mendicant*, is in my office today. Bart's come to Yuma to ask me personally for permission to film his next blockbuster. With him is Mr. Jiro Isuzu, who is a producer with the Nishitsu Corporation. I see from the brand names on some of your video equipment that you probably know more about Nishitsu than I do."

The mayor laughed heartily, and alone. He went on. "They have selected Yuma out of dozens of American cities as the location for Bart's new film. You may now ask questions, if you'd like."

There was an embarrassing silence. The print press looked at their notebooks. The TV crews hesitated. Bronzini had seen it all over the world. His reputation intimidated even the usually bold TV crews.

"Maybe I should be asking the questions," Bronzini quipped. "Like, how hot does it get this time of year?"

No one even smiled. He hated it went they didn't smile.

Finally a pert blond who identified herself as the

entertainment reporter for one of the TV stations piped
up. "Mr. Bronzini, tell us about your new film."

"It's a Christmas movie. It's about—"

"And what do you think of Yuma so far?"

"It's hard to form much of an impression when all
you've seen is the airport and the mayor's office."
Bronzini beamed sheepishly. He waited for a follow-up
question, but they shifted their attention to Jiro Isuzu.

"Mr. Isuzu. Why did you pick Yuma?"

"It perfect for our needs," Isuzu said.

"Mr. Isuzu, do you think that Americans will go to
see a Japanese-made movie?" "Mr. Isuzu, how do you
feel about the current Japanese economic dominance in
the Pacific?" "Mr. Isuzu . . ."

And so it went. The press rattled on about every
conceivable angle that had to do with Yuma and several
that did not. When their stories ran, some within hours,
they would all play up the banal local angle. Nowhere
would it be mentioned that this role was a significant
departure from Bartholomew Bronzini's flex-and-pecs
screen roles. Nowhere would it be mentioned that he
had written the script. He was lucky if his two de-
clarative-sentence comments would be reported accur-
ately.

He hated it when they did that, too.

Finally the TV people began packing up their equipment and the print reporters shuffled out of the room,
casting curious glances at him over their shoulders. He
overheard one woman tell another, "Can you believe
it? He's going to make over a hundred million on this
movie and he can barely speak three words in a row."

After the reporters had gone, the mayor of Yuma
came up to him and shook his hand again.

"You were wonderful, Bart. Mind if I call you Bart?"

"Go ahead. You're already in practice."

"Thank you, Bart. I'm up for reelection next year and
this is going to kick off my campaign like a football."

"You have my vote," Bronzini joked.

"Oh, are you registered in this city?"

"It was a little joke," Bronzini told him. "Very little."
The mayor looked blank. His expression wondered,

"Can this Neanderthal make jokes?" Bronzini hated that expression.

"Oh," Mayor Cloves said. "A joke. Well, it's good to see that you have a sense of humor."

"It's an implant," Bronzini said.

"You wirr see to permissions?" Jiro Isuzu put in quickly.

"Yes, yes, of course. And let me be the first to welcome your production to our fair city."

Bronzini shook the mayor's hand in relief. That was it? A photo op? Maybe this wouldn't be so terrible.

"Oh, before you go," the mayor said quickly, "could I have your autograph?"

"Sure," Bronzini said, accepting a pen and a photograph of himself torn from a fan magazine.

"Who do I make it out to?" he asked.

"Make it out to me. But it's for my daughter."

"Yeah," Bronzini sighed as he autographed the photo. He signed it, "To the mayor of Yuma, from his good friend Arnold Schwarzenegger."

The mayor read it without batting an eye. Just as Bronzini had known he would.

Out on the street, Bronzini growled a question to Jiro Isuzu. "Is that it? Am I outta here now?"

"No, we have many more visits to make. First we go to hotel."

"Why? Is the cleaning staff demanding a lock of my hair?" Bronzini said, hopping onto his bike.

Bartholomew Bronzini followed the van to the Shilo Inn, an elegant adobe hotel on Route 8. The lobby entrance was blocked by marching picketers. They carried placards and signs reading "Bronzini Unfair." "Bronzini Is Un-American." "Bronzini the Traitor."

One man carried a *Grundy III* poster showing Bronzini, his long hair held in place by a headband. The tagline read "Bronzini Is Grundy." The last word was crossed out and replaced with the word "Grungy."

"What the hell is this?" Bronzini shouted.

"Union," Isuzu told me. "They protest."

"Damn it. This is supposed to be a union film."

"It is. Japanese union."

"Listen, Jiro. I can't do a nonunion film. My name will be mud. I'm a hero to the working guy."

"That was before *Ringo V*, when Ringo kirred in boxing match. But you are stirr big hero in Nippon. Your future is there. Not here. Americans tire of you."

Bronzini put his hands on his hips. "Stop beating around the bush, Isuzu. Why don't you come out and speak your mind?"

"So sorry. Not understand. Have spoken mind."

"You don't understand. I'm not turning my back on everything I represent. I'm Bartholomew Bronzini, the rags-to-riches personification of the American dream."

"Those are Americans," Isuzu said, indicating the marchers. "They do not carr you hero."

"That's because they think I've double-crossed them. And I won't. I'm done here." He started for his bike.

"Schwarzenegger wirr do movie for ress," Isuzu called after him. "Perhaps better."

"Then get that Black Forest bozo," Bronzini barked.

"We wirr. And we will pay his sarary out of rawsuit damages from suing you for breach of contract."

Bronzini froze with his hands touching the handlebars of his bike. One leg was poised to mount the saddle. He looked like he was doing an imitation of a dog about to relieve himself against a fireplug.

The thought of Schwarzenegger being paid out of Bronzini's own pocket stopped him cold. Reluctantly he lowered his leg. He walked back to Jiro Isuzu. The Japanese's composed face looked faintly smug.

"You understand now?"

"Jiro, I'm starting not to like you."

"Production office in this hoter. We must go there. Many terephone carr to make. Much problem to work out if we are to start shooting on schedule." He pronounced it "sked-oo."

Bronzini looked at the circling pickets. "I've never crossed a picket line in my life."

"Then we go in side door. Come."

Jiro Isuzu started off, trailed by a cluster of functionaries. Bronzini looked at the picketers, who were so busy shouting slogans that they weren't aware that the object of their displeasure was standing only yards away.

Never one to back away from a challenge, Bronzini decided to reason with them. He started for the picket line, when a heavyset man noticed him.

"Hey, there he is!" the man shouted. "The Steroid Stallion himself. Bronzini!"

The catcalls followed. "Boo!" they hooted. "Bronzini! Go back to Japan."

"Hear me out," Bronzini shouted. His words were drowned out. The picketers—they belonged to IATSE, the International Alliance of Theatrical Stage Employees —interpreted Bronzini's angry face to suit themselves.

"Did you hear what he called us?" one cried indignantly.

That did it. They started for him en masse.

Bronzini stopped. He folded his arms. He was going to hold his ground. What was the worst they could do?

The worst they could do, it turned out, was to surround him in a shouting, haranguing circle.

"Down with Bronzini! The Bronze Bambino has feet of clay!"

"Listen to me," Bronzini shouted. "I just want to talk to you about this. I think we can reason this through."

He was wrong. They were not listening. Camera crews were moving up to get a picture of the world-renowned Bartholomew Bronzini held hostage by two dozen protesters armed only with placards.

When the cameras started taping, one of the protesters called out, "Hey, watch this!"

He whacked Bronzini with his placard. The broomstick broke against Bronzini's muscular shoulder. He barely felt it, but that didn't matter. Bartholomew Bronzini had grown up in a rough Italian neighborhood where turning the other cheek was the kiss of death.

He decked his assailant with a roundhouse right.

The protesters turned into a mob. They descended on Bronzini like a fury. Bronzini returned blow for blow. He started laying protesters out on the blacktop of the parking lot. A wild grin cracked his Sicilian face. This was something he understood. A bare-knuckled fight.

But as he mashed a man's nose flat, he wondered if he wasn't on the wrong side of this brawl.

The question was answered for him when the horde of Japanese men piled out of the lobby. Some of them, on orders from an excited Jiro Isuzu, pulled pistols from under their coats. Bodyguards.

"Stop them," Isuzu shrieked. "Protect Bronzini. Now!"

The bodyguards waded in. The protesters turned on them too. Bronzini tried pushing his way clear of the mob, but there were too many of them. He took one of the protesters by the throat.

Then a shot rang out. The man in Bronzini's metallic grasp gasped once and went limp. He fell. His head made a cracking sound when it hit the ground.

"What the fuck!" Bronzini yelled. "Who fired that shot? Who?"

It was obvious in another moment. Bronzini felt something yank on his belt. He struggled. It was one of the Japanese bodyguards.

"Let go of me," Bronzini snarled. "He's hurt bad."

"No. You come."

"I said let me—"

Bronzini never got the next word out. The sky and ground swapped perspectives. He was suddenly on his back. The shock blew the air out of his lungs. Stunned, he wondered if he had caught a stray bullet. And as other gunshots sounded in the background, he was lifted by several husky Japanese and dumped into the waiting Nishitsu van.

He was whisked from the Shilo Inn at high speed.

"What happened?" Bronzini asked the hovering Jiro Isuzu in a dazed voice.

"Judo. Necessary."

"The fuck."

4

It was dawn when Remo Williams was dropped off in front of his Rye, New York, home by taxi.

Remo handed the driver a crisp hundred dollar bill.

"Merry Christmas," Remo said. "Keep the change."

"Hey, Merry Christmas to you too, buddy. You must be expecting a whale of a holiday yourself."

"Nah. I'm on an unlimited expense account."

"Thanks just the same," the cabby said, pulling off.

It was not snowing in Rye, New York. The storm that had blanketed New England had passed through New York State the previous day. The town had already cleared the sidewalk with a small tractor snow blower. Its caterpillar tracks had left their unmistakable imprints.

But Remo's walkway was buried.

Remo placed one foot on the crust of snow that covered the walk. His breathing changed. His arms seemed to lift slightly from his sides as if they were filled with air instead of bone and blood and muscle.

Remo walked across the thin frozen crust of the snow without breaking through. He felt light as a feather. He *was* a feather. He thought like a feather, moved like a feather, and the thin hard crust reacted to him as if each foot was a feather duster.

Remo went in his front door with the expression of a man who had slogged through a sloppy wet snowbank in his stocking feet, not one who had executed a feat that other men would have scorned as impossible.

Even the novelty of having a home to come back to for the first time since he joined the organization did not lift his spirits. The living room consisted of bare walls, a hardwood floor, and a big-screen TV. Two straw mats sat on the floor before the screen.

Somehow, it was not very homey.

Remo walked to his bedroom. It, too, was only four

walls and a bare floor. A futonlike mat stretched out in one corner. His wardrobe, consisting of six pairs of chinos and an assortment of black and white T-shirts, lay neatly folded at the bottom of a closet. On a shelf above a cluster of empty wire hangers were racked a dozen pairs of handmade Italian leather loafers.

From the other bedroom came a series of long, drawn-out sounds, like a goose honking.

"*Braaawwwwkkkk!*"

"*Hnnnnkkkkkkk!*"

Snoring.

Remo decided he wasn't sleepy. Turning on his heel, he made for the door.

Remo later pulled up in front of an all-night drugstore, asked the woman behind the counter if she accepted credit cards, and when he got a yes in return, he went straight to the Christmas-decoration shelf. There were more bulbs, candy canes, and tinsel than he could carry at one time, so he took hold of the shelf at each end and applied pressure. The crack was instantaneous.

Remo carried the entire shelf to the cash register.

"Oh, my God," the girl said.

"Put all this stuff on my card," Remo said, slipping the plastic onto the glass counter.

"You broke the shelf."

"Yeah. Sorry about that. Just add it to the bill."

Outside, Remo set the shelf on the hood of his Buick. He opened the trunk, and balancing the shelf carefully, upended it over the open trunk. The packages rattled down the shelf like coal down a cellar chute.

Remo tossed the shelf into a cluster of trash barrels and closed the trunk.

His next stop was at a used-car lot with a banner that said "Christmas Trees Cheap." The lot hadn't opened for the day, so Remo took his time examining the stock. The first one he liked looked too tall for his living room. The second left dry pine needles in his hands when he grasped one of the branches experimentally.

Remo went through every tree on the lot and de-

cided that if the cars for sale were in the same shape as
the trees, the driving public was in mortal peril.

"Nobody respects Christmas anymore," Remo growled
as, one by one, he picked up the trees by their bases
and, like a farmer shucking corn, stripped them of their
branches with one-handed sweeps.

Remo left a note that said, "I got carried away with
the spirit of the season. Sorry. Send me a bill." He
didn't sign it or leave an address.

Disgusted, Remo next drove to the golf course that
spawled behind his house. There he picked his way
among the evergreens. He found a young one he liked
and, kneeling beside it, felt all around the base to get a
sense of its root system. When he found a weak point,
he used the side of his hand to sever the root.

By the time he was done, the evergreen came out of the
frozen ground as easily as a daisy. Remo carried it to his
back door over his shoulder like Paul Bunyan. He got it
through the door so expertly he lost only three needles.

Remo set the tree in one corner of the room. It
balanced perfectly, even without a stand. Remo had
flattened out the roots to form a natural base.

Getting the decorations from the car, he proceeded
to decorate the tree. He took his time with it. After two
hours, the tightness began to leave his face and the
beginning of a contented smile crinkled the corners of
his deep-set eyes. In another minute he would have
begun to hum "Little Drummer Boy."

That moment never came.

From out of the bedroom, the continued adenoidal
goose honking abruptly died down, to be replaced by
the rustle of silk. And then, so softly that only Remo's
ears could have heard, came the shuffle of sandals.

Chiun, Reigning Master of Sinanju, looked into the
room. His eyes alighted on the lean, muscular back of
his adopted son. Momentary pleasure illuminated his
wise hazel orbs. Remo was home. It was good to behold
him once more.

Then he noticed what Remo was doing.

"Pah!" he spat. "I see that it is Jesus Time again."

"It's called Christmas," Remo said over his shoulder,

"and I was just getting into the mood before you mouthed off."

"Mouthed off!" Chiun squeaked. "I did not mouth off, whatever that is." The Master of Sinanju was old. Only his eyes looked young. He was a tiny Oriental with only smoky puffs of white hair over his ears and another wisp at his chin. He wore a yellow silk kimono. His hands were joined within its linked sleeves.

"I did not mouth off," Chiun repeated when Remo ignored him and returned to stringing lengths of silver wire on the evergreen tree. Remo said nothing.

"Trees belong outdoors," Chiun added.

Remo sighed. "This is a Christmas tree. They're for indoors. And if you don't want to help, fine. Just stay out of my way. This is our first Christmas in our new home. I'm going to enjoy it. With or without you."

Chiun meditated on the matter. "This tree reminds me of those magnificent ones which dot the hillsides of my native Korea," he pointed out. "The scent is very much the same."

"Then pitch in," Remo said, mollified.

"And you have killed it for your pagan ceremony," Chiun added harshly.

"Keep it up, Chiun, and there won't be any presents under the tree with your name on them."

"Presents?" Chiun gasped. "For me?"

"Yeah. That's the tradition. I put presents under the tree for you and you put them under the tree for me."

Chiun looked down at the foot of the tree. He saw no presents. "When?" he asked sharply.

"What?"

"When will these alleged presents appear?"

"Christmas Eve. That's Sunday night."

"You have bought them?" Chiun asked skeptically.

"No, not yet," Remo answered vaguely.

"I have bought none for you, you know."

"There's time yet."

Chiun examined Remo's tight profile curiously.

"In past years you were not so obsessed by this Christmastime," he ventured.

"In past years I never had to kill Santa Claus."

"Ah," Chiun said, raising a long-nailed finger. "At last we come to the heart of the matter."

Remo said nothing. He lifted a spindle-shaped ornament from its box and plucked straw packing from dangling silver bells.

"Your mission," Chiun said expectantly, "it was successful?"

"He's dead if that's what you mean." Remo reached up and pulled the flexible treetop down. He slipped the ornament over the top. When he let go, it sprang erect. The tiny bells tinkled merrily.

"You do not look happy for one who has avenged the children of this land."

"The killer was a child himself."

Chiun gasped. "No! You did not kill a child. It is against everything I taught you. Children are sacred. Say this is not so, Remo."

"He was a child in mind, not body."

"Ah, one of the many mental defectives that populate America. It is sad. I think this stems from the hamburgers everyone devours. They destroy the brain cells."

"I wanted to kill this guy so bad it hurt."

"Your job is not to hate, but to eliminate your emperor's enemies with dispatch and professionalism."

"I did it right. He didn't suffer."

"But you did."

Remo stopped what he was doing. He put aside a box of silver-blue bulbs and sat down on a tatami mat. Quietly, fervently, he told the Master of Sinanju what he had encountered. When he was done, he asked a question: "Did I do the right thing?"

"If a tiger turns man-eater," Chiun intoned sagely, "he must be hunted down and destroyed."

"A tiger knows what he's doing. I'm not sure he did."

"If a tiger cub mauls a child, he too must be put down. It matters not whether he knows that what he did was wrong, for he has tasted blood, and the taste will never cease haunting him. So, too, was it with this unfortunate cretin. He committed great evil. Some might not judge him harshly, but in truth that is not the issue. He had tasted blood. Better that he be liberated from his physical prison and be free to return to earth in another life, to atone for his transgressions."

"You sound like Shirley MacLaine."

"I will take that as a compliment."

"Don't."

"Then I will assume it is an insult," Chiun snapped, "and leave you to your misery, you who would rather suffer in ignorance than be unshackled by wisdom."

And with that, the Master of Sinanju jumped to his feet and flounced back to his room. The door closed so hard it made a breeze that ruffled Remo's hair. Oddly, for all that violence, the door closed without a sound.

Remo went back to his tree. But his mind was troubled. The phone rang. Remo went to answer it.

"Remo. I need to see you," the lemony voice of Dr. Harold W. Smith told him. Smith was the head of CURE, and Remo's boss.

"Don't you want to hear about the mission?"

"No, I assume that if it had gone awry, you would have reported it before I called."

"Take me for granted, why don't you?"

"I have something more important. Please come to Folcroft at once."

"Chiun and I will be there in a half-hour."

"No," Smith said hastily. "Just you. Please leave Chiun out of this."

The door to Chiun's bedroom opened suddenly. The Master of Sinanju appeared, his mien hard.

"I heard that!" he said loudly.

"I guess you just stepped in it, Smitty," Remo said.

Harold Smith sighed. "Contract-renewal time is coming up. I wanted to avoid premature negotiations."

"No negotiations are premature," Chiun announced, loud enough to carry to the receiver.

"Are you using a speakerphone?" Smith asked sharply.

"No. You know Chiun can hear an insult clear across the Atlantic Ocean."

"One-half hour," Smith said. "Good-bye."

"That man is growing more impossible with each passing day," Chiun said huffily.

"What are you trying to bag him for this year?

Disneyland again? Or are you still trying to get him to match Roger Clemen's salary?"

"Our Disneyland negotiations have collapsed."

Remo feigned horror. "No!" he gasped.

"Smith claims that the current owner refuses to sell," Chiun said bitterly. "I, however, may bring it up again. For too many years have I accompanied you on your missions for insufficient recompense."

"I thought we were co-equal partners, to use your own phrase."

"True, but that is an understanding that exists between you and me. It has nothing to do with Smith. For the purposes of contract negotiations, I am the Master and you the pupil. I have been trying to impress this upon Emperor Smith, but to no avail. The man is invincibly dense."

"Is that why you didn't go to Providence with me?"

"Possibly. It might have helped my cause had you failed miserably. But I do not hold your uncharacteristic success against you. I am certain it is not deliberate."

"Nice of you to be so understanding, but I do feel like I failed miserably."

"May I quote you? To Smith?"

"Do what you want," Remo said. "I'm leaving."

The Master of Sinanju hastily padded after him.

"And I am accompanying you," he said. "Perhaps Smith has an assignment for you of such magnitude that he will beg me to accompany you. For a suitable price, of course."

Remo cast the half-decorated tree a wistful glance as he left the house. He had no inkling that by the time he would see it next, all the needles would have dried up and fallen to the floor.

Bartholomew Bronzini left the Yuma police station in smoldering silence. He was escorted out by a trio of Nishitsu Corporation Lawyers. Jiro Isuzu led them.

At the bottom of the steps, Jiro Isuzu turned to Bronzini and said, "Authorities wirr not make trouble now. Don't want to roose movie. Also, promise to use porice in firm." He pronounced it "fir-em."

"Why didn't you let me speak up back there? I wanted to tell my story."

"Not necessary. Situation under contror now. Porice brame picketers."

"Hey, I had a part in that little fracas. I got in their faces. I'm as much responsible for what happened as anybody. And what the hell did you think you were doing by ordering your goons to open fire like that?"

"Your rife in danger."

"The hell it was. I was decking them reft and light—I mean left and right."

"Action necessary to save your rife. Also to discourage picketers."

"They had a right to picket. This is America."

"Arso this is Japanese production. No bad pubricity must attach itself to our work."

"No bad publicity! Four IATSE protesters are dead. You think that won't get in the newspapers?"

"Porice have agreed to hold suspects untir firm complete."

"What? You can't hide a thing like this forever."

"Not forever. For two week."

"Two weeks!" Bronzini exploded. "That's our shooting schedule? It's im-fuckin'-possible. Pardon my French."

"We do outdoor scenes first," Isuzu explained. "Break production into nine units, arr shoot at once. Other actors fry in to do their work. This way, we come in under budget in ress than arrotted time. Now prease forrow."

"Where to?"

"Other probrem need fixing. Prease forrow van."

The Nishitsu team loaded into the waiting van. Bronzini straddled his motorcycle, waiting for them to start. "This isn't right. None of it," he muttered.

But when the van started off, he followed it through the gridlike streets, out of the center of town, and along a dusty desert road. They were leaving the city proper. The high battlements of the Chocolate Mountains loomed in the distance. On either side of the road, stucco and exposed-beam houses gave way to endless beds of lettuce fields, one of Yuma's principal crops. In the distance a chevron of F/A 1-18's etched silent contrails against the cloudless sky.

Then the lettuce beds gave way to scrub desert and sandhills. The hardtop road stopped but the van kept going. It wound in and around the sandhills and Bronzini wondered where they were going.

They passed through a chain-link fence guarded by Nishitsu personnel and up a dusty road. Behind a cluster of hills lay a group of candy-striped tents. Bronzini recognized it as a location base camp. But what was it doing way out here in the desert?

The van turned into the base camp and parked beside a row of Nishitsu RV's and Ninja jeeps.

"What's this all about, Jiro?" Bronzini demanded as he dismounted.

"Base camp for firm."

"No shit. Isn't this a little out-of-the-way?"

"We are firming in desert."

"You are what!" Bronzini ground out. "What are you going to do, paint the sand white and pretend it's snow? I got news for you, it won't wash. And I won't stand for working on a stupid backlot street set either. We film in the city with real buildings and local people as extras. My films are known for their authenticity."

"Crimax of firm set in desert. We wirr shoot it here."

Bronzini threw up his hands. "Wait a minute, wait one little minute here. I want to see the script."

"Script sent yesterday. You no get?"

"My agent got."

"Oh," Jiro said. "One moment, prease." He went to one of the RV's and returned with a copy of the script.

Bronzini snatched it from his hands. He looked at the cover. The title was visible in a cutout window.

"*Red Christmas!* What happened to *Johnny's Christmas Spirit?*"

"Title change in rewrite."

Bronzini flipped through the pages until he found some dialogue featuring his character, whose name was Mac. The first words he came to were "Up yours, you Christless commie bastards!"

"What!" Bronzini shouted. "This isn't my script."

"It is rewrite," Isuzu said calmly. "Character names are same. Some other things changed."

"But where's the little boy, Johnny? I don't see any lines for him."

"That character die on page eight."

"Dies! He's the focus of the story. My character is just the catalyst," Bronzini shouted. He pointed to a page. "And what's this crap here? This tank fight?"

"Johnny die in tank fight. Very heroic scene. Very sad. Defends home from Red Chinese invader."

"*That* wasn't in my script either."

"Story improved. Now about Red Chinese invasion of Yuma. Set on Christmas Eve. Much tinser. Many carors sung. Very much rike American Christmas story. It very beautifur."

Bronzini couldn't believe his eyes. He was reading a scene in which Christmas carolers were blown apart by Chinese shock troops throwing hand grenades.

"The fuck. Why don't you just call it *Grundy IV* and be done with it?"

"Nishitsu not own Grundy character. We try to buy. Owner refuse to serr. It important you not wear head-band in this firm. Rawsuits."

"That's the least of your problems, because I'm not doing this piece of regurgitation. If I wanted to do *Grundy IV*, I would have signed for *Grundy IV*. Savvy?"

"You sign for Christmas story. We wirr firm same."

"No chance, sake breath."

Jiro Isuzu's blank eyes narrowed at Bronzini's epithet.

Bronzini raised a placating hand. "Okay, okay, okay, I take it back. I'm sorry. I got carried away. But this isn't what we agreed to."

"You sign contract," Isuzu told him blandly. "If there is something in contract you not agree to, take up with rawyer tomorrow. Today you talk to Indian chief. Make him agree to arrow firming in varrey."

"Indian chief?"

"Rand needed in Indian reservation. Onry place to firm. Chief say yes, onry if you ask personarry. We go to meet him now."

"Oh, this just gets better and better."

"I am happy you say so. Cooperation essentiar to maintain shooting schedule."

Jiro Isuzu smiled as Bartholomew Bronzini leaned against the van and set his broad forehead against its sun-heated side. He shut his eyes.

"How could I get into a situation like this?" he said hollowly. "I'm the world's number-one superstar."

"And Nishitsu soon to be world's number-one firm company," Izusu said. "You wirr have new, greater career with us. American pubric not care for you anymore. You wirr talk to chief now?"

"All right, all right. I've always been as good as my word. Or my signature."

"We knew that."

"I'll just bet you did. But as soon as I can find a phone, I'm firing my agent."

5

Most babies are pink at birth. A few are as red as a crab.

Dr. Harold W. Smith was blue. He had blue eyes, which the doctor who had delivered him did not consider unusual. All human babies, like kittens, are born with blue eyes. Blue skin was another matter. At birth, Harold Smith—he didn't become a Ph.D. until much later in life, although it was a matter open to debate among his few friends—was as blue as a robin's egg.

The Vermont obstetrician told Smith's mother that she had given birth to a blue baby. Mrs. Nathan Smith politely informed him that she understood all babies cried at birth. She was confident her Harold's disposition would improve.

"I don't mean that he's a sad baby," the doctor said. "In fact he's the most well-behaved baby I've ever seen. I was referring to his medical condition."

Mrs. Smith had looked blank.

"Your son has a minor heart defect. It's not at all rare. Without going into the pathological details, his heart is not pumping efficiently. As a result, there's insufficient oxygen in his bloodstream. That's why his skin has that faint blue tinge."

Mrs. Smith had looked at her little Harold, who was already sucking his thumb. She firmly pulled the thumb out. Just as firmly, Harold stuck it back in.

"I thought it was these fluorescent lights," Mrs. Smith said. "Will he die?"

"No, Mrs. Smith," the doctor assured her. "He won't die. And he'll probably lose that blue tint in a few weeks."

"What a shame. It matches his eyes."

"All newborns have blue eyes. Don't count on Harry's staying blue."

"Harold. I think Harry sounds so . . . common, don't you agree, Doctor?"

"Er, yes, Mrs. Smith. But what I'm trying to tell you is that your son has impaired heart function. I'm sure he'll grow up to be a wonderful boy. Just don't expect much of him. He may be a little slow. Or he may not develop as soon as his friends, but he'll get along."

"Doctor," Mrs. Smith said firmly, "I will not allow my Harold to be a slacker." She pulled his thumb from his mouth again. After she had turned away, Harold availed himself of his other thumb. "He is heir to one of the most successful magazine publishers in this country. When he comes of age, he must be able to fulfill his responsibility to the Smith family tradition."

"Publishing isn't very strenuous," the doctor said musingly. "I think Harold will do fine." He patted Mrs. Smith on one bony knee with a familiarity the New England matron resented deeply but was too well-bred to complain about, and walked away thanking his lucky stars that he had not been born Harold W. Smith.

He winced at the small slap that sounded from her room. Mrs. Smith had caught Harold sucking on his other thumb.

Harold Smith's eyes turned gray within a matter of days. His skin remained blue until his second year, when, as the result of exercises his mother insisted he perform every day, it assumed a more normal hue.

Normal for Harold Smith, that is. Mrs. Smith was so pleased with his fishbelly-white complexion that she kept him indoors so he wouldn't lose it prematurely.

Harold Smith never went into the family publishing business. World War II had broken out and he went off to war. His cool, detached intellect was recognized early on and he found himself in the OSS, working in the European theater of operations. After the war, he switched to the new CIA, where he remained an anonymous CIA bureaucrat right through the early sixties, when CURE was founded by a young President only months before he was cut down by an assassin's bullet.

Originally set up to fight crime outside of constitutional restrictions, CURE had over the course of two decades grown into America's secret defense against internal subversion and external threats. Operating with a vast budget and unlimited computer resources, Smith was its first and so far only director. He ran CURE as he had always done, from his shabby office in Folcroft Sanitarium, CURE's cover and nerve center.

The desk had not changed in those years. Smith still held forth in the same cracked leather chair. The computers in the basement had been upgraded several times. Presidents had come and gone. But Harold Smith went on as if embalmed and wired to his chair.

If Smith could have been accused of having sartorial concerns, a person meeting him for the first time might have assumed that he selected his gray three-piece suit to go with his hair and eyes, both of which were a neutral gray. The truth was that Smith was by nature a colorless and unimaginative person. He wore gray because it suited his personality, such as it was.

One thing had changed. As he grew older, Smith's youthful pallor had darkened. His old heart defect worsened. As a consequence, his dry skin looked as if it had been dusted with ground pencil lead.

On another man, gray skin would have looked freakish. Somehow the coloring fitted Smith. No one suspected that it was the result of a congenital birth defect, any more than anyone would have believed that this harmless-looking man was second only to the President of the United States in the raw power he wielded.

But for all his power, Smith trembled inwardly this day. It was not from the awesome responsibility that weighed on his coat-hanger-like shoulders. Smith was ordinarily fearless.

This morning, Dr. Smith dreaded the imminent appearance of the Master of Sinanju, with whom he was deep in contract negotiations. It was an annual ritual, and it wrung more from his constitution than would entering an Iron Man competition.

So when Smith heard the elevator outside his second-floor Folcroft office hum as it ascended, he looked around his room for a place to hide.

Smith gripped the edges of his desk with white-knuckled intensity as the door opened.

"Greetings, Emperor Smith," said Chiun gravely. His face was an austere network of wrinkles.

Smith rose stiffly. "Master Chiun," he said in his lemony New England voice. He sounded like a dish-washing liquid. "Remo. Good morning."

"What's good about it?" Remo growled, throwing himself onto a couch. Chiun bowed and Smith returned to his seat.

"I understand you have an assignment for Remo," Chiun said distantly.

Smith cleared his throat. "That is correct," he said.

"It is good to keep him busy. For he could lapse into indolence at any time. As he was before I accepted the thankless responsibility of training him in the art of Sinanju."

"Er, yes. Well, the assignment I have in mind for him is rather unusual."

Chiun's hazel eyes narrowed. Smith recognized that narrowing. Chiun was looking for an opening.

"You have heard, perhaps, of Remo's most recent assignment," Chiun began.

"I understand it went well."

"I killed Santa Claus," Remo growled.

"That was your job," Smith told him.

"Yeah," Remo said vehemently, "and you have no

idea how much I looked forward to it. I wanted to wring his neck!"

"Remo," Chiun said, shocked. "One does not dispose of an emperor's enemies the way one would harvest a chicken. Death is a gift. To be bestowed with grace."

"I put him down with a heart-stopping blow. And that's what it felt like, putting down a dog."

"The enemies of America are all dogs," Chiun sniffed. "And they deserve to die like dogs."

"I happen to like dogs," Remo said. "This was like drowning a puppy. It made me sick. New rule, Smitty: in the future, I don't work Christmas week. Or Easter. You'll be sending me after the Easter Bunny next."

"What has that vicious rodent done now?" Chiun asked seriously. He was ignored.

Smith cleared his throat. "The assignment I had in mind should not involve any killing."

"Too bad," Remo said sourly. "I still want to dismember him. Or somebody."

"Ignore my pupil, Emperor. These moods come upon him every year at this time."

"I had a rough childhood. So sue me."

Chiun drew himself up proudly. "Since Remo's last mission went so well, I see no reason that I accompany him on this new assignment," he said, watching for the effect this opening gambit would have on Harold Smith, the inscrutable.

Smith relaxed perceptibly. Chiun's brow wrinkled.

"I am glad to hear that, Master Chiun," Smith told him. "This particular assignment is an awkward one. Your presence would be difficult to manage."

Chiun's papery lips compressed. What was this? Had Smith said such a thing merely to counter his negotiating position? How would he succeed in raising the year's tribute for his village if the Master of Sinanju's role in future assignments did not become a bargaining chip?

Chiun decided that Smith was bluffing.

"Your wisdom is insuperable," he said broadly. "For should Remo fail in his mission, should harm befall him, then I stand in readiness to complete his mission."

"Don't listen to him, Smitty," Remo warned. "He's trying to reel you in."

"Remo! I am negotiating for my village, which will be your village one day."

"You can have it."

"Such insolence!"

"Please, please," Smith pleaded. "One thing at a time. I thank you for your offer to stand in readiness, Master Chiun."

"Subject to proper compensation," Chiun added hastily.

And Smith knew there was no getting away from negotiation here and now.

"Disneyland is out of the question," Smith said quickly. "The owners say it is not for sale at any price."

"They always say that the first time," Chiun insisted.

"That was the third time."

"Those shylocks! They are trying to force you into making a wildly extravagant offer. Do not let them, Emperor. Allow me to negotiate on your behalf. I am confident that they will come to terms."

"Say good-bye to Mickey Mouse," Remo said.

Chiun turned like a silk-covered top. "Hush!" he hissed.

"However," began Smith as he opened a desk drawer, "I did manage to obtain a lifetime pass."

Chiun's face widened in pleasure. He approached Smith. "For me?" he asked, impressed.

"As a token of good faith," Smith told him. "So that this year's negotiations begin on a trustworthy note."

"Done," said the Master of Sinanju. He snatched the pass from Smith's outstretched hand.

"Nice going, Smitty," Remo said. "You're learning after all these years."

Remo braced for a rebuke from Chiun, but instead he floated up and waved the pass under his nose.

"I am going to Disneyland," Chiun said solemnly. "And you are not."

"Whoopdee doo." Remo made a circle in the air.

"I hope that the assignment Smith has for you takes

you to a harsh, inhospitable climate," Chiun said haughtily.

"As a matter of fact," Smith said, "I am sending Remo into the desert."

"A fitting place for one who is barren of respect and the milk of human kindness. I recommend the Gobi."

"Yuma."

"Even worse," Chiun cried triumphantly. "The Yuma Desert is so remote that even *I* have not heard of it."

"It is in Arizona, down by the Mexican border."

"What's down there?" Remo wanted to know.

"A movie."

"Can't I wait till it opens locally?"

"I meant that they are filming a movie in Yuma. You've heard of Bartholomew Bronzini? The actor?"

"No," Remo said, "I've heard of Bartholomew Bronzini the accountant, Bartholomew Bronzini the lingerie salesman, and Bartholomew Bronzini the sequin polisher. The actor I've never heard about. How about you, Chiun?"

"The famous Bronzini family is well-known for its many Bartholomews," Chiun said sagely. "Of course I am familiar with him."

"Well, I'm convinced," Remo said brightly.

"This is serious, Remo," Smith said. "Bronzini is filming his latest production in Yuma. There are labor troubles. The production is backed by a Japanese conglomerate. The film industry's main crafts union, the International Alliance of Theatrical Stage Employees, has been frozen out of the production. They are very upset. But the Japanese production is perfectly legal. Yesterday there was an altercation between a number of IATSE picketers and Bronzini himself. Several union members were killed. Bronzini himself was roughed up."

"Knowing Bronzini, he probably started it."

"You know Bronzini?" Smith asked in surprise.

"Well, not personally," Remo admitted. "But I read things about him. When he goes to a restaurant, they have to set an extra place for his ego."

"Gossip," Smith said. "Let's deal with the facts."

Remo sat up. "This doesn't sound like our job."

"It's very important. A film of this scale involves million-dollar expenditures. If this is successful, other Japanese films may be made in the United States. It could go a long way toward correcting our current trade imbalance with the Japanese."

"I got a better idea. We ship back all their cars. They all look alike anyway."

"Racist!" Chiun hissed.

"I didn't mean it the way it came out," Remo said defensively. "But isn't this a little out of our league?"

"Do not listen to him, Emperor," Chiun said. "He is trying to get out of this obviously important mission."

"I am not. If Smith says go, I'll go. I've never seen a movie made. It might be fun."

"Good," Smith said. "Your job will be to keep an eye on Bronzini. Make certain nothing happens to him. His acting career may be on the decline, but to many people he symbolizes the American dream. It would be very damaging if he were to come to harm. I've spoken to the President about this and he agrees that we should give this high priority, despite what would seem to be a situation not within our normal operating scope."

"Okay," Remo said. "I'm a bodyguard."

"Actually," Smith put in, "we've made arrangements for you to join the production as a stunt extra. It was the easiest way. And they are desperate for professionals willing to cross the picket lines."

"Does that mean I get to be in the film?" Remo asked.

Before Smith could answer, the Master of Sinanju cried out in a stricken voice.

"Remo is going to be in the movies!"

"Yes," Smith admitted. Then he realized what he had said and to whom, and hastily added, "In a manner of speaking."

Chiun said nothing. Smith relaxed again. Then Remo came up behind Chiun and tapped him on the shoulder. When the Master of Sinanju flounced around, Remo said in a taunting voice, "I'm going to be in a movie and you're only going to Disneyland."

Chiun whirled on Smith in a flurry of silken skirts.

"I demand to be in this movie as well!" he cried.

"That's impossible," Smith said sharply. He glowered at Remo through his rimless eyeglasses.

"Why?" Chiun demanded. "If Remo can go, I can go. I am a better actor than he will ever be."

Smith sighed. "This has nothing to do with acting. Remo will be a stunt extra. Their faces are never seen on the screen."

"That may be good enough for Remo. But I insist upon co-star billing."

Smith buried his pinched face in his hands. And it had gone so well until now. . . .

"Master of Sinanju," he said wearily, "please go to Disneyland. I cannot get you onto that movie set."

"Why not? I will accept a reasonable explanation."

Smith lifted his head. It appeared as bloodless as a turnip. His face was faintly lighter than his gray eyes.

"Believe it or not, most big-budget film sets have tighter security than our top military installations. Film people need to safeguard their ideas from competitors. Even the smallest film these days is a multimillion-dollar undertaking. The profits they realize can easily go to eight figures. I can get Remo onto that set because he's a white male. You, on the other hand, are Korean."

"I asked you for a reasonable explanation and you offer me bigotry. Are you saying that these movie people are prejudiced against Koreans?"

"No, what I am saying is that you're not appropriate as a stunt person, for obvious reasons."

"The reasons are not obvious to me," Chiun insisted.

"Remo, could you please explain it to him?"

"Sure," Remo said brightly. "It's very simple, Little Father. I'm going to make a movie and you're going to Disneyland and hang out with the mice and the ducks."

"What manner of white logic is this?" Chiun shrieked. "You are both conspiring to deny me stardom."

"You're right, Chiun," Remo said flatly. "It's a plot. I think you should wring the truth out of Smith while I'm in Yuma. You both enjoy your negotiation now. . . ."

Remo started for the door. Smith shot out of his seat as if it had sprouted porcupine quills.

"Remo," he begged, "don't leave me alone with him."

Remo paused at the door. "Why not? You two deserve one another."

"You'll need your contact's name," Smith pointed out.

"Damn," Remo said. He had forgotten that little detail.

"There!" Chiun cried. "Proof that Remo is incapable of fulfilling this mission without my help. He very nearly went off willy-nilly, without direction. He would no doubt have blundered into the wrong movie and ruined everything."

"Earlier, you told me that Remo didn't require you on missions," Smith pointed out in a reasonable voice.

"Ordinary missions," Chiun flung back. "This is an extraordinary mission. Neither of us has made a movie before this."

"I'm sorry."

"I am willing to dispense with the requirement that my presence on future assignments receive extra compensation," Chiun said stiffly.

"That's very generous of you, but my hands are tied."

"Then I will pay you. I can make up the difference when I am cast in a movie of my own."

"Nice try, Little Father," Remo said, "but I don't think it will wash. Smitty looks like he's made up his mind."

Smith nodded. "None of us have any choice in this matter. I'm sorry, Master of Sinanju, I have no way of getting you onto the set."

"That is your final word?" Chiun asked coldly.

"I am afraid so."

"Then send this white ingrate on his way," Chiun said brusquely. "And prepare yourself for a negotiation the likes of which you have never before faced."

"Sounds grim, Smitty," Remo joked. "Better tell the wife to hold supper until the new year."

"Just be certain not to specify *which* year," Chiun added darkly.

Smith went ashen. Woodenly he took a folder from his desk and slid it across to Remo.

"Everything you need to know is there," Smith told him.

Remo picked up the folder and opened it.

"I didn't know I was in *King Kong Lives*," he said.

"You were?" Chiun asked, shocked.

"Phony background," Remo explained. "According to this, I'm Remo Durock. Well, I guess I'm off to seek my fortune."

"Break a leg," Chiun called tightly.

"They say that to actors," Remo said. "I'm a stunt man. It has a whole different meaning for stunt men."

"Then break an arm, ingrate."

Remo only laughed. The door closed after him and the Master of Sinanju abruptly turned to face Smith. The elemental fury on his visage was tightly reined in, but it was all the more frightening for that reason.

Without a word, Chiun settled onto the bare floor.

Smith took a yellow legal pad from his desk, two number-two pencils, and joined him there.

"I am ready to begin negotiations," Smith said formally.

"But are you ready to negotiate?" Chiun asked flintily. "*That* is the true question."

6

Senator Ross Ralston was not above what he jokingly called "a little honest influence peddling," but he drew the line at selling out his country. Not that anyone had ever asked him to sell out America. But if they had, Senator Ralston knew what he would say. He had served his country in Korea. He still had his Purple Heart to prove it. Probably no one had been more surprised than Lieutenant Ross Ralston that day in 1953 when his Purple Heart came in.

"What's this for?" asked Ralston, who was division liquor officer in Mansan, a rear area.

"Your eye injury."

"Eye injury?" Ralston had nearly burst out laughing. He had sustained it in the mess hall while attempting to crack a soft-boiled egg. The thing wouldn't budge. He gave it a good whack with a spoon and pieces of shell flew in all directions. One got into his right eye. A medic removed it with saline solution.

"Yeah, eye injury," the major said. "According to this, you caught a shell fragment. If this is another Army snafu, we can send it back."

"No," said Lieutenant Ralston quickly. "Shell fragments. That's right. I got hit by a shell fragment. Sure. I just didn't expect a Purple Heart out of it. I was hit pretty bad, sure. But it's not like I'm blind or anything. In fact, the dizzy spells have almost stopped. So what are you waiting for? Pin that baby on."

It wasn't technically a lie. And Ross Ralston consoled himself with the knowledge that he hadn't put in for the medal. It had been automatically processed from the medic's routine notation. Ralston knew that in his plum station—arranged for by his father, Senator Grover Ralston—he couldn't hope to steal a Purple Heart.

For Ross Ralston, it had started with that Purple Heart. The little evasions, the minor distortions. A career in politics and a steady but inevitable walk to the U.S. Senate. But Arizona Senator Ralston knew where to draw the line. He did it every day. He was a member of the Senate Foreign Relations Committee. He was willing to do favors, but only as long as they didn't compromise the higher interests of the United States.

Senator Ralston never realized that the trouble with being only a little dishonest was that it was like being only a little pregnant. It was either all or nothing.

So when he was asked by no less than superstar Bartholomew Bronzini to bend the Gun Control Import Act of 1968 just a hair, he had no hesitation. Everyone knew that Bronzini was a patriot. Everyone who had seen him in *Grundy I, II,* and *III,* that is. No question of conflict of interest here. The man was as American as apple pie, even if he did look like a sicilian leg-breaker with a chromosome imbalance.

"Tell me again why you need this waiver," Ralston prompted.

They were seated in Senator Ralston's well-appointed Capitol Hill office. There was a tiny Christmas tree on his desk made of glazed clay and plastic ornaments.

"Well, sir,"—Ralston smiled at the idea of being called sir by Bronzini—"it's like this. I'm making a movie in your home state. In Yuma."

"Is that in Arizona?" Ralston asked.

"Yes, sir, it is."

"Oh. I don't get back home much anymore. Washington keeps me pretty busy."

Bronzini went on. "It involves a lot of combat situations with extras firing automatic weapons and throwing hand grenades. We can't bring these weapons into the country without a waiver from the State Department."

"I thought that you people had warehouses full of these props." He emphasized the word "props" so Bronzini would know they spoke the same language.

"We do, sir, but in this particular film we need Chinese-made AK-47's."

"Ah, I see. The recent bans."

"Actually, Senator, those are semiautomatic weapons that have been banned. We need the fully automatic versions. You see, a prop rifle is usually a fully operational weapon. It's the loads that are blanks."

"Yes, I see your difficulty, Bart. May I call you Bart?"

"You can call me Mary if it will get me the waiver. I'm in a jam here. Filming starts in two days and the only way we can get these weapons to our location in time is with a State Department waiver."

Senator Ralston was amazed at Bronzini's quiet demeanor. He half-expected him to come charging into the room screaming his demands at the top of his lungs. The man knew the cardinal rule for tapping into the Washington power flow: if you can't buy it, suck up to it.

"Bart," the senator said, jumping to his feet, "I think I can do something for you on this."

"Great," Bronzini said, cracking a relieved smile.

"But you gotta do something for me in return."

"What's that?" Bronzini asked, suddenly wary.

The senator put a friendly arm around Bronzini's shoulders.

"I'm going to have to go into these infamous smoke-filled rooms we got here in the capital and go to bat for you," he said seriously. "It would help a lot if I had a lever with my fellow committee members."

"Anything," Bronzini said. "Anything I can do, I will."

Senator Ralston smiled expansively. This was going to be easier than he had expected.

"Would you mind posing for a photo with me?"

"Oh, absolutely."

"Sally, will you come in here? And bring the camera."

Breathlessly the senator's secretary flew into the room, clutching an expensive Japanese camera. Bronzini noticed almost with a start that the red letters over the lens read "Nishitsu."

"Christ, what don't those people manufacture?" he mumbled.

"Stand right here," Senator Ralston was saying happily. He was thinking about how this photo would look framed on his office wall. For in Washington, power was in whom you knew. Connections. Now, an actor like Bartholomew Bronzini might not have much clout among his fellow power brokers, but impressing them was two-thirds of the game.

Bronzini posed for so many shots he began to feel like a *Playgirl* centerfold. The senator put his arm around him. They shook hands in three different poses. And when it was over, Senator Ralston personally saw the famous actor to the door.

"A pleasure doing business with you," he said broadly. "You'll have that waiver by close of business tomorrow."

"Thank you, sir," said Bartholomew Bronzini in his sincere but flat voice.

"Sir," Senator Ralston said to himself as he watched the actor depart, ponytail switching. "Bartholomew Bronzini called me sir."

He never dreamed that for a handful of snapshots he had just struck a deal to arm an occupying army.

Bartholomew Bronzini entered his suite at the Lafayette Hotel. Jiro Isuzu was waiting for him. Jiro bounced from his chair with the expectant look of a faithful dog presenting himself to his master.

"Yes?" he asked. It sounded like a cat's hiss.

Bronzini nodded. "Yes. He promised us the waiver by tomorrow."

"This is most excerrent, Bronzini san."

"He didn't even ask me about the production."

"I tord you my presence was unnecessary. Your name arone open many door."

"Yeah, I noticed," Bronzini said dryly. "So we have the waiver. Can you get the guns to Yuma in time for the first day's shooting?"

Jiro Isuzu smiled tightly. "Yes, guns are in Mexican depot. Arrive from Hong Kong today. Easy to get across border now that waiver is certainty. Unrike tanks."

"Tanks?"

"Yes, we require many, many Chinese tanks."

"I didn't ask him about any tanks."

"Senator not one to ask, Bronzini san. Customs. We go there now. Prease to forrow."

Bronzini arrested the wiry Japanese by grabbing a handful of his coat collar.

"Hold on Jiro," he said. "We got a waiver on the machine guns only because I promised to export them when filming's over. Tanks are another matter altogether. I don't know if this is possible."

"You have used tanks in your firms before?" Isuzu said, prying Bronzini's fingers from his person.

"Sure, but I filmed *Grundy III* in Israel. The Israelis let me use all the tanks I wanted, but they're in a perpetual state of war over there. They're used to tanks in the streets. If you want to shoot tank scenes, I suggest we move filming to Israel."

"These tanks farse."

"Farce? Did we take a sudden turn into comedy?"

"Not farce, farse. Not real. Props. Customs men, once they see this, will happiry agree to their import."

"Oh, false! You really gotta work on your L's Jiro. It's gonna hold you back later on in life."

"Japanese take pride in not pronouncing retter L." He pronounced it "eru."

"We all have our crosses to bear. So where do we go from here—or do you want me to talk to the President while I'm in town? Maybe ask him to repeal daylight-saving time for the duration of production."

"You know American President?" Isuzu asked.

"Never met the guy. It was a little joke."

"Not see humor in terring rie," Isuzu said stiffly.

"Why should you be any different?" Bronzini muttered to himself. "So what's next?"

"We meet with customs man. Then we return to Arizona, where we wirr personarry oversee the movement of these prop tanks."

"Okay, you read, I forrow," Bronzini said, gesturing broadly to the door.

As they stepped out into the plush hotel hallway, Jiro Isuzu turned to Bartholomew Bronzini.

"You have become very cooperative since we arrive in Washington, D.C. Why change of attitude?"

"It's like this, Jiro," Bronzini said, stabbing the elevator's down button. "I don't like the way I was conned into this. No shit, okay? I do *not* like it. But that's my name on that contract. I'm a man of my word. If this is the movie you want, this is the movie you get."

"Honor is a very admirable trait. We Japanese understand honor, and varue it highry."

"Good. Do you understand elevators? I'm getting old waiting for this one. What's the Japanese name for elevator anyway?"

"Erevator."

"No shit. Sounds like the American word, give or take a consonant."

"It is. Japanese take many things from American curture. Reject only what is bad."

"Which brings me to the other reason. Everywhere I turn, I see the name Nishitsu. You guys may be the wave of the future, and if you're going to be doing movies, I'm your boy."

"Yes," Jiro Isuzu said as they stepped into the elevator. "You are our boy indeed, Bronzini san."

The director of U.S. Customs was an easy man to deal with. He settled for an autograph.

"But you realize that these tanks will have to be exported when you're finished." He laughed self-consciously. "Not that we think you're trying to put one over on us—after all, what would a movie company want with actual combat vehicles? And everyone knows that the Japanese are among the most peace-loving peoples on the face of the earth. Especially after we dropped the Big One on them, eh, Mr. Isuzu?"

When Isuzu did not join in the customs director's nervous laughter, the latter recovered and went on.

"But you *do* understand that we do have regulations that must be adhered to. I can only expedite the process. The inspection procedure must be observed. It's for everyone's benefit."

"I understand perfectly, sir," Bartholomew Bronzini assured him. He shook the man's hand.

"Nice meeting you too, Mr. Isuzu. Sorry about my little joke there."

"Don't mind Jiro," Bronzini quipped. "His funny bone was surgically removed at birth."

"Oh," the director of customs said sincerely. "Sorry to hear that."

The T-62 tanks and armored personnel carriers were stored at a Nishitsu warehouse in San Luis, Mexico. They had been dismantled and shipped to Mexico as farm equipment and assembled there by Nishitsu employees. The Mexican authorities had been paid off in Nishitsu merchandise. VCR's were the most popular. Hardly anyone took any of the Nishitsu Ninja jeeps because even the Mexicans had heard about their tendency to tip over on sharp turns. The Mexican road system was almost all sharp turns.

Customs Inspector Jack Curry's knees shook as he

went through the rows of tanks in the Nishitsu warehouse with no less than Bartholomew Bronzini. They did not shake from the fearsomeness of these war machines. Although they looked pretty awesome with their long smoothbore cannon and Chinese Red Army star on the turrets. They were painted in chocolate-and-vanilla desert camouflage striations.

"This is really something," he said.

"I can hardly believe it myself," Bronzini said. "Look at these monsters."

"I didn't mean the tanks, Mr. Bronzini. I'm just so surprised that you'd actually be here in person."

Bronzini recognized a cue when he heard one.

"This is important to me, Mr. Curry. I just want everything to go smoothly."

"I can understand that. It's obvious that these tanks must have cost thousands of dollars apiece, even if they are props." Curry experimentally rapped the fender of one of them. It rang with a solid metallic sound.

"Our finest machinists assembre these," Jiro Isuzu put in proudly.

"Yes, well, if it wasn't for the fact that this is a movie, I'd almost think they were real."

"These Japanese copies of Chinese battre tank," Isuzu supplied. "Tanks are supposed to look . . . What is word?"

"Realistic," Bronzini supplied.

"Yes, rearistic. Thank you. You inspect now?"

"Yes, of course. Let's get to work."

At a signal from Isuzu, Nishitsu mechanics fell on the tank like white ants. They popped the hatches and one of them slid into the driver's compartment. He started the engine. The tank growled and began spewing diesel exhaust in the cramped confines of the warehouse.

The tank shifted its tracks, and eased from its slot. It rolled to a halt in front of Bronzini and the others.

Jack Curry entered the turret with his big flashlight. He speared light over the interior. He inspected the big cannon. It lacked a breech. Obviously a dummy. It could not possibly fire without the missing components.

The turret-mounted .50-caliber machine gun was also apparently a shell. There was no firing mechanism.

Curry wriggled his way into the driver's pit. It was so cramped he got tangled in the handlebarlike steering yoke. He poked his head up from the driver's hatch.

"It looks fine," he said. "I take it these things are completely self-propelled."

"Yes," Jiro Isuzu told him. "They wirr run like rearistic tank, but cannot shoot."

"Well, in that case, there's only one thing that prevents me from passing these things."

"What that?" Isuzu asked tightly.

"I can't seem to get out of this hatch so I can sign the proper forms," Curry said sheepishly. "Would someone give me a hand here?"

Jack Curry was amazed when Bronzini himself offered him a leather-wristband-supported hand.

"Here, just take it slow," Bronzini told him. "Put your foot on that bar." Bronzini pulled. "There. Now the other one. Uhhh, there you go."

"Thank you, gentlemen," Curry said, stepping off the hull. "Guess I'm not as spry as I once was."

"Tanks buirt for Japanese extra. Much smarrer than American," Isuzu said with a rapid-fire bowing of his head.

Bronzini thought he was going to throw his head out of whack, he was bobbing it so much.

Customs Inspector Jack Curry gave the rest of the tanks and APC's a cursory glance and then he produced a sheaf of documents. He set them on the tank's fender and began stamping them with a little rubber stamp.

When he was done, he handed them to Bronzini.

"There you are, Mr. Bronzini. Just have your people show these at the place of entry and you should have no trouble. By the way, how are you going to get them into the U.S.?"

"Don't ask me. That's not my department. Jiro?"

"It very simpre," the Japanese answered. "We wirr drive them across border into desert."

"There," Bronzini said. "Now, is there anything else?"

"No," Curry replied, grabbing Bronzini's hand with both of his and shaking it vigorously. "I would just like to tell you what a genuine thrill it was to meet you. I

really loved that scene in *Grundy II* where you said,
'Blow it out your bazookas!' to the entire Iranian Navy."

"I was up two nights writing that line," Bronzini said,
wondering if the guy was ever going to let go. Finally
Curry disengaged and left the warehouse, walking backward. He said good-bye at least thirteen times. He was
so impressed he never thought to ask Bronzini for his
autograph. It was a first. Bronzini was almost disappointed.

The tanks rolled across the border that night. They
crossed arid desert to the checkpoint, where they
stopped, forming a long snakelike column. They grumbled and coughed diesel fumes.

Customs gave the documents a cursory examination,
stamped them as "Passed," and without a fight waved
through the first invading force to cross into U.S. territory since the British Army took Washington in 1812.

The customs officials gathered around to watch. They
smiled like boys watching a parade. The Japanese drivers, their helmeted heads poking up from the drivers'
compartments like human jack-in-the-boxes, waved.
Friendly salutes were exchanged. Nishitsu cameras on
both sides flashed, and more than one voice asked, "Do
you see Bronzini? Is he in one of those things?"

7

Remo changed planes in Phoenix for Yuma. He was not
surprised, but neither was he happy to see that the Air
West plane that would take him to Yuma was a small
two-prop cloudhopper seating, at most, sixteen people
in an incredibly narrow cabin. And no stewardess.

The plane took off and Remo settled back for the
bumpy ride. He dug out Smith's folder to read his
professional credits—or rather, Remo Durock's professional credits. Remo was amazed to read that he had
been a stunt man in everything from *Full Metal Jacket*

to *The Return of Swamp Thing*. He wondered how the hell Smith could expect him to get away with that, but then remembered that one of the cardinal rules of stunt performing was to keep your face from the camera.

Remo's International Stunt Association card was clipped to the folder. He pulled it out and inserted it into his wallet. Remo was interested to read that he had won a Stuntman Award certificate for his work on *Star Trek: The Next Generation*. He had never watched *Star Trek: The Next Generation*. He looked to see if he had won an Oscar and was disappointed to find that he had not.

Less than ten minutes into the flight, the terrain under the plane's wing abruptly changed. Phoenix's suburbs gave way to desert, and the desert to mountains. The mountains were surrounded by more desert. For miles in every direction there was nothing but desolation. Only the rare ruler-straight road, passing through nothing and apparently going nowhere.

Then Yuma came into view like a surprise oasis. For the city was a virtual island in a sea of sand. It was green around the edges, thanks to the nearby Colorado River, and Remo's eyes, zeroing in on the flat lushness, recognized expansive lettuce beds fed by blue irrigation pipes. Beyond the lettuce fields, Yuma looked like any other desert community, except it was much larger than he had expected. Many of the homes had clay-red roofs. And almost every yard had a swimming pool. There were as many blue pools as red roofs.

Yuma International Airport—so called because it was a way station between the U.S. and Mexico—was much smaller than Remo had expected. The plane alighted and rolled to the tiny terminal.

Remo stepped out into the clear dry air that, even in late December, was immoderately warm. He followed the line of passengers into a terminal that seemed to consist of a gift shop around which someone had added a single ticket counter and a modest security and waiting area as an afterthought.

There was no one waiting for him in the waiting area, so Remo walked out the front entrance and looked for a studio representative.

Almost instantly a station wagon slithered up to the curb. An outdoorsy young woman with a cowboy hat over her long black hair leaned out of the window. She wore a fringed buckskin vest over a T-shirt. The shirt depicted two skeletons lounging on lawn chairs under a broiling sun and the words "But it's a *dry* heat."

"Are you Remo Durock?" she called in a chirping voice. Her eyes were gray in her open face.

Remo grinned. "Do you want me to be?"

She laughed. "Hop in, I'm Sheryl, unit publicist for *Red Christmas*."

Remo climbed in beside her.

"Where's your luggage?" she asked.

"I believe in traveling light."

"You should have brought your boots," Sheryl said as she piloted the station wagon onto the main drag.

"I thought it didn't snow in the desert," Remo remarked as he took note of the plasticky Christmas decorations that festooned the windows of every business establishment that whipped past them. They were identical to the decorations he had seen back east. Somehow, they looked tackier here in sun-soaked Arizona.

"It doesn't," Sheryl was saying. "But there are snakes and scorpions where you'll be working."

"I'll watch my step," Remo promised.

"This must be your first location shoot," Sheryl prompted.

"Actually I've been in a lot of stuff. Maybe you saw me in *Star Trek: The Next Generation*."

"You were in that? I've been a Trekker since I was six years old. Tell me which episode? I've seen them all."

Remo thought fast. "The one with the Martians," he ventured.

Sheryl's attractive face puckered. "Martians? I don't remember any Martians. Klingons, Romulans, Ferengi, yeah. But no Martians."

"They must not have aired that one yet," Remo said quickly. "I was the stunt double for the guy with the pointy ears."

Sheryl's eyes widened. "Not Leonard Nimoy?"

The name sounded familiar so Remo said, "Yes." He regretted it instantly.

"Leonard Nimoy's going to be in a *Next Generation* episode? Wow!"

"It was just a cameo role," Remo said, glancing into the file folder and the glossary of movie terms Smith had provided. "I was actually the stunt cameo double."

"I never heard of such a thing."

"I pioneered the concept," Remo said soberly. "It was quite an honor. I have my heart set on an Oscar."

"You mean an Emmy. Oscars are for films, not TV."

"That's what I meant. An Emmy. I almost got an Oscar, but some guy named Smith beat me out of it."

Sheryl nodded. "Too bad," she said. "But count yourself lucky. Unit publicists don't get Emmys or Oscars or any of that stuff. Actually, this is my first film. Until last week I was a cue-card girl at one of our TV stations here. It's such a hot potato that an experienced publicist wouldn't touch it, so I applied and here I am."

"Because of the union trouble?"

"You know it. You'll see when we get out to the location. We'll be running the gauntlet. But it's worth it. This film is going to be my ticket out of Yuma."

"Is it that bad?" Remo asked as they passed through the city and out into the desert. Remo saw lettuce beds on either side of the dusty road. They were the same beds he had seen from the air.

"It's a big, growing city, but it's in the middle of nowhere. Always has been, always will be. Uh-oh."

Remo had been watching Sheryl's chiseled-in-sandstone profile as they talked. He looked out the windshield to see what had brought the frown to her pretty face.

The road ahead was a swirl of boiling dust. Visible through it were the backs of several ponderous tracked machines. They were barely moving.

"Are those tanks?" Remo asked.

"Tanks they are. Hang on. I'm going to try to get around these dusty brutes."

Sheryl sent the car onto the soft shoulder of the road and crept around the tanks. They had stopped now, exhaling fumes into the settling dust. Remo rolled up his window.

As they sped past, Remo watched the inscrutable faces of the tank drivers that poked up from the drivers' compartments.

"Unfriendly fellows, aren't they?" Sheryl said.

"Who are they?"

"Those are the Chinese extras."

"I hate to be the one to rain on anyone's fantasy, but those guys are Japanese."

"Almost everyone on the shoot is Japanese. As for the extras, who's going to notice or care?"

"You'd think a Japanese production would be more picky about details like that. Won't *Red Christmas* play over there too?"

"You're right. I hadn't thought of that. But that's not my problem. I handle all U.S. publicity. Bronzini hired me himself. Although so far, there hasn't been much for me to do, which is why I'm making gofer runs half the time. No offense."

"None taken. Is Bronzini as big a jerk as I've heard he is?"

"I've barely spoken two words to him. But he reminds me of Grundy. He's just like him. Except for the headband. But you know, it's funny, I read everything I could on the fella before I started, and he's swearing up and down that he'd never do another Grundy movie. So I show up the first day, and what is it? A Grundy movie! They just call the character Mac. Go figure."

"Just what I thought," Remo said. "The guy's a jerk."

They cleared the line of tanks and the reason for the bottleneck became immediately apparent.

"Oh, damn, they're out in full cry today, aren't they?" Sheryl said ironically.

They stood two deep, their arms linked in front of an open chain-link fence that bisected the road. Remo wondered what a fence was doing out here in the desert, but the thought evaporated as the driver of the lead tank climbed down a track and started yelling at the picketers. He was screaming at them in Japanese. Remo didn't know Japanese, so he didn't understand what was being said. The protesters shouted back at the driver. They were making themselves perfectly understandable. They called the Japanese tank driver a gook and a slant-eyed chink. Obviously they couldn't tell a Chinese from a Japanese either.

"The little Japanese fella sure looks like he's coming to a slow boil," Sheryl mused. "Just look at his neck get red. He is *not* a happy camper."

"Wonder what he's going to do?" Remo asked as the driver clambered back into the tank. The tank engine started to run. Diesel exhaust spewed in noxious clouds.

Jerkily the tank started inching forward.

"Someone should be filming this," Sheryl said under her breath.

Remo's eyes were on the tanks. "I don't think these guys are in any mood to back down," he said.

"Which? The Japanese or the union folks?"

"Both," Remo said worriedly as the tanks churned toward the line of protesters. The protesters linked arms defiantly. If anything, they shouted louder.

As they inched past, the profiles of the drivers looked as determined and inflexible as robots. The tanks were now less than ten feet from the human bulwark.

"I don't think they're bluffing," Sheryl said in a distressed voice.

"I don't think anyone is bluffing," Remo said, suddenly grabbing the wheel. Sheryl's foot was resting on the accelerator. Remo placed his foot over hers and pressed hard.

The station wagon spurted ahead. Remo spun the wheel, sending the car skidding in front of the lead tank.

"Hey! Are you trying to get us killed?" Sheryl yelled.

"Hit the brake."

"Are you loco!"

Remo reached over and yanked the hand brake. The car lurched to a stop between the tank's rattling tracks and the linked pickets.

Sheryl found herself on the tank side. She saw the tank looming up on her like a wall on wheels. The turret cannon slid over the car roof.

"Oh, my God," she said, paralyzed. "They're plumb not stopping."

Remo grabbed Sheryl and kicked his door open. He yanked her out of the seat and flung her to one side.

Remo spun around and sized up the situation. The tank tracks were almost on top of the station wagon. Remo had a choice. He decided it would be quicker to stop the tank than to break up the protesters.

As Sheryl gave an anguished cry, the churning tank started to climb the station-wagon flank. Thick windows crunched like glass in monster teeth. Metal squealed and folded.

Remo slipped up to one side of the tank. It was tilted nose-up, and its multiton body slowly began to compress the light car down. Tires blew. The hood ruptured. Taking care not to be seen by the drivers of the other tanks, Remo took one tread in both hands while it was momentarily immobile. The track consisted of linked metal parts. Quickly Remo ran sensitive fingers along the segments. The tracks were really just a sophisticated chain of articulated steel segments, blocks, and rubber pads. He was looking for the weakest link.

He found it. A block connection. He chopped at it. It took only one chop. The metal parted and Remo backpedaled because he knew what could happen when the track began to move again.

The first sound was surprisingly like a pop. The second was a vicious whiplike rattle. The tank, stressed, had thrown its left track. The track lashed the concrete, creating a small crater that would have taken a jackhammer two minutes to excavate.

Rolling on only one track, the tank shifted suddenly. Balanced precariously atop the station wagon, it began listing to port. Remo stepped in and gave it a push.

The driver realized his problem too late. The tank toppled. It went over on its turret like a big brown turtle. The driver tried to scramble free, but all he succeeded in doing was to push his head out of his cockpit so that when the tank went over, it hit the ground sooner than it would have. He hung out of the pit, upside down. He didn't move.

Remo slipped under the tank and felt the man's

pulse. It was thready. Concussion. Remo pulled him free and stretched him out on the road.

"Is he dead?" Sheryl asked in horror. The picketers stood back, their eyes shocked. They said nothing.

"No, but he needs medical attention," Remo said.

Sheryl was about to say something when the other tank drivers marched up, and one roughly pushed her to one side. Remo came to his feet as if sprung and grabbed her attacker by the arm.

"Hey! What's your problem?" he demanded.

The Japanese hissed something Remo didn't catch and slid one foot between Remo's legs. Recognizing the beginning move of an infantile ju-jitsu maneuver, Remo allowed a cool disarming smile to warp his face. The Japanese kicked. And fell over. Remo had moved his legs aside so swiftly that his opponent's foot missed.

Remo unconcernedly stepped on his chest on his way to Sheryl's side.

"You okay?" he asked quietly.

"No, I am *not* all right. What the hell is going on here?" she raged. "They were going to run those union people right over. And look at the car. They pulverized it. That's my car, too, not a studio loaner."

The other drivers quietly lifted their unconscious comrade onto the back of the second tank. One of them shouted to the others. The one Remo had incapacitated picked himself up and, casting an angry glance in Remo's direction, hurried to his machine with disciplined alacrity.

The tanks started up again. This time they crawled around the disabled tank and the ruin that had been Sheryl's station wagon.

"Oh, my God. They're going to do it again," Sheryl moaned.

"Everyone link arms!" one of the picketers shouted. "We'll show them how Americans stand up to bullies."

Not every protester obeyed. A few retreated.

Remo dived into the picketers.

"I've got no time to argue with you people," he said. "Another place and time, maybe. But not today." He grabbed wrists and squeezed nerves. Union members yelled and screamed as if stung. But they ran in the direction Remo propelled them. In moments, the gateway was clear of human obstruction.

The tanks wound around the road and through the open fence. Once the first one passed, no one had the stomach to get in their way again. The line seemed to go on forever. The drivers looked neither to the right nor to the left. They might have been components of their tanks, and not the operators.

"This is crazy," Sheryl said in an incredulous voice. "What got into them? This is only a movie."

"Tell them that," Remo said.

Sheryl spanked dust off her hat.

"You did a nice job of breaking up those picketers, by the way," she said. "I'd swear they would have run them down like yellow dogs."

"I wonder," Remo said.

"Wonder what?"

"I wonder if we're not on the wrong side of this dispute."

He was watching the chocolate rump of the last tank as it spilled sand from its rolling tracks. It looked as inexorable as the wheel of fate.

"Well, come on, then. We'll have to hoof it on to base camp. Jiro's going to hear about this."

"Who's Jiro?"

"Jiro Isuzu. The executive producer. He's a stiff-necked SOB. Makes those tank guys seem like little old ladies. Except Jiro's so polite you want to bust him in the mouth sometimes. I know I do."

8

"Please, Master of Sinanju," Harold Smith said in a dry, cracked voice. "It's nearly three A.M. We can continue negotiations tomorrow."

"No," replied the Master of Sinanju. "We are nearly done. Why break off such delicate talks now, when we are so close to an understanding?"

Dr. Harold W. Smith didn't feel close to an understanding. He felt close to exhaustion. For nearly nineteen hours the Master of Sinanju had led him through the most Byzantine contract negotiations of their long and difficult association. It would have been difficult enough, Smith thought, but they were conducting these negotiations on the hard floor of Smith's office because, as Chiun explained it, although Smith was the emperor and Chiun merely the royal assassin, in honest negotiations, all such distinctions were dispensed with. Smith could not sit on what Chiun insisted was his throne, and Chiun would not stand. So they sat. Without food, without water, and without bathroom breaks.

After nearly all night, Chiun still looked as fresh as an origami sunflower. Smith's leaden face was the color of a clam's shell. He felt dead. Except his stomach. The combination of no food and nervous distress had triggered a flow of stomach acid and was eating into his peptic ulcer. If this didn't end soon, Smith feared, he would have no stomach lining left.

"This year," Chiun recited, looking at the half-curled scroll that was held to the floor by tiny jade weights, "we have agreed to a modest ten-percent increase in the gold payment. In consideration of the new situation."

"Explain to me again why I must pay more gold if the new arrangement does not require you to accompany Remo on his assignments," Smith said dully. "Shouldn't that realistically mean less service on my part?"

Chiun raised a wise finger. "Less service from the Master of Sinanju, yes. But more service from Remo. You will be working him harder; therefore he is worth more."

"But shouldn't we first deduct the additional expense you insisted upon when we originally settled on your expanded role and then negotiate Remo's price?"

Chiun shook his aged head. "No. For those are the terms of the old contract. Since we are entering into an entirely new arrangement, they will only cloud the issue."

"I feel the issue is already clouded," Smith said unhappily. His patrician face looked like a lemon that had been sucked of all moisture.

"Then let me clarify it for you," Chiun went on, adding in a low voice, "once again. Ten percent more gold for Remo's added burden. And then, in the form of precious stones and bolts of silk and weights of rice, there is my new fee."

"If you are not taking part in Remo's missions," Smith wondered, "what *is* your part? I completely fail to understand."

"While Remo is enjoying the broadening effects of travel to exotic far-off lands like Arizona—"

"Arizona is a western state," Smith interjected sharply. "It is hardly exotic."

". . . far-off western states, exotic by Korean standards," Chiun continued, "to partake of their splendid sights . . ."

"A desert. It's in the center of wilderness and desolation."

". . . meeting famous personalities, such as Bartholomew Banzini . . ."

Smith sighed. "Bronzini. And I wish you would stop throwing that back in my face. It was your idea that Remo undertake the Santa Claus assignment alone."

"A mistake on my part," Chiun allowed. "I am willing to admit it—if you will make certain concessions."

"I cannot—repeat, cannot—get you on that movie set," Smith said firmly. "You must understand the security problems. It's a closed set."

Chiun's parchment face fell into a frown.

"I understand. We will speak no more of it."

Smith's tensed shoulders loosened. They tightened again when Chiun resumed speaking.

"The stipulated amount is to cover my new added burdens."

Smith loosened his Dartmouth tie. "New burdens?"

"The burdens I assumed during Remo's last assignment," Chiun said, knowing that the unloosened tie was the first crack in the man's stubborn armor.

"You stayed home," Smith protested.

Chiun raised a solemn finger. Its long nail gleamed.

"And worried," Chiun said morosely.

The yellow pencil in Smith's bony fingers snapped.

"Perhaps there is a way," he groaned. "There *must* be."

Chiun's agate-hard eyes glistened. "There is always a way," he intoned. "For a ruler as resourceful as you."

"Allow me to use the telephone."

"I will waive the no-telephone rule," Chiun said magnanimously. "Provided it furthers swift resolution of our talks."

Smith started to push himself to his feet. He froze. He looked down at his crossed legs in constipated bewilderment.

"They won't move," he croaked. "They must have fallen asleep."

"You did not feel them falling asleep?" Chiun asked.

"No. Can you help me?"

"Certainly," said Chiun, rising. He stepped past Smith's offered hand and to his desk, where he reached for the telephone. He paused. "Which telephone instrument do you wish?" he inquired.

"I really wish to be helped to my feet," Smith said.

"In good time. You required a telephone. Let us deal with your paramount desire first, then the lesser ones."

Smith wanted to tell the Master of Sinanju—no, he wanted to scream at the Master of Sinanju—that right at this moment, more than anything else he desired the use of his legs. But he knew that Chiun would only evade the issue. He saw the telephone as the most direct indirect path to his goal.

"Give me the ordinary phone," Smith said.

The Master of Sinanju ignored the dialless red telephone that was Smith's direct line to the White House and lifted the more elaborate office telephone. He placed it at Smith's angular knees with a magnificent flourish.

Smith lifted the receiver and began dialing.

"Hello, Milburn?" he said. "Yes, I know it's three o'clock, but this could not wait until morning. Please do not shout. This is Harold."

Chiun cocked a delicate ear in the direction of the conversation.

"Your *cousin* Harold," Smith repeated. "Yes, *that* Cousin Harold. I have a very big favor to ask of you.

Are you still publishing those . . . er, magazines? Good. I have a person here who is interested in writing for you."

"Tell him I am an accomplished poet," Chiun hissed, not understanding what this had to do with going to Arizona, but hoping that Smith knew what he was doing and had not cracked from the strain of negotiations.

"No, Milburn. I *know* you don't publish poetry. This man is very versatile. If you can provide him with a press pass to his latest film, I am certain he can get an interview with Bartholomew Bronzini."

Chiun smiled happily. Smith had not cracked. Although he was babbling.

"I didn't realize there was no such thing as a press pass to get on a movie set. Oh, is that how it works? Yes, well, if you can work out the details, I can guarantee that Bronzini will accept. My friend is very, very hard to refuse."

Chiun beamed. He gave Smith the American A-okay symbol. Smith put his finger in his ear to hear better. Chiun wondered if that was a mystic countersign or an expression of annoyance.

"His name is Chiun," Smith went on. "That *is* his first name. I think." Smith looked up.

"It is my name," Chiun told him. "I am not a Bob or a John or a Charlie who requires an additional name so that no one will confuse him with other persons."

"It is his pen name," Smith said, fearful of extending an already too-involved conversation. "Yes, thank you. He'll be there."

Smith hung up with nerveless fingers.

"It is all arranged," he said. "You'll have to go through the formality of an interview."

"Of course. I am certain if these people want me to write their movie script, they must be assured of my unsurpassed talents to undertake so illustrious a task."

"No, no, you don't understand. You won't be writing any such thing. My cousin Milburn publishes movie fan magazines. You will be going to the set of *Red Christmas* as a correspondent for one of their magazines."

"I will be writing letters?" Chiun squeaked. "To whom?"

"Not that kind of correspondent. I will be glad to explain this to you in greater detail if you will just help me to my feet."

"At once, Emperor," Chiun said happily. He knelt before Smith and inserted long fingers into the back of Smith's knees.

"I feel nothing," Smith said when Chiun's hands withdrew.

"That is good," Chiun assured him.

"It is?"

"It means that when I lift you, there will be no pain."

And there wasn't. Smith didn't even feel the usual creaking in his arthritic knee when Chiun assisted him to his feet and into his leather chair. Relieved, Smith briefed the Master of Sinanju on his job interview. Then, going to his computer terminal, he began inputting through the keyboard.

"What are you doing?" Chiun asked.

"The editor who will interview you requires clips of your past articles."

"I have written no articles. Only poetry. Shall I go home and bring them?"

"No, don't even mention your poetry. My computer is faxing him copies of your articles, which will be fabrications, of course."

When Chiun opened his mouth as if to protest, Smith added hastily, "It will get you to Arizona faster."

"I will submit myself to your greater judgment."

"Good," said Smith as he shut down his computer. "Tickets will be waiting for you at the local airport. Now, if you'll excuse me, I'm going to stretch out on the couch and try to get some sleep."

"Very well, Emperor," said the Master of Sinanju, bowing as he slipped from the room in monklike silence.

Smith wondered why the Master of Sinanju left without the formalities of farewell he usually overindulged in.

He found out ten minutes later when, just as he was about to drop off, he got a charley horse in his right leg.

"Argghh!" Smith howled. The pain increased until he thought he could not stand it anymore. Then his other leg began to clench up.

The cab deposited the Master of Sinanju at the address on lower Park Avenue. He took the elevator to the eighth floor and turned right until he saw the red-and-blue neon sign that said STAR FILE GROUP.

Chiun's nose wrinkled. Was this a magazine publisher or a Chinese restaurant?

Chiun approached the receptionist's desk and bowed.

"I am Chiun, the author," he said gravely.

"Mr. Chiun to see you, Don," the receptionist called over her shoulder so loudly the Master of Sinanju winced with the gracelessness of it all.

"Send him in," a pleasantly grumpy voice called from an open office.

Head erect, Chiun floated into the room. He bowed to the young man who sat at a corner desk. He looked like a koala bear that had been rolled in brown sugar. Chiun saw that the illusion was helped by noticeable beard stubble. He suddenly noticed the walls. They were covered with posters of famous people. Nearly nude women wrestlers predominated. Chiun averted his eyes from the wanton display.

"Sit down, sit down," the man said diffidently.

"You are Donald McDavid, the famous editor?" Chiun inquired.

"And you must be Chiun. Happy to meet you."

"Chiun, the *author*," Chiun corrected with a finger.

"Milburn gave me your clips this morning. I've been looking them over. Very interesting."

"You like them?"

"The pictures are nice," Donald McDavid said.

"Pictures?" Chiun asked, wondering if he should have introduced himself as Chiun the author and artist.

He accepted a manila folder filled with magazine clippings. The photographs showed scenes from American films. The copy, however, appeared to be excerpts from a Korean personal-hygiene manual. Was Smith mad? Insulting him with such tripe?

"You *do* write in English, don't you?" McDavid asked as a curly-haired young man came in with a tray containing a Dr. Pepper and a mug of black coffee.

"Of course," Chiun said.

"Good, because I can't read Chinese, and neither can our readers. They're fussy about stuff like that. We'd get letters."

"This is Korean," Chiun told McDavid as he sipped his coffee experimentally. He fingered an ice cube from his Dr Pepper and plopped it into the coffee. He let both sit.

"I can't read Korean either," he said dryly.

Chiun relaxed. It was amazing. This white was nearly illiterate, yet he edited important magazines. Chiun made a mental note to take the folder with him. He would not have his reputation as a poet sullied by Smith's nonsense.

"Well, I can't tell a thing from these clips, but that's your byline on them, and Milburn says you come highly recommended. So you're hired."

"In my field, I am the best," Chiun assured him.

"I've spoken with the publicity people on *Red Christmas*. They're not real high on letting anyone on set so early. But Bronzini overruled them. So you're in. I've put together some assignment sheets. We'll want an interview with Bronzini, as well as a set-visit piece, a director's profile, and whatever else you can get. See who's on the set when you get there. Talk to them. We'll sort it out when you get back."

Chiun leafed through the assignment sheets. His eyes narrowed when he saw the payment rates.

"Do you publish poetry?" he asked suddenly.

"No one publishes poetry anymore."

"I do not speak of common American poetry, but the finest Korean poetry. Ung."

"God bless you."

Chiun's face expressed indignation. "Ung is its name," he said. "I have recently been composing an ode to the melting snowcap on Mount Paektusan. That is a Korean mountain. It is currently 6,089 stanzas long."

"Six thousand stanzas! At a dollar a word, it will eat up half the yearly budget on one of our magazines."

"Yes," Chiun said hopefully.

"Sorry. We don't publish poetry." McDavid indicated a corkboard on the wall over his desk.

Chiun peered up at it. Rows of cover proofs hung from hooks. The latest *Star File* cover showed a half-nude white female draped over a spaceship. Beside it was a magazine called *Fantasmagoria*. A man in a dried-skin mask was butchering a young woman on that cover. It looked very real, and Chiun wondered if it was for cannibals. Beside that was something called *Gorehound*, which Chiun took to be aimed at pit bulls. Or possibly their owners. And next to that was *Stellar Action Heroes*.

"Do people read these?" Chiun sniffed.

"Most just look at the pictures. That reminds me. I'd better give you a few issues so you know our house style. Write in the present tense. Lots of quotes."

Chiun accepted a stack of magazines. He surreptitiously slipped Smith's folder of spurious clippings into the stack.

"I will give these my undivided attention," Chiun promised.

"Fine," said Donald McDavid, reaching for his coffee. He took a sip.

"Ugh. It's cold," he said. He tried the Dr Pepper and pronounced it flat.

Leaning back in his chair, Donald McDavid called through the door, "Eddie, can you get me a milk?

"Milk is bad for you," Chiun pointed out. "It suffocates the blood vessels."

"I'm working on my first heart attack," Donald McDavid said. "One last thing. We buy all rights."

"That is your privilege," said Chiun, adding, "My right to vote is yours for a dollar a word."

Donald McDavid burst out laughing as he accepted a glass of milk from his assistant. He sipped it experimentally, made a face, and reached for a salt shaker that stood beside the telephone. As Chiun watched in horror, he salted his milk and drained it down without stopping.

"I'll want your first copy on my desk in two weeks," he said, wiping milk from a nearly invisible mustache.

"In case you are not here then, who is your next of kin?" Chiun asked.

Outside the building, Chiun hailed a taxi. The driver took him to LaGuardia Airport. At his terminal, Chiun counted out the fare in coins.

"What, no tip?" the driver barked.

"Thank you for reminding me," Chiun said. He handed the driver a stack of magazines.

"*Gorehound!*" the driver called after him. "What the hell am I supposed to do with these?"

"Study them. Learn from them. Perhaps you too may rise to the exalted station where a dollar a word is your lot in life."

9

Jiro Isuzu was very, very apologetic.

"So very sorry," he said. He bowed from the waist, his eyes downcast. The wind was picking up, blowing loose desert sand into his dry mask of a face. Remo wondered if his downcast eyes reflected humility or the need to protect them from the abrasive sand. They stood in the shelter of the base-camp tents.

"They acted like they plumb owned the road," Sheryl shouted.

"Japanese extra not speak Engrish," Isuzu said. "I wirr reprimand them in crear terms."

"So what about my car?" Sheryl asked sternly.

"Studio wirr reimburse. You may have car of choice. If you wirr accept a Nishitsu wagon, we will throw in furr option package."

"All right," Sheryl said in a half-mollified voice. "But I don't want one of your Ninjas. I hear they tip whenever the wind changes direction."

"Excerrent. And I am again sorry for your inconvenience. Now, if you prease, there is a problem for you to dear with. A correspondent from *Star Fire* magazine is on way. I did not want press, but Bronzini san insist. Stuck. You take care of this man, okay?"

"Good. I'd like to do something other than the daily Fedex run."

"Shooting schedule moved up, by the way. Camera rorr tomorrow."

"Tomorrow is two days before Christmas. This isn't going to sit well with the crew."

"You forget, crew Japanese. Not care about Christmas. If American crew unhappy, they may find work ersewhere. Firming begin tomorrow."

At that, Jiro Isuzu walked off. His spine didn't waver a millimeter from the vertical.

"What American crew?" Sheryl muttered. "There's Bronzini, the military technical adviser, the stunt coordinator, and little old me." She sighed. "Well," she said to Remo, "now you've met Jiro. Quite a piece of work, isn't he?"

"Nishitsu makes cars?" Remo asked blankly.

"They make everything. And they act like they hung the moon and optioned the sun. Well, I guess I've got a reporter to contend with. See you around the set."

"Where do I find the . . ." Remo looked into his folder. ". . . stunt coordinator?"

"You got me," Sheryl said, starting for one of the striped tents. "Find an A.D. with a walkie-talkie and ask for Sunny Joe."

Remo looked around. The tents had been set up in a shallow arroyo created by bulldozers. One was still throwing up sand to form bulkwarks against the wind. Men rushed in all directions, like ants. Every one of them was Japanese.

Remo collared one with a walkie-talkie.

"Help me out, pal," he said. "I'm looking for Sunny Joe."

"Sony Joe?"

"Close enough."

The man touched the walkie-talkie clipped to a nickel-cadmium belt battery pack and began speaking in rapid guttural Japanese into the microphone suspended before his mouth. He listened to his earphones. The only thing Remo understood was the name "Sony Joe."

Finally the man pointed north.

"Sony Joe that way. Okay?"

"Thanks. What does he look like?"

The Japanese shook his head curtly. "No Engrish speakuu. Okay?" Remo took that to mean he didn't speak English.

Remo trudged off in the direction indicated. He peeked into his folder and learned that an A.D. was an assistant director. He wondered how someone could be an assistant director on an English-language film and not speak English.

As he walked along, he kept his eyes open for Bartholomew Bronzini. There was no sign of the world-famous actor. Remo was also surprised to see no cacti. This was scrub desert. Just sand and the occasional dry bush. He looked back and noticed that he wasn't leaving footprints. He decided that someone might notice, so he began walking on the balls of his feet. That way, he left the same impression as a twelve-year-old boy.

Remo climbed a sandhill and was surprised to see a vast panorama of tanks and armored personnel carriers arrayed in a flat area entirely surrounded by fresh sandhills. Men in Chinese military uniforms were wiping down the machines, which had already picked up a dusting of beige sand.

Remo decided that the group of uniformed men who were practicing falls from a nearby hill were stunt men. One of them had to be the one he wanted.

As he approached, Remo saw, behind a flat rock, a man aiming a rifle. The man was white, with a weathered face and sun-squint eyes. He pulled the trigger.

Suddenly one of the Japanese extras clutched his chest. Red fluid gushed from between his fingers.

Remo floated to the base of the sandhill and floated around it. He slipped up behind the man just as he squeezed off a second shot.

Remo took him by the back of the neck. He tried to bring him to his feet, but found his arms were only long enough to bring him up to eye level. The man topped him by three heads.

"Give me that," Remo growled, grabbing the weapon. It looked homemade, like an antique.

"What's your problem, friend?" the man demanded.

"I saw you shoot that man."

"Good for you. Now, if you'll give it back, I'll go shoot a few more."

"This isn't how we settle union disputes in America."

"Union! You don't think . . ." The man started laughing. "Oh, this is rich," he burst out.

"What's so funny?" Remo asked. He let the man drop and broke open the weapon. It had a stainless-steel drum magazine on top. Instead of bullets, it contained glass marblelike objects. They sloshed with reddish liquid.

"You are. You think I really shot that guy. That's an air gun."

"A BB rifle can kill if you hit a soft spot," Remo said, lifting out one of the marbles for a closer look.

"Be careful with that. The prop master will have my hide if you break it. That thing is handcrafted. Only sixteen like it in the world."

One of the Japanese extras came down the sandhill.

"Sunny Joe. Why you stop?" he called. Remo saw the splash of red that marred his blouse front.

"Wait a minute," Remo blurted out. "*You're* Sunny Joe?"

"That's what they call me. So who are you?"

"Remo."

The man called Sunny Joe seemed startled by the name.

"What's your last name?" he asked.

"Durock," Remo said after a pause.

Sunny Joe looked disappointed with Remo's answer. That expression gave way to an annoyed one.

"How the hell long you been in this business, son?" he barked. "Not to know an air gun when you see one?"

"Sorry," Remo said. "With all the union troubles, I guess I jumped to a conclusion."

"No harm done, I guess," Sunny Joe relented. He searched Remo's face as if looking for his soul. "And I can use a paleface. Half these damn Japs can't speak

English. Come on. We're doing practice bullet hits. Let's see what kind of moves you got."

Remo followed the man up the sandhill.

"The thing you gotta remember, Remo," he was saying, "is that Bronzini likes to be as realistic as possible. You stand right here. I'll drop back and pop you one. When you take the hit, don't fall, corkscrew. Pretend you're being hit by a sledgehammer, not a bullet. We want real impact up on that screen."

Remo shrugged as Sunny Joe loped back to his shelter. He was a tall man, Remo saw. Nearly seven feet tall, and while he looked imposing, Remo noticed that he had lanky limbs. He was sixty if he was a day, but he moved like a man ten years younger.

Sunny Joe dropped into a crouch and took aim. The gun coughed. Remo's acute vision perceived the red sphere zip toward him. He set his feet.

But Remo had been trained for years to move out of the way of bullets. Even harmless ones. Reflexively he sidestepped the bullet. To cover himself, he twisted and hit the sand. He looked up.

Sunny Joe lumbered up to him, anger on his face.

"What the hell happened?" he bellowed.

"I corkscrewed."

"You corkscrewed *before* the round struck. I didn't see the blood splatter. What's the matter with you? Bucking for an Oscar?"

"Sorry," Remo said, brushing sand off his clothes. "Try again?"

"Right. This time, wait for the round."

As they returned to their marks, a trio of helicopters clattered overhead. Their noise filled the valley floor like jangling scrap metal.

"Damn," Sunny Joe muttered. "They're gonna be doing that all through production. Choppers from the Marine Air Station, I'll bet. Joyboys with nothing better to do than overfly the shoot. They're probably asking themselves which tiny speck is Bronzini. Damn fools."

"They'll get tired of it sooner or later," Remo ventured.

"Sure, they will. But that's just the Marines. There's an Army proving ground a few miles north, and ol'

Luke Air Force Range is due east of here. We'll have F-16's up the wazoo from now till Valentine's Day."

"You don't sound like you enjoy your work much."

"Work, hell, I was retired until the Japs came along. I'm over sixty, man. This industry feeds off youth, even in the stunt profession. I came back to the reservation to wither away, so to speak. Then Bronzini came along and asked to use this part of the reservation."

"This is Indian land?"

"Damn straight. Bronzini has been pulling strings everywhere to mount this production. Had everyone eating out of his hand. Until he slammed into the chief. The chief knew who he was, of course, but wouldn't let on. He said part of the price of letting the reservation be used was my participation. I'm a proud man, but I got this business in my blood, so I said what the hell. I took it. Maybe it'll lead to something."

"You don't look Indian."

"Not many Indians look Indian anymore, if you want to know the truth of it."

"What tribe?"

"You never studied them in school, I'll tell you that much. We're practically extinct. My Indian name is Sunny Joe. It's kind of a tribal nickname, I guess you'd have to say. My legal name's Bill Roam. But call me Sunny Joe. Everyone does. That's Sunny with a U, not an O. Okay, get on your mark."

Remo took his position. This time, when the pellet gun coughed, he closed his eyes. The bullet took him square in the chest. He twisted, fell, and rolled.

"Better," Sunny Joe called out to him. "Now, one of you others give it a try."

None of the Japanese on the sandhill moved.

Sunny Joe got up from his marksman's crouch and tried to make his desires known with sign language. Finally he took one of the Japanese by the scruff of the neck and marched him to the mark.

Remo thought the Japanese extra was going to punch Sunny Joe in the stomach. He didn't look happy to be manhandled. Remo decided that he was just touchy.

He settled back to watch, thinking that he had a lot to learn if he was going to pass as a stunt professional.

Bartholomew Bronzini was surprised to see that the usual IATSE protesters were not picketing the entrance gate to the Indian-reservation location site. He wondered if it had anything to do with the upended tank and the crushed station wagon.

He horsed his Harley around the wreckage and raced up the winding road to the base camp. He didn't bother stopping in front of the production tent. He slammed the Harley through the flap and crashed into a table.

Bronzini leapt free of the bike before it slid into the tent wall. The candy-striped fabric tore with a shivery rip. But no one noticed that, least of all Jiro Isuzu.

Isuzu found himself staring into the wrathful Neapolitan visage of Bartholomew Bronzini, the Bronze Bambino. And there was nothing baby-faced about him today.

"What the hell is going on?" Bronzini thundered.

"Prease to speak in respectfur tone," Jiro said. "I am producer."

"You're the fucking line producer," Bronzini snarled. "I want to speak to the executive producer."

"That Mr. Nishitsu. Not possible to speak to him. In Tokyo."

"They don't have phones in Tokyo? Or doesn't he speak English either?"

"Mr. Nishitsu in secrusion. Not a young man. He visit set once camera rorr. You wirr meet him then."

"Yeah? Well, you deliver him a message for me."

"Gradry. What is message?"

"I don't like being conned."

"Not know that word."

"Lied to. You understand 'lie'?"

"Prease to exprain," Jiro Isuzu said stiffly. Bronzini noticed he was not backing down. Bronzini respected that. He lowered his voice, although still angry.

"I was just on the phone to Kurosawa."

"That is breach of protocor. You not directing this firm."

"Here's a flash, Jiro, baby." Bronzini sneered. "Neither is Kurosawa. In fact, he never heard of *Red Christmas*. Not only that, but he sounded pretty fucking vague about the concept of Christmas all by itself."

"Ah, I understand now. There was a probrem. Kurosawa unabre to direct *Red Christmas*. Have been meaning to inform you of this unhappy act. So sorry."

"Don't 'so sorry' me. I'm sick of 'so sorry.' And I'm still waiting for that explanation."

"I was assured by Mr. Kurosawa's representative that he wourd be abre to direct firm. It appears we were misinformed. Serious breach of etiquette, for which satisfaction wirr be demanded and aporogies no doubt tendered by the responsibre persons."

"Satisfaction! My only satisfaction would have been working with Kurosawa. He's a master."

"This very regrettabre. Mr. Nishitsu himserf wirr no doubt convey his regrets to you when he arrive."

"I can hardly fucking wait," Bartholomew Bronzini said acidly. He threw up his hands. "So who *is* directing?"

Isuzu bowed. "I have that honor," he said.

Bronzini stopped dead. His droopy dachshund eyes narrowed, if that was possible. His wildly gesticulating hands paused in the air, as if captured in amber.

His "You?" was very tiny but very, very vehement.

Jiro Isuzu took an involuntary step backward.

"Yes," he said softly.

Bartholomew Bronzini stepped up to him and leaned over. Even leaning, he towered over the Japanese. And Bronzini was not very tall.

"How many films have you directed, Jiro, baby?"

"None."

"Then it's real sporting of you to offer to pick up the pieces," Bronzini said airily. "After all, this is only a fucking six-hundred-million-dollar epic. It's only my comeback film. It's not even important. Hell, why bother with a director at all? Why don't we all just jump in the sand and play until we get enough footage to edit down into a cartoon? Because that's what this is developing into—a fucking joke."

"I wirr do good job. I promise."

"No. No chance. I'm putting my foot down now. Production stops. We do a search. We find an experienced director. Then we start. Not before. You read me?"

"No time. Camera rorr tomorrow."

"Tomorrow is the day before Christmas Eve," Bronzini told him as if speaking to a very slow child.

"Mr. Nishitsu move up schedule."

"Let me see the shooting schedule."

"Not avairabre. So sorry."

"Fine. Excellent. It's not available. There's no shooting schedule, no director. All we have is a star, more tanks than Gorbachev, and you. Wonderful. I'm going back to the hotel and ask the head chef to help me hold my head in the oven, because I'm so blind pissed off, I'd probably screw it up."

Fists clenched, Bronzini started for the tent flap.

"No," Jiro said. "We need you."

Bronzini halted. He whirled. He couldn't believe Isuzu was pressing the point. The guy had nerve.

"For what?" he asked flatly.

"Talk to Marines and Air Force."

"About what?"

"Because we start earry, not arr extra arrive from Japan. We wirr ask to use American servicemen. Arso, equipment. Big parachute drop shoot tomorrow."

"I don't remember a parachute drop."

"Parachute drop in new draft. Written rast night."

"Who put that in?" Bronzini asked in a suspicious voice.

"I do so."

"Why aren't I in the least surprised, Jiro? Tell me that. Why?"

Isuzu coughed into his hand. "Script mine," he said defensively. "Mine and Mr. Nishitsu's."

"Let's not forget who wrote the first draft," Bronzini said bitterly. "You remember the pre-tank draft, the one set in Chicago?"

"You will receive proper screen credit for contribution, of course. Come. Prease to forrow me."

"You want my help, you gotta help me in return."

"Beg pardon?" Isuzu said.

"This union thing. I want it solved. By tomorrow. That's my price for my cooperation."

Jiro Isuzu hesitated. "Union dispute wirr be sorved before camera rorr. Acceptabre to you?"

Bronzini blinked. "Yeah. It is," he said, taken by surprise.

Jiro Isuzu stepped from the tent smartly. Bronzini followed him with his volcanic blue eyes. With a grunt of surprise, he wrestled his Harley up from the ground and pushed it from the tent.

On his way out, he nearly ran down Sunny Joe Roam, who was trailed by several Japanese extras and one American.

"I got them to corkscrew just like you said, Mr. Bronzini," Sunny Joe rumbled.

"Fine. Now go learn Japanese," Bronzini said as he mounted the bike and kicked the starter. "Because you're going to need it."

Roam laughed. "Once you get to know him," he whispered to Remo, "he's a great kidder. Here, let me introduce you. Bart, I want you to meet Remo. He's our stunt American. He'll be doubling for you."

Remo put out his hand, thinking that if he was going to watch over Bronzini, he'd better swallow his dislike for the man and make friends.

"I'm a big fan," he lied.

"Then why don't I feel a breeze?" Bronzini sneered, ignoring the offered hand. He roared off after a Nishitsu production van.

"Wonder what's eating him?" Sunny Joe said.

"He always acts like his jockstrap is too tight," Remo said. "I read it in a magazine."

The base commander of the Yuma Marine Air Station was stoic when Bartholomew Bronzini stepped into his office. Jiro Isuzu hung unobtrusively behind him.

"Let me say from the start," Colonel Emile Tepperman said brusquely, "that I've never seen one of your films."

Bartholomew Bronzini allowed a sheepish expression to settle over his hangdog face.

"It's not too late," he quipped. "They're all on video."

His crooked grin was not returned. He wasn't sure if that was because the Marine officer was a no-nonsense type, or that this was further proof, if any was needed, that Bartholomew Bronzini's strong suit was not stand-up comedy. He also wasn't sure why he was playing along with this dog-and-pony show. As angry as he felt, he was a professional. He was going to finish this movie on schedule—whatever the schedule was—and get the hell out.

"Sit down and tell me what it is you want the Corps to do for you," Colonel Tepperman suggested.

"We'd like the use of your base for a day or two," Bronzini said. "Starting tomorrow."

"Funny time to be starting a film. So close to the holidays."

"We'll be shooting through the holidays," Bronzini told him. "Can't be helped, sir. I figure it might be less disruptive with your soldiers on leave."

"I don't have the authority to grant such permission," the colonel said slowly, eyeing Isuzu. "We have an ongoing signals intelligence operation at this base."

"Who does have the authority?" Bronzini asked coolly.

"The Pentagon. But I hardly think they'd entertain—"

"So far, we have received great cooperation from your State Department, Congress, and rocal raw authorities," Jiro Isuzu broke in urgently.

The colonel considered the Japanese's words.

"I suppose I could make a phone call," he said reluctantly. "How many days would this entail?"

"Two," Isuzu said. "Not more than three. We would also require the use of uniformed personnel."

"For what?" Colonel Tepperman asked suspiciously.

"As extras."

"You want to use *my* people in *your* movie?"

"Yes, sir," Bronzini said, catching the ball. "I did it all the time in the *Grundy*s. Hollywood extras don't move or act like real soldiers. They don't know how to handle weapons realistically."

The colonel nodded. "I stopped going to war movies years ago. Couldn't stand the imbecilic things I saw. You know, in one film they had some idiot running around with an U.S. M-120 grenade launcher attached to a Kalashnikov rifle."

"That will never, repeat, never happen in this film," Bronzini promised. "We know our weapons."

Colonel Tepperman reached for his telephone.

"Okay. I'll make that call," he said decisively. "Do you have a part for a Marine colonel in this movie of yours?"

Bronzini looked to Jiro with a raised eyebrow.

"Yes," the Japanese said smoothly. "This very ambitious firm. We have parts for as many men as you have. But they must bring own weapons. We wirr need many authentic American weapons."

"We have all you need."

"Of course, they must be roaded with prop burrets."

"Damn straight," Colonel Tepperman said as he listened to the ringing in his phone receiver. "Hello, put me through to the commandant of the Marine Corps."

The base commander at Luke Air Force Range was stubborn.

"I'm sorry, gentlemen, but I can't allow this," said Colonel Frederick Davis. "I appreciate what you have in mind, but I can't have a movie crew tramping all over my base. Too irregular."

"We wirr not require to be on the base for very rong," Jiro Isuzu said eagerly. "An afternoon at most." Bronzini noticed the Japanese was sweating. On a shooting schedule this tight, it was no wonder.

"No, I doubt it," Colonel Davis was saying. "I'm sorry."

Bronzini broke in. "What we want to do, sir, is a massive parachute drop, using as many airmen as you can spare."

"You want me to provide airmen?"

Bronzini nodded. "In full gear."

"We wirr suppry the parachute, of course," Isuzu said. "And pay arr operating expense. Okay by you?"

"And a *per diem* for everyone," Bronzini added. He noticed a faint gleam appear in the colonel's evasive eyes.

"My God, man, do you realize what's involved? You'll need C-130 Hercules transports."

"We'd like three," Bronzini said with calm assurance.

"We want to have the men drop into the Yuma Desert. Naturally, we'll need to film the planes taking off from here. And the operation in its entirety."

"Sounds spectacular," Colonel Davis mused. He had never been in combat, never participated in a military operation on the scale this flat-cheeked actor was describing.

"Think of the publicity for the Air Force," Bronzini said. "In the script, they are the forces that engage the invading Chinese on the ground and destroy them."

The colonel thought long and quietly.

"You know," he said, sitting up in his chair, "our recruitment people tell me that every time you do a *Grundy* film, enlistments go up twenty percent in all branches of the service."

"Maybe this time it'll be thirty. Or forty."

"Sounds tempting. But it is a lot to ask. I don't think I could get the Pentagon to go along."

"Marines arready say yes," Jiro Isuzu inserted.

The colonel's face clouded over. "Those jarheads," he muttered. "What kind of parts are *they* getting?"

"Their base is overrun by Chinese Red Army in first reer," Jiro told him.

"He means the first reel," Bronzini translated.

"I might be persuaded to make a few phone calls," Colonel Davis said. "But you'll have to do something for me in return."

"Name it," Bronzini said. "An autograph? A photo?"

"Don't be absurd, man. I don't want any of that worthless junk. I want to be the first man out of the plane."

"Done," said Bartholomew Bronzini, rising to his feet. He shook the colonel's hand. "You won't regret this, sir."

"Call me Fred, Bart."

10

Sheryl Rose wondered what kind of a name Chiun was as she pulled up to the Yuma International Airport terminal. It sounded Asian. Probably Japanese. He'd almost have to be to cover this film. She parked the studio van at the curb and stepped inside.

There was only one man waiting inside. He was about five feet tall and wore a colorful silk robe. He looked lost, and Sheryl's heart went out to him.

"Are you Mr. Chiun?" she asked.

The tiny Asian man turned stiffly and said, "I am Chiun."

"Well, howdy, I'm Sheryl. From the studio."

"They sent a woman?"

"I'm the only unit publicist on *Red Christmas*," she said pleasantly. "Take me or leave me, but I hope you like me."

"Who will carry my luggage?" the little Asian asked plaintively. Sheryl noticed his shiny head, bald but for little cloudlike puffs over each fragile ear.

"No hat? Didn't your editor tell you that the sun is very, very strong in Arizona? You'll get a terrible sunburn going around like that."

"What is wrong with my attire?" demanded Chiun, looking down at his robe. It was cactus green. Scarlet and gold dragons marched across the chest.

"You'll need a hat."

"I am more concerned about my luggage."

"Now, don't you fret, I'll take care of it. Meanwhile, why don't you step into the gift shop and treat yourself to some headgear?"

"My head is fine."

"Oh, don't be shy," Sheryl told the sweet old man. "The studio will be glad to pay for it."

"Then I will be happy to take you up on your generous offer. My luggage is in that corner," he said, gesturing with his impossibly long fingernails to several lacquered trunks stacked at odd angles in the waiting area. Then he disappeared into the gift shop.

Sheryl touched one experimentally. It felt like it was filled with hardened concrete.

"Me and my helpful mouth," she said as she struggled to wrestle the top trunk to the floor.

An hour later, she had got the final trunk to the curb.

"Perhaps you need assistance from a man," Chiun said. His head was tilted back so he could see over the floppy brim of a ten-gallon cowboy hat.

"Do you see any stray helpful males?" she asked him, looking around.

"No. Perhaps I should help?"

"Oh, I can handle it," Sheryl puffed, thinking: What a sweet little man. He looked positively frail enough to break in a stiff breeze. God knew what would happen if he tried to pitch in. He might have a heart attack or some such thing.

Finally she hoisted the last trunk into the back.

"Do you always travel with five steamer trunks?" she asked as she climbed behind the wheel, checking the rearview mirror to grimace at the dusty sweat-streaked mask her face had become.

"No. Normally it is fourteen."

As she drove away, Sheryl breathed a prayer of thankfulness that he had decided to travel light this time.

"I'll bet you're excited about interviewing Bronzini," Sheryl said as they pulled onto the desert location twenty minutes later.

"Which one is he?" Chiun asked as base camp came into view. His hazel eyes narrowed at the sight of so many uniformed men.

"I don't see His Bronzeness at the moment," Sheryl said, looking around.

"I am unfamiliar with that form of address."

"It's just a little joke around the set. They call Bronzini the Bronze Bambino. Some of the trades refer to him as 'Your Bronzeness.' I thought everyone knew that."

"I do not. But then, I am not everyone," Chiun said haughtily, "I am Chiun."

"O-kay." Sheryl cranked down her window and spoke to a Japanese grip. "Where's Bronzini?"

"Overseeing setup on first unit," she was told.

"Thanks," Sheryl said, setting the van in motion. They bounced and weaved into the vast arroyo where the tanks were arrayed. "This is where they'll be filming the main desert battle sequences between the Chinese invaders and the American defense forces," she explained. "Do you know the story line?"

"No," Chiun said distantly. He was looking at the milling Japanese. They stared back with suspicious eyes.

"Maybe you should take notes. Or do you use a tape recorder?"

"I use my infallible memory, which requires neither sharpening or batteries."

"Suit yourself."

"Why are those men wearing Chinese uniforms?"

"Those are the extras. They play the Chinese invasion force."

"But those are Japanese!" Chiun hissed.

"Do tell. Almost everyone on this set is Japanese."

"This is foolishness," Chiun sputtered. "How can they expect people to believe their story when they have crafty Japanese pretending to be lazy Chinese?"

"I take it you belong to neither category," Sheryl remarked dryly.

"I am obviously Korean," Chiun said testily.

"I did notice that you can handle your L's," Sheryl said. "I guess people from your side of the world notice the difference better than we Americans." She pulled the van into the shadow of a sandhill.

"A worm would notice the difference. A grasshopper would notice. An American possibly would have to have it explained to him. Twice."

"Well, come on. Let's find Bronzini. It shouldn't be hard. He'll be the one with barbells in each hand."

As they stepped from the van, a red-and-white Bell Ranger helicopter lifted over a ridge and orbited the arroyo. It settled down in the clearing, rotors kicking up sand. A door popped open.

"That's the camera ship and there's his Bronzeness, making another spectacular entrance," Sheryl pointed out.

Two men stepped from the helicopter.

"I must interview him. At once," Chiun said firmly.

"Wait a sec. You don't just walk up to him. First, I have to clear it with Jiro. Then he has to take it up with His Bronzeness. He tells me, and I tell you. That's the way it works around here."

"He will speak to me," said Chiun, storming for the helicopter, where the two men stood engaged in earnest conversation. The Master of Sinanju ignored the shorter man, and accosted the taller one.

"I am Chiun, famous author," he said in a loud voice. "The readers of my magazine are clamoring for an answer to the most pressing issue of the day. Namely, how can you expect to have any properly colored persons take your movie seriously if you insult their intelligence with Japanese pretending to be Chinese?"

Bill "Sunny Joe" Roam looked down at the querulous face and said, "You're barking up the wrong tree, chief."

"Something I can do for you?" Bartholomew Bronzini asked, his face quirked with amusement. He looked down at a ten-gallon hat that might have belonged to a rodeo clown.

Sheryl Rose broke in.

"I'm sorry, Mr. Bronzini," she said hastily. "He got away from me. This is Mr. Chiun, from *Star File* magazine."

"Now you call him Mr. Bronzini," Chiun said huffily. "A moment ago he was His Bronzeness."

Sheryl's eyes widened in horror. But before Bronzini could react, the little Asian stepped back so he could see past his hat brim.

"You!" the Master of Sinanju gasped. Quickly he composed his features and executed a formal, if stiff, bow. "I am surprised to see you here, great one," he said guardedly.

"I'm still getting used to it myself," Bronzini grunted. "Mind if we do this later? The interview, I mean."

"As you wish," said Chiun, bowing once more. He held his hat before him in working fingers.

As the two men trudged off, Sheryl stepped in front of the Master of Sinanju and put her hands on her hips.

"You never, *ever* approach a star of Mr. Bronzini's magnitude again," she scolded. "And you don't repeat anything I tell you off the record."

"He is amazing," Chiun said, watching Bronzini walk away.

"He's very powerful. He could make or break my career. I hope you can regain your composure when he okays the interview. If he ever does."

"He is the very image of Alexander."

Sheryl blinked. "Alexander?"

"Now I understand," Chiun said, gesturing to the array of soldiers and military equipment that ringed the arroyo. "No wonder he makes films such as these. They remind him of his glory days. It is sad that he should have come to this, however."

"Come to what? Who's Alexander?"

"The Great," said Chiun.

Sheryl pursed her lips. "Yes . . . ?" she prompted. "The great what?"

Chiun's eye met Sheryl's. "Alexander the Great."

"What on earth are you going on about?"

"That man," Chiun said as he watched Bronzini's retreating back, "is the reincarnation of Alexander the Great. What else would explain his mania for reenacting the fury of battle?"

"Oh, I'd say the twenty million dollars they pay him per film might have something to do with it."

"He looks exactly like Alexander," Chiun went on. "The straight nose. The sleepy eyes. The sneering mouth."

"Actually, I always thought of him as having Elvis Presley lips," Sheryl remarked. "And I take it you knew Alexander personally."

"No, but one of my ancestors did. I wonder if Bronzini would remember."

"I doubt it."

"Good. That way he cannot bear a grudge against my house."

"Okay, I'll string along a little further. What house?"

Chiun's hazel eyes narrowed. "I am forbidden to say, for I am here under cover. But one of my ancestors slew Alexander."

"Really? Fancy that."

"Oh, it was nothing personal, I assure you. I am glad that I met this Bronzini. And I look forward to speaking with him at length. It is very seldom that one encounters the truly great in the modern world."

"Well, this is fascinating," Sheryl said distantly as she looked around the location, "but why don't we get started on the interviews? Let's see . . . who can we set up first? I don't see Jiro. Bronzini's personal technical adviser won't be here till tomorrow. You already met Sunny Joe, our stunt coordinator. That was him with Bronzini."

"Yes," Chiun said quickly. "I would like to interview one of the stunt persons."

"Anyone in particular?"

"Yes. The name is Remo."

"Remo. Remo Durok? You want to start with him?"

"Yes, please upset it."

"Set it up, you mean."

"I mean what I say. Let others interpret it as they will."

"Remo doesn't have a speaking role. He's really unimportant."

"Can I quote you?" Chiun asked.

"No! Don't quote me about *anything*!"

"I will promise that if you take me to Remo." Chiun beamed.

Sheryl looked around, biting her lower lip. "I don't see him anywhere. Let's head back to base camp. Someone must know where he is."

At base camp, they were serving lunch in an orange-and-white-striped mess tent. Crewmen and extras lined up at a food-dispensing trunk.

"Let's see what's for lunch, shall we?" Sheryl suggested.

Chiun sniffed the air. "It is rice," he said.

"How do you know that?"

"They are Japanese. They eat rice. It is the only thing about them I do not detest."

"Did your editor know about your . . . uh . . . attitude toward the Japanese when he sent you to this shoot?"

"He is barely literate. Besides, I am not hungry."

"Suit yourself. Let's see if there's anything we can do. Maybe there's something going on in the director's office."

The director's office was the last in a line of Nishitsu RV's. It was emblazoned with the *Red Christmas* logo, a Christmas tree bedecked with hand grenades and crossed ammunition belts superimposed over a mushroom cloud. Sheryl knocked on the door. Getting no answer, she turned to Chiun. "Guess it won't do any harm to poke our heads in."

She opened the door and let Chiun go first.

The Master of Sinanju found himself in a sparsely furnished interior. The walls were covered with long rice-paper strips on which Japanese ideographs made vertical lines. Papers lay on a desk.

"Not as neat as I expected," Sheryl noted.

"The Japanese never show their true faces in public. This rat's nest you see is how they are when they think no one is looking."

"I've seen worse," Sheryl said, looking around. "I guess this here's a copy of the script." She opened it up. "Now, don't this beat all? It's in Japanese too. Maybe there's an English translation somewhere about."

Chiun went from strip to strip, reading. "These are accountings of provisions," he told Sheryl.

"Doesn't surprise me none. It takes a lot to mount a movie of this scale. It's practically an epic."

"Many weapons, much ammunition, and supplies. They have a great deal of rice."

"They eat a lot of rice. You know that."

"How long will this film take to finish?"

"They told me the shooting schedule is four weeks."

"Then they lied to you. According to this note, the shooting schedule is five days."

Sheryl put her head next to Chiun's. She examined the paper.

"You must be reading it wrong," she said. "You can't hardly film a sitcom in that time."

"Are you conversant with Japanese writing?"

"Well, no," Sheryl admitted.

"I speak and read it fluently, and this stipulates that they will take Yuma in five shooting days."

"Take?"

"I am giving the literal translation. Is 'take' a movie term?"

"Yes. But a take is a good scene. One they'll use. I can't imagine what they could mean by taking Yuma. I know they'll be filming in the city later on, but that can't be it."

"I will gladly listen to your translation," Chiun told her coolly.

"Don't be silly. Someone just made a mistake. This is a four-week production."

"They have rice for nearly six months."

"Says who?"

"Says I. Just now." Chiun tapped another rice-paper strip. "According to this, they have rice for six months. Twice the amount they believe they will require."

"Well, there you go. The other thing must be wrong, then. They wouldn't have a six-month supply of rice for a five-day shoot, now, would they?"

"They would not have such a supply of rice for a four-month shooting schedule either," Chiun said slowly. "Why do they call it a shooting schedule?"

"You've heard of shooting a picture?"

"I have heard of taking a picture. Is that the 'take' they meant?"

"No. When they film, they call it shooting a movie. Therefore, shooting schedule. Wait a minute. You should know that! You're a film correspondent."

"I know it now," Chiun said, turning abruptly. "I would like to see their rice supply."

"Why, for Pete's sake?"

Before the Master of Sinanju could reply, a Japanese crewman leapt into the trailer.

"What you do here?" he barked. "Off rimits!"

"Oh, we were just looking for Jiro," Sheryl said.

"Off rimits!" the Japanese repeated spitefully.

"I don't think he speaks English," Sheryl whispered.

"Allow me to answer this," Chiun said. He lapsed into guttural Japanese. The other man's face quirked in astonishment. He grabbed for the Master of Sinanju. Chiun sidestepped the thrust. The Japanese kept going. He fell on his face. He bounced to his feet and made another move toward the tiny Korean.

"You cut this out, both of you!" Sheryl said, getting between the two of them. "This here's Mr. Chiun. He's with *Star File* magazine. You behave yourself."

The Japanese pushed her aside roughly and lunged at Chiun.

Smiling, Chiun spoke a simple, pungent word in Japanese. "*Yogore.*" His opponent howled and lunged.

The Japanese went sailing past him, his feet tripping on the RV's steps. They scrambled for footing, but to no avail. He fell facedown into the gritty sand.

Calmly the Master of Sinanju walked down his legs, over his back, and stepped off his head to alight on the sand. He turned.

"Why do you loiter?" he asked Sheryl. "He will be awake soon."

Sheryl looked around. There was no one in sight. "I'm with you," she said as she stepped over the man.

As they slipped to the cluster of tents, Sheryl said in a tight voice, "You know, sometimes the atmosphere around here is so tense you can break off pieces and chew them instead of gum. If this is how these folks make movies, God help us if they ever take over our movie companies. I, for one, will be looking for a new line of work, thank you."

The food-provision tent faced the busy food-service truck. Chiun and Sheryl ducked behind it.

"How are we going to get in?" Sheryl asked, feeling the coarse fabric.

"You will stand guard?"

"Sure as shootin'."

After Sheryl had turned her head, the Master of

Sinanju plunged a fingernail into the cloth and slashed downward so swiftly the rip sound was compressed into a rude bark. He masked it by feigning a cough.

"What's the matter, poor thing?" Sheryl asked. "Inhale some sand?"

"Behold," Chiun said, pointing to the cloth. At first Sheryl couldn't see what he was talking about, but when Chiun touched the fabric, a vertical slit appeared as if by magic.

"Well, how about that?" she said. "Must be our lucky day."

For the long tear exactly followed the line where a white stripe joined an orange one. Chiun held the tent open for her.

"Must be a defect in the workmanship," Sheryl said when Chiun joined her inside the cool tent.

" 'Workmanship' is not in the Japanese vocabulary," Chiun sniffed. He walked around the tent. It was crammed with burlap sacks. He touched one, and felt the hard-packed rice grains give like gravel.

"There is enough rice here to maintain many men for many months," he said gravely.

"There you go. What'd I tell you?"

"More than four weeks' supply. More than four months. Depending on the numbers of persons involved, perhaps nearly six months."

"So, they're prepared. Like the Boy Scouts. Films do run beyond their shooting schedules."

"It is not good that Bronzini leads them."

"Why not?"

"In his earlier existence, he was a dangerous man," Chiun mused. "He aspired to conquer the known world. Many suffered, not the least of which was my village in Korea. There was no work for as long as he massed his forces and conquered empires."

"Look, I'm going to ask this straight out because it's starting to drive me crazy, but you aren't from the *Enquirer*, by any chance, are you?"

"No. I am here officially from *Star File* magazine, although if the truth be known, I am a poet. In fact, I am thinking of writing of my experiences here in Ung poetry. The short form, of course. Regrettably, *Star File* magazine does not publish two thousand-page issues. I am thinking of calling it *Chiun Among the Yumans*. Perhaps I will consent to sell the movie rights now that I have contacts in this industry."

"Look, we really shouldn't be here. Especially if we're going to be talking this trash. Let's skedaddle."

"I have seen what I wish. Now I must speak with Remo."

"Okay, great. Let's find him."

None of the A.D.'s could locate Remo, although their walkie-talkies crackled messages all over the location area.

Finally the word came back.

"Remo gone to Ruke," the A.D. informed them, and walked away.

"Okay," Sheryl told Chiun. "You speak Japanese. You translate."

"Is there a place known as Luke near here?" Chiun asked.

"Luke? Sure, Luke Air Force Range. That must be it. Remo and Sunny Joe probably went there to do preproduction on the parachute drop they got set for tomorrow. If you don't mind waiting till tomorrow, we can watch them film it."

"Perhaps I should speak to the Greekling," Chiun said.

"The which?"

"Bronzini."

"He's Italian."

"Now. Before, he was a Greekling."

"Which movie was that?"

"When he was Alexander."

"I have a crackerjack idea," Sheryl said suddenly. "Let's get out of this sun. I think if we sat in the shade a spell, it would clear our heads right quick."

The Master of Sinanju looked up at Sheryl inquisitively.

"Why?" he asked. "Has the sun affected your mind?"

Lee Rabkin thought it was the strangest negotiation session he had ever taken part in. As the president of the IATSE local, he had been involved in many bitter union disputes.

He had expected the usual. After all, *Red Christmas* was a Japanese production. They did things a little differently. So when Rabkin received a call at two A.M. from producer Jiro Isuzu that the production, bending to Bartholomew Bronzini's preferences, had reconsidered their nonunion stand, and could he bring his negotiators to the location immediately—Isuzu had pronounced it "immediatry"—Lee Rabkin was up and banging on the others' doors before Isuzu heard the phone click.

Nishitsu vans were waiting for the sleepy union protesters. They were driven in silence to the location and let off at a base camp of circled tents and RV's.

Somewhere nearby, a portable gas generator started up with a coughlike complaint.

Jiro Isuzu stepped out of an RV and bowed so low that Lee Rabkin took it as a sign of total surrender.

"Ready to play ball, Isuzu?" He sneered.

"Barr? Not understand. Brought you here to negotiate union rore in firm."

"That's what I meant," Rabkin said in a superior voice, thinking: Boy, this Jap is dumb. No wonder he tried to dance around the union.

"Forrow, prease," Isuzu said, turning smartly on his heel. "Negotiation trench has been prepared."

"Trench?" someone whispered in Rabkin's ear.

Rabkin shrugged unconcernedly and said, "Hell, they sit on the floor at mealtime. I guess they negotiate in trenches."

They followed Jiro Isuzu beyond the base-camp tents and a short way into the desert. It was an eerie sight by moonlight. Hollows lay in impenetrable shadow and the gentle dunes resembled silvery frosting. Up ahead, three men stood in silhouette, AK-47's cradled to their chests.

"What's with the guns?" a union member asked nervously.

"It's a war picture," Rabkin said loud enough for everyone to hear. "Maybe they're rehearsing."

Isuzu suddenly disappeared. Rabkin hurried to catch up and found that Isuzu had simply walked down a plank and into an eight-foot-deep trench in the sand. Shovels stood chucked on one side of the freshly dug pit.

Isuzu called up, "Come, prease."

"When in Rome, I guess," Rabkin muttered. He went in first. A guard hurried off to the generator.

"They must be going to rig lights," Rabkin told the others following him into the trench.

"Good. It's as black as a snake's asshole in here."

When at last everyone was standing in the dark trench, Jiro Isuzu barked a quick command in Japanese.

"Well, do we sit, or what?" Rabkin demanded, trying to see Isuzu's face in the murk.

"No," Jiro Isuzu told him in a polite voice, "you simpry die."

And then Lee Rabkin's eyeballs seemed to explode from within. He felt the electric current ripple up through the soles of his feet and he fell on his face. His nose completed the circuit and fried his brains like scrambled eggs and cooked his corneas cataract white.

Jiro Isuzu watched the bodies jerk and fall disinterestedly. They smoked like bacon even after the electric current was shut off from the metal plates under the sand at their feet. Although it was again safe for him to walk from the trench, he preferred not to step over so many white-pupiled corpses and accepted the hands that reached down to pull him off the protective rubber mat that was the same beige shade as the sand.

Isuzu threw another order over his shoulder and walked off without a backward glance. Dawn was only an hour away, and there was still much to do. . . .

11

On the morning of December 23, a Canadian cold front descended on the United States of America, plunging the nation into below-zero temperatures. On this historic day, the two warmest cities of the country were

Miami, Florida, and Yuma, Arizona. And it was not warm in Yuma.

When the morning sun broke over the Gila mountains, Bartholomew Bronzini had been up an hour. He had a quick breakfast in the Shilo Inn restaurant, then returned to his room to do his morning workout.

When he stepped out of the lobby, two things surprised him. The first was the cold. It felt like forty degrees. The other was the absence of union picketers.

Bronzini ducked back into the lobby.

"No pickets today?" he asked the girl at the registration desk. "What goes on?"

The receptionist leaned closer. "I have a girlfriend at the Ramada," she whispered. "That's where they're staying. She says they left in the middle of the night without paying their bill."

"Probably ran out of money. Thanks."

There were no picketers at the location access road when Bronzini blasted his Harley-Davidson onto it. He passed the checkpoint, which consisted of two Japanese guards standing near the destroyed T-62 tank.

The guards attempted to wave him to a stop. Bronzini didn't bother to slow down.

"They must be joking, trying to keep me off my own set," he muttered. "Who do they think they're dealing with? Heather Locklear?"

The base camp was deserted. Off in the near distance, one of the prop tanks was chugging back and forth in the sand. It had a bifurcated plow blade mounted on the front. The tank used the blade to make piles of sand and push them into a hole.

Bronzini sped up to the main-unit location. He got a surprise when he turned the corner.

There were over a thousand men lined up in battalion formation. They wore brown People's Liberation Army uniforms and stood with their AK-47's at parade rest. On either side of them, the tanks and APC's had been lined up in ruler-straight rows. Tank commanders and crewmen clustered in front of the waiting machines.

Jiro Isuzu stood facing them, his back to Bronzini.

Bronzini dismounted and walked up to him.

"Bronzini san," Isuzu demanded hotly, "what you do here so earry?"

"Nice uniform, Jiro," Bronzini said coolly. "If you're going to be an extra too, who'll be directing? A gaffer?"

Isuzu's face darkened. "I wirr direct from within shot at times. You are famiriar with technique."

"I've directed myself," Bronzini admitted. "Never with a sword, though."

Jiro Isuzu grasped the scabbard of his ceremonial sword. Bronzini knew swords. It was not Chinese, but a samurai sword. It looked authentic, too.

"Sword bring good ruck. In famiry many generation."

"Try not to trip over it," Bronzini told him. He indicated the phalanx of extras. Several of the crewmen were going from man to man, distributing Federal Express envelopes.

"We are firming Chinese sordier preparing for battre," Jiro said unctuously. "Not need you yet."

"Yeah?" Bronzini noticed the Japanese crewmen were also in uniform. Several were filming the proceedings with hand-held Nishitsu video cameras. A big yellow Chapman crane lifted a thirty-five-millimeter film camera over the men, capturing a breathtaking panoramic shot of the formation.

"Cameraman in uniform too?" Bronzini said quietly.

"We need every man. Not enough extras."

"Uh-huh." As Bronzini watched, the soldiers squatted in the sand and, removing knives from belt scabbards, started paring their fingernails. They next chopped off a lock of hair. The clippings and hair were carefully deposited in the Fedex envelopes and sealed.

"What the heck is this about?" Bronzini asked.

"Chinese war custom. Sordiers going into battre send home parts of serves to be buried in famiry urn if they not return."

Bronzini grunted. "Nice touch, but don't you think the Fedex envelopes are a bit of a stretch?"

Uniformed groups went through the formation as the extras climbed to their feet. They collected the envelopes.

At a nod from Isuzu, they raised their fists and shouted, "Banzai!"

"Banzai?" Bronzini said. "Stop me if you've heard this one before, Jiro, but 'banzai' is Japanese."

"Extras get carried away. We edit out. Okay?"

"I'll want my technical adviser to okay all this stuff. He's due in today. I won't have my name on a piece of shit. Understand?"

"We arready reave message at hoter. Ask him to meet us at airdrop site. Okay?"

"Not okay. I read the script last night. I know this is a Japanese film, but does my character have to die?"

"You hero. Die tragic heroic death."

"And the part about the Americans nuking their own city really bothers me. What do you call that?"

"Happy ending. Evil Red Chinese die."

"So does the civilian population. How about a rewrite?"

"Rewrite possibre. We talk rater."

"Okay," Bronzini said, eyeing the soldiers in formation. "This is amazing. How many people you got here?"

"Over two thousand."

"Well, I hope they're cheap. This is the kind of thing that put *Grundy IV* over budget."

"We are under budget. And on schedule. Prease to wait at base camp."

"A couple of questions first. What were they burying by the base camp?"

"Trash."

"Uh-huh. The Indians are sure going to appreciate turning their reservation into a dump site."

"Indian paid off. No trouble from Indian. Arso, have reached understanding with union. They agree to stay out of this firm, we use them in next. You go now."

"Let me know when you're ready for the first setup." Bronzini looked at his watch. "This time of year, there's only twelve hours of daylight till magic hour."

"Magic hour?"

"Yeah. After the sun goes down, there's an hour of false light before it gets dark. On American productions, we call it magic hour. It gives us extra shooting time. Don't tell me you never heard the term."

"This first firm for Nishitsu."

"No shit," Bronzini said, vaulting onto his bike. "And you know, Jiro, I think it's going to be your last. I just hope you don't drag my career down with yours."

Bronzini sent the Harley rocketing back to base camp.

Remo Williams arrived at Luke Air Force Range at eight A.M. He stopped his rented car at the checkpoint. An airman stepped up to the car.

"I'm with the movie," Remo told him.

"Your name, sir?"

"Remo Durock."

The guard consulted a checklist.

"My name should be easy to find. I think there's only four or five non-Japanese with the film."

"Yes, sir. Remo Durock. You're free to pass. Take a right, then two lefts. It's the red brick building."

"Much obliged," Remo said. He parked his car in front of the red brick building. It was near the airfield. A small propeller-driven plane was idling on the flight line. It looked ridiculously tiny when compared to the hulking C-130 Hercules transports parked wing to wing on the near side of the tarmac.

Remo went inside, showed a fake photo ID in the name of Remo Durock to a desk sergeant, and was directed to a room.

"Hey, Remo. You're late." It was Bill Roam.

"Sorry. I had trouble finding the main gate," Remo said. He noticed a heavyset man in a khaki safari jacket and bush hat with Roam.

"Remo, meet Jim. This is Bronzini's technical adviser, Jim Concannon."

"How're you doing?" Remo asked.

"Outstanding," Concannon replied.

"Jim's our all-around expert on military matters," Roam explained. "He worked with Bronzini on all the *Grundy* flicks. Right now, he's walking me through checkout on these Japanese parachutes."

Remo noticed that the room was filled with parachute packs. Hundreds of them. They were black.

Concannon was unpacking one now, untying the canvas covers to examine the nylon chute bell. He examined the fabric carefully, holding it up to the light.

"You check every stress point," Concannon was explaining. "Don't worry about any little holes you find in the canopy. Just make sure the shroud lines are anchored firmly and not tangled up."

"Right," Bill Roam said. He tossed a pack to Remo. Remo caught it. "Lend a hand, son. It's your ass that's gonna be dangling from one of these Nipponese umbrellas."

Remo set the pack on the long table and undid the flaps. He checked the lines, tested the fabric. It felt sound.

"Hell of a point to come to," Bill Roam was saying as Jim showed them how to repack the chutes. "I can remember a time when Japanese products were the joke of the Western world. And today I'm working for a Japanese film company and booting several hundred Air Force boys out the back of a transport with Japanese parachutes strapped to their backs."

"Okay," Jim said. "These appear to be strack. Now, who wants to be the guinea pig?"

"Hell, man. Not me. I'm too old," Bill Roam said.

"I haven't jumped from a plane since Korea," Jim added.

They both looked at Remo.

"You game?" Bill Roam asked him.

"Why not?" Remo said, pulling the chute onto his back.

They walked out to the idling prop plane. An airman was at the controls. He wore aviator sunglasses and chewed gum vigorously. Remo climbed in.

Jim Concannon clapped him on the back.

"You be sure to let us know if it doesn't open, hear?"

Everyone laughed but Remo. The door was slammed on his impassive face. Providence was still on his mind.

The plane hummed down the runway and lifted awkwardly. It climbed up and out over the desert.

The pilot spoke up over the engine drone. "I'm going

to stay as close to the base as I can. Not much wind right now. So you ought to land close enough to be picked up by helicopter. That okay with you?"

"Sure," Remo said. He pushed open the passenger door, placed a foot on the wing, and as the plane tipped that wing to earth, Remo launched himself into space.

As he fell, the sleeves of his Air Force uniform chattered wildly. The vast expanse of southwestern Arizona hurtled up to meet him. Remo reached for the D-ring and pulled.

The pack vomited a cloud of black nylon. The updraft filled it, and Remo was yanked back violently. Then he swung like a pendulum. He looked up.

The big black bell was floating above him. He looked past his boots and saw the sand rising to meet them.

When Remo hit the ground, he rolled and shucked off the parachute webbing all in one motion.

A helicopter rattled overhead moments later. It settled several yards distant. Its rotors blew sand in every direction, kicking up a momentary sandstorm. Remo shut his eyes until it subsided. Then he ran for the waiting chopper and ducked under the rotor.

Sunny Joe Roam put out a big hand and pulled him aboard.

"Nice jump," he said. "You know your stuff. Military background?"

"Marines," Remo admitted.

Jim Concannon grunted. "Jarheads," he said. He said it with a smile.

"Don't mind ol' Jim," Roam laughed. "He's ex-Army. He may talk like a grunt, but there's none finer. Speaking of which, Jim, we gotta get you over to that drop 'ite. You'll be with the desert drop unit today."

"Where will Bronzini be?" Remo asked in concern.

"Search me," Roam told him. "Latest I hear, filming's split into nine units. We'll be with the parachute-drop unit. Bronzini will probably be with the tank units at the Marine Air Station. We'll have the fun. All they're doing is running tanks in and out of the main gate. Anyway, much obliged for doing the drop. I'd have sent up an airman, but if we'd lost him, they would have held it against us, probably. Right, Jim?"

The two men joined in good-natured laughter as the helicopter lifted off.

"What about the other parachutes?" Remo wondered.

"Hell," said Sunny Joe. "What do you want, to go jump in every dang one of them?" Their laughter increased. "They looked sound and yours tested out. They work."

"That's the problem with parachutes," drawled Jim. "They're like condoms. Good for that first plunge, but I wouldn't want to depend on them a second time."

"Well," Remo said, looking back at the deflated mushroom of his parachute as it flapped in the rotor wash, "we know that one worked." His face was worried. Not about the parachute drop, but over the fact that he wouldn't be working near Bronzini this first day. Maybe that wouldn't be a problem. He hadn't seen any picketing outside the hotel or at the air-base gate.

The camera crews were the first to enter the Yuma Marine Corps Air Base gate outside the city limits.

Colonel Emile Tepperman was there to greet them. He wore his best utilities, and a pearl-handled sidearm at his hip. It was loaded with blanks.

The Chapman crane came next. It was a four-wheeled vehicle with a telescoping boom-mounted camera. The cameraman wore an authentic-looking People's Liberation Army uniform, down to the sidearm. The crane positioned itself on one side of the approach road.

A half-dozen Japanese piled out of a van, lugging Nishitsu video-cameras. They deployed snappily, impressing Tepperman with their near-military discipline.

Then came the Nishitsu car carrying Jiro Isuzu. He was swiftly passed through the gate. Emerging from the car, he walked up to Tepperman, trailed by a retinue of men in desert camouflage carrying leather cases.

"Good morning, Mr. Isuzu," Tepperman said heartily. "Great morning for it, isn't it?"

"Yes, thank you. We are ready to begin."

"Where's Bronzini?"

"Bronzini san in read tank. On way. We wish to firm tank entering base. Your men fire on them. Tank fire back. Then you surrender."

"Surrender? Now, wait a minute. This isn't consistent with the image of the Corps."

"This earry in firm," Isuzu assured him. "Rater we firm Marines crushing wicked Chinese Red Army."

"Well, in that case," Tepperman said, "as long as the Corps emerges victorious, I'll go along."

"Excerrent. Stand very stirr, prease."

Two uniformed Japanese began clipping metallic buttonlike objects to Tepperman's uniform.

"What are these little doodads? Acting medals?"

"Squibs. When we fire, they break. Spirr fake brood. very convincing."

"Does it wash off?" Tepperman asked, thinking of the dry-cleaning bill.

"Yes. Very safe. You have brank sherr?"

"Beg pardon?"

"Brank sherr," Isuzu repeated. "You have?"

"I don't quite get your drift," Tepperman admitted.

Jiro Isuzu thought before speaking again. Then he said, "Brank burret."

"Oh, bullet. You mean blank shells!"

"Yes. Brank sherr."

"Yes, I received them. My men have them too. Don't worry. There'll be no accidental shooting on this base."

"Exerrent. We begin soon."

Isuzu turned to go, but Tepperman caught him by the sleeve.

"Hold on. What about my mark?"

"Mark?"

"You know. I understand that the first thing an actor has to learn is how to find his mark."

"Ah, that mark. Yes. Hmmmm. Here," Jiro said, picking a squib from Tepperman's uniform. He dropped it and stepped on it.

"You stand there," he said, pointing to the bloody blotch.

Tepperman gave a relieved smile. He hadn't wanted

to look like an idiot. A lot of his relatives were moviegoers. "Great. Thanks," he said.

Colonel Emile Tepperman stepped onto the blotch. He placed his hand on the flap of his side holster, and struck a rakish pose as he awaited his international film debut.

On either side of the approach road, his Marines were positioned, their M-16's in hand. Japanese special-effects technicians finished applying blood squibs to their clothes.

Finally the grumble of the tanks came from beyond the perimeter fence. A wide grin broke out on Emile Tepperman's face. Through the dust, he could see Bart Bronzini in the lead tank. He was standing up in the open turret hatch. Tepperman wondered if he would be visible when the tank rolled by. He would really enjoy being in the same scene with the Steroid Stallion.

The tanks stopped.

Jiro Isuzu looked up at the camera operator perched on a saddle at the end of the Chapman crane boom.

Someone ran up and placed a clapper board in front of the camera. Tepperman smiled. It was just like he'd seen in movies about movies.

"Rorring!" Jiro called.

The clapper clapped. The man dropped it and ran to retrieve an assault rifle he'd left leaning against the guard box. The camera panned toward the tank line.

They started up the road, a rumbling line of clanking machinery, dust tunneling in their wake.

Tepperman felt a thrill of expectation course through him. So real. He saw his men tense expectantly. He had lectured them last night about looking sharp. And not looking into the camera. He had read somewhere that that was a no-no, the mark of an amateur actor. Tepperman took pride in the professionalism of his men. He just hoped they had sense enough not to upstage him.

The tank column turned into the gate, and on cue the guard fired his M-16 three times, and it occurred to Tepperman for the first time that if this was supposed to be the enemy rolling in, why was the hero standing in the lead tank? He decided the plot must be more complicated than he'd been led to believe.

Tepperman watched as the guard went down in a return hail of fire. Blood squirted from the radio-controlled squibs. He threshed wildly as he went down, and Colonel Tepperman made a mental note to reprimand the guard for overacting.

The tanks split into two columns. Isuzu raised his sword and brought it down with a flourish.

That was Tepperman's cue.

"Return fire!" he thundered, dropping into a crouch. His weapon came up in his hand. He snapped off eight rapid shots, hoping the pearl handles showed up on camera. Tepperman noticed with a frown that none of the Chinese troops hanging off the tanks were going down.

"Dammit!" he muttered. "Where's the realism?" He saw Marines drop all around him, their shirts spattered with realistic-looking blood. One man was really yelling his head off. "Damn these overactors," Tepperman grumbled, reaching for another clip.

Tepperman squeezed off another shot, trying to knock off a tank machine-gunner. He didn't go down, which of course he would not: Tepperman was not using live ammunition. He hoped someone would blow this take, so he could tell Isuzu that what this scene really, really needed was for the heroic base commander to score a few hits. For the good of the story line, of course.

Tepperman was screwing his face into a heroic grimace when he felt something clutch his ankle.

He turned, still crouched on his haunches.

A pain-racked face stared up at him. It was a Marine. He was on his stomach. He had crawled from the side of the road to his commander's side, leaving a very realistic trail of blood.

"Nice touch, son," Tepperman hissed. "The old dying soldier trying to warn his superior officer. Good. Now play dead."

But the Marine clutched Tepperman's ankle more tightly than ever. He groaned. And through the groan came rattling words that were audible above the percussive cacophony of gunfire and tank clatter.

"Sir . . . the bullets . . . real," he choked out.

"Get a grip on yourself. It's only a movie. What have you been smoking? Loco weed?"

"I'm wounded . . . sir. Bad. Look . . . blood."

"Squibs, man. Haven't you ever seen special effects before?"

"Sir . . . listen . . . to . . . me. . . ."

"Calm down," Tepperman said savagely. "That's Bart Bronzini in that lead tank. Get a grip on yourself. You'd think a Marine could stand the sight of fake blood. You make me sick to my stomach."

The Marine let go of Tepperman's ankle and reached under himself. He grimaced. When his hand came away, it was covered with dripping red matter.

"Here . . . proof," he croaked. Then his cheek dropped to the ground.

Colonel Emile Tepperman looked at the red matter that had been plopped into his hand. It looked astonishingly like human viscera. On impulse, Tepperman sniffed it. It smelled like an open bowel wound; Commandant Tepperman knew that horrid smell well. He had done a tour in Vietnam.

Tepperman jumped to his feet, horror making the points of his mustache quirk like cat whiskers.

"Stop the action!" he cried. "Hold it! Something's gone wrong! This man is really wounded. Someone must have mixed up the ammunition."

The firing roared on, directed by Jiro Isuzu with an upraised sword.

"Isuzu! Bronzini! Bronzini!" Tepperman hollered hoarsely. "For God's sake, can't anyone hear me?"

Not thinking, Commandant Emile Tepperman stepped off his mark. Unexpectedly, the blood squibs in his uniform erupted in all directions. He ignored them.

"Stop this. Turn off those cameras!" Tepperman bellowed, without result. "Dammit," he muttered. "What's the word they use? Oh, right." He cupped his hands over his mouth. "Cut! Cut!"

But the shooting continued. Marines fell. Some of

them spurted red fluid in ways that were obviously
special effects, but others went down with arms and
legs suddenly bent at weird angles. A Marine's head
exploded in a halo of blood that no Hollywood special-
effects shop could duplicate—because it was horrify-
ingly real, as Colonel Emile Tepperman now knew.

The tanks rolled over many of the bodies with callous
disregard for human life. Some of the men were already
dead. Others simply played dead, not realizing that the
script had been changed. The expressions on their faces
when they felt the bite of steel tank tracks was horrible,
their screaming inhuman.

It was completely out of control.

Tepperman yelled "Cut!" until his voice cracked. He
stumbled between the tanks and the broken bodies
until he reached Jiro Isuzu. He grabbed the Japanese
by the shoulder and whirled him around.

"Stop this!" Tepperman thundered. "I order you to
stop this at once. What are you doing?"

"We are firming," Jiro said. He pointed above their
heads. A big square camera lens was focused on them.

"This is carnage, slaughter, and you're filming it."

"Branks," Isuzu told him, smiling toothily. "Not to
worry."

"Those tanks aren't blanks. They're real. They're crushing people. Listen to those ungodly screams."

"Perhaps mistake has been made. Gun, prease. I check."

Dazedly Colonel Tepperman allowed Jiro Isuzu to
take his sidearm. The Japanese was so calm and unruf-
fled that for a moment Tepperman doubted the reality
—or unreality—of what was going on all around him.

Isuzu placed the muzzle to Tepperman's forehead.

"Now, for camera. Do you surrender this base?"

"Uh, yes," Tepperman stammered.

"Say the word, prease."

"I surrender," Tepperman said.

"Now I wirr purr trigger. Not to worry. Brank. Okay?"

Tepperman steeled himself. He knew that a blank
shell could not hurt him. He never learned differently.
For when the trigger was pulled, it was as if a sledgehammer had struck Tepperman between the eyes.

The explosive force of the gunpowder had punched a hole in his skull. Propelled by expanding gases, the paper wadding penetrated his brain. He hit the ground as dead as if shot by a steel-jacketed round. The only difference was that there was no exit wound.

"You never surrender," Jiro Isuzu told his unhearing ears, as the last involuntary twitching of his leg muscles died down. "It is shameful."

12

Bartholomew Bronzini had been accused of many things during his cinematic career. He had been criticized for making too much money, usually by the rich. He had been criticized for his monotone delivery, usually by out-of-work off-Broadway actors. He had been criticized for being prolific, usually by someone who had never done anything more creative than listing a Cocker Spaniel as a dependent on a Form 1040.

Bronzini got used to those things. They were the price of fame. Like signing autographs for people who insisted they wanted them for relatives.

But the criticism that really perplexed Bartholomew Bronzini was the accusation that he was somehow a phony when he played the American war superhero Dack Grundy without ever having served in the U.S. military himself.

The first time he fielded that question during a TV interview, Bronzini replied "What?" in a dumbstruck voice. The interviewer assumed that was his definitive answer and went on to the subject of his latest multimillion-dollar divorce settlement. By the time he was asked it again, Bronzini had formulated a ready-made answer. "I'm an actor playing a part. Not a soldier playing at acting. I'm a John Wayne, not an Audie Murphy."

Bartholomew Bronzini was not acting now.

He was perched on the sloping turret of the lead

T-62 tank rolling along the main road of MCAS Yuma. Behind him, a Japanese crewman stood in the turret well and sprayed the air with the swivel-mounted .50-caliber machine gun. Defending Marines were corkscrewing more realistically than any extra. Heads exploded. Arms were sawed off by bullet streams.

Bartholomew Bronzini was no fool. He might never have seen combat, but he had made a lot of war movies. He realized before anyone else that this was no movie. This was real.

Yet they were filming it. It made no sense. Isuzu had told him that they were going to make a grand entrance to impress the Marines, and that Bronzini should ride on the lead tank. But as soon as the column passed the gate, the Marines had opened up. With blanks. Then all hell broke loose.

Even though it wasn't in the script, Bronzini leapt upon the machine-gunner. The Japanese released the gun's trips and tried to rabbit-punch the powerful actor. Bronzini took the man by the back of the head with one hand and pummeled his flat features to a pulp with the other. Then he knocked the Japanese off the tank and took the .50-caliber in hand.

Bronzini swept the gun muzzle around. He had never fired a loaded .50 caliber. But he had fired many blanks. Pulling the trigger was no different. It was what came out the barrel that counted. He pulled the trigger.

The face of the Japanese driver in the following tank disintegrated. He slumped forward. Out of control, the tank veered left, cutting off the tank behind it. The tracks merged and began shredding one another.

Bronzini swiveled his .50 toward the Japanese foot soldiers. He cut them down with a long burst. A Japanese popped out of the turret of his own tank. Bronzini didn't waste any bullets on him. He yanked the .50-caliber's muzzle around and brained the soldier with it, putting him over the side. As he lay stunned, the second tank crushed his legs with a splintery sound.

Bronzini looked around. He saw Jiro Isuzu off to one side of the entrance, his samurai sword high in the air.

He was directing the action in a style that was half-Hollywood and half-military.

Bronzini sighted on his open mouth and pulled the trips. Nothing happened. He spanked the breech with the heel of his hand, saying, "Come on, you mother!"

Then he saw that the feed belt was empty.

A bullet spanged off the turret by his boot with so much force Bronzini felt the impact in his clenched teeth. Another round went past his ear. It made an audible crack as it split the air.

"The fuck!" Bronzini said, seeing AK-47's in the Japanese hands lining up on him. He was no soldier, but he knew that when you're taking fire, you seek shelter. He dived into the turret.

He found himself sprawled behind the cannon breech. Obviously, the tanks had been restored to fully operable condition before they crossed the border. Beside it was the open hatch that led to the driver's cockpit, which was set forward, inside the hull.

Bronzini crawled to the hatch. The driver was down in his seat, peering through the periscope as he guided the tank by its handlebarlike lateral controls.

Bronzini silently unshipped the combat knife sheathed in his boot. It was no prop. He reached in and took the driver by the throat and ran the knife into his kidneys. The Japanese thrashed, but there was nothing he could do in the cramped driver's cockpit except sit and struggle against the remorseless hand that found his mouth with a stifling hold as the knife was slowly turned clockwise, and then counterclockwise, until he was dead.

Bronzini pulled him back and squeezed into the blood-soaked driver's seat. There was no time to sort this out. Bronzini was on automatic pilot, going on pure instinct, the very thing that had guided his career.

Bronzini realized that he couldn't hope to fight the Japanese from the driver's seat. He had no gun or cannon control. He'd need a tank crew for that.

So he jammed the lateral to the left, sending the tank pivoting on one locked track. The perimeter fence came into view. Beyond it was an endless expanse of sand.

Bronzini lined up on the fence. There were knots of crouching Japanese soldiers between him and freedom.

"Fuck 'em," Bronzini said, sending the tank clanking ahead, "and the rats they rode in on."

Bronzini kept the fence in view. The Japanese saw him coming. They scattered. He heard frenzied screaming as his tracks caught a running man's boot and pulled him into the rollers. Bronzini kept going. Somewhere in the din of gunfire, he could hear Jiro Isuzu shouting the name "Bronzini" over and over.

Two Japanese suddenly appeared in the periscope. They set themselves against the fence and, firing single shots, tried to hit Bronzini through the periscope.

Bronzini hunched down and floored the gas. The T-62 surged ahead like a steel-plated charger.

The tank's smoothbore cannon went between the soldiers, collapsing the fence like so much mosquito netting. The soldiers, lashed by Isuzu's harsh voice, held their ground, trying to put their shots into the bouncing periscope port. One went in. It missed Bronzini's head and ricocheted once, digging a furrow across the top of the seat back.

Then the tank rolled over the fence. And the two men. Their screams were cut off very quickly.

Bronzini sent the tank across the road. The clatter of its tracks on asphalt turned with a gritty growl as it dug into the sand. Bronzini put the tank on a straight heading.

He abandoned that tactic when a geyser of sand and fire exploded thirty yards in front of him. A dull boom echoed in the cockpit.

Bronzini threw the tank sharply to the right, then to the left. Another cannon shell struck off to starboard. Sand particles peppered the hull like a fine dry hail.

Bronzini zigzagged across the desert. He popped the driver's hatch and craned his head out. Back at the ruined fence, two T-62's were elevating their 125-millimeter smoothbore cannon. One cannon spit a flash of fire. The recoil sent the tank rolling back.

The shell overshot Bronzini's tank by an easy hundred yards. The wind kicked up and began dispelling the floating sand cloud. But more sand blew in with it. Bronzini buttoned up the hatch.

"Sandstorm," he muttered, grinning like a wolf.

He sent the tank into the obscuring storm. Sand came in through the port, making it impossible to see where he was going. But Bronzini didn't care. A cannon boomed far behind him, and was answered by an equally distant detonation. If anything, the shell had fallen further away than the last one.

Bronzini set his tank on a straight line and held it. The Japs could empty their cannon all over the desert, for all he cared. He was driving a sand-colored tank through a sandstorm. It couldn't be more perfect than if he'd written the script.

Then Bronzini realized that in a way he had. His Sicilian face darkened with wrath. Hunched under the sand-spitting port, he fumbled for the protective goggles he knew every tank carried. He found them and yanked it over his eyes. They afforded him no more visibility than he'd had before, but at least he could look out the periscope. Sand stung his face like hot needles, but Bronzini felt a different kind of pain.

Somewhere beyond the haze lay the city of Yuma and help. Bartholomew Bronzini vowed he wasn't going to stop until he reached the city.

"I should have known!" he muttered. "Nobody pays an actor a fucking hundred million dollars for a one-picture deal. Not even me."

The C-130 Hercules transports were warming up, their rear drop gates down and gaping like maws as First Assistant Director Moto Honda pulled up in a microwave-equipped TV transmission van.

Air Force Rangers stood waiting under Colonel Frederick Davis' proud steely gaze.

"Snap to it, men," he barked. "It's showtime."

The airmen were attired in their camouflage utilities. First A.D. Moto Honda approached Colonel Davis with a hard face that might have been formed out of a block of dog chewbone.

"You men ready, Coronel?" he demanded brusquely.

"Just say the word," Colonel Davis returned. "Just don't forget—I jump first."

"Understand," Honda said, bowing. "You jump first. Be first to hit ground."

"Real fine," Davis said. "How're the Marines doing?"

"Not werr. Base has farren to invader."

"That's what I like. Hardheaded realism." Davis noticed the camera being set up. Another camera was being lugged by another uniformed Japanese crewman. "So shall we go for a take?"

"One moment. Sright change in script. Propman make mistake with parachute."

"Which one?"

"Arr parachute." When Davis looked his lack of comprehension, he added, "Every one."

"Oh. I understood they were thoroughly checked by your people as well as my own. Where's that stunt guy of yours, Sunny Joe?"

"Here!" Sunny Joe Roam called. He loped up to the knot of men. "There a problem, Colonel?" he asked.

"Smarr probrem," Honda said. "Change in script. We wirr not firm parachute drop as night scene. Parachute must be . . . What is word?"

"Substituted?"

"Yes. Thank you, substituted. Instead of brack parachute, we issue white day parachute."

Colonel Davis looked at Sunny Joe Roam.

"What do you think?" he asked uneasily. "My people found them shipshape."

"They're good chutes," Roam admitted.

Honda spoke up. "New chutes from same factory, Nishitsu. Only finest materiars. But we must hurry."

"Hold your water," Roam snapped. "I'm responsible for the safety on this shoot."

"We lose much money by deray," Honda pointed out. "Shooting schedule tight."

"Damn!" Roam said distractedly. "Sure wish Jim was here. Well, trot them out. We'll both look 'em over. That good enough for you, Colonel?"

"Yes. Anything to keep the film on schedule."

Honda led them to the back of a van filled with

packed parachutes. They were so tightly jammed into the van that Sunny Joe Roam and Colonel Davis had difficulty extracting a pair. Finally, two came loose. They knelt on the ground and opened them.

"Looks good to me," Roam said, running his fingers between shroud lines.

"I'm satisfied," Colonel Davis agreed.

Honda grinned tightly. "Very good," he said. "Have men rine up for exchange."

Colonel Davis returned to his men. Sunny Joe Roam stood by his side, his face troubled, his big arms folded over his chest.

"Listen up, men," Davis bellowed. "There's been a script change. We're getting new chutes. Each drop team will form a line at that van." He pointed back to the van, where uniformed crew members were hastily dumping parachutes onto the ground. They set several of these aside. No one noticed that this weeding-out included only the chutes that had formed the exposed group from which the test samples were selected.

Three lines of airmen formed up. They shucked off their chute rigs and traded them for white packs.

Remo Williams was at the end of one of the lines. He caught Sunny Joe's eye. Sunny Joe sidled up to him.

"What's going on?" Remo whispered.

"Another damned script change. They were going to film the scene with filters to make it look like a night drop. Now they want a day drop. So out go the black parachutes and in come the white parachutes."

"Anybody test these things?" Remo asked worriedly.

"The colonel and I looked a couple of them over."

"That's it?"

"They're as good as the others. If you're worried, think of it like this. Out of five hundred chutes, how many of them could go bad? One, maybe two. The odds of your getting a bad one are pretty damn slim."

"Whatever you say," Remo said. He was still concerned. He hadn't expected filming to be this immense and fragmented an operation. How the hell was he going to protect Bronzini if they kept getting separated? Not that Remo cared much about Bronzini. The guy was obviously a stuck-up jerk. But an assignment was an assignment.

Remo was the last in his line to pick up his chute. He buckled it on and tested the webbing straps. They seemed solid.

As three lines formed near the three droning transports, Colonel Davis looked to First A.D. Honda.

Honda was looking through the lens of the camera. He looked up and nodded to Davis. Sunny Joe ducked into one of the transports to get out of camera range.

"Action!" Honda called.

Another crewman warned, "Rorring!"

Davis turned and shouted a command to his men over the climbing whine of the transport turbines.

The airman teams turned snappily and humped up the ramplike drop gates. As they crouched down on the floor of cargo bellies, the gates rose like hydraulic jaws.

Remo watched the sunlight being swallowed by the closing gates and felt the plane shudder as the brakes were released. He felt like Jonah being swallowed by a whale. The noise was overpowering until the Hercules lifted off the flight line.

Sunny Joe Roam hunkered down beside Remo.

"You go last!" he shouted over the engine sound.

"Is that an honor?"

"No, you're the only civilian on the jump. If something goes wrong, the others will catch you." Roam clapped Remo on the back. Remo was not amused and said so.

"What's eating you?" Roam asked.

"Never mind. Let's say this wasn't what I expected."

The flight was short. When the pilot called back that they were over the drop zone, Bill Roam worked his way forward to the cockpit. He looked out the window.

Down on the desert floor, a worm of purple smoke lifted lazily. It showed perfectly against the color of the sand. He spotted the green-and-white tent where the ground camera crew was positioned, and a pair of APC's.

"Try to find the camera ship," Roam told the pilot.

"Got it." The pilot pointed to a tiny red-and-white dot at one o'clock. It was the Bell Ranger helicopter.

Roam nodded. "Okay. Radio the other pilots to drop their gates when I give the word."

"Roger." The pilot spoke into his microphone. Then he handed it to Roam, saying. "You're all set."

Bill Roam watched the mountainous expanse of the Yuma Desert roll down below.

"This is your jumpmaster," Bill Roam said in the mike. "Stand up!"

Instantly, in each Hercules transport, airmen jumped to their feet and formed three lines down the center of the cargo bay.

"Hook up!" Roam called.

The airmen attached their chute lines to the nylon static lines suspended the length of the cargo belly.

"Drop gates!"

As the grinding sound of hydraulics came from in back, Bill Roam saw the two leading transports start to open up. Then he called "Jump!" and rushed back to the cargo belly.

"You're on," he told Remo, as wind rushed into the cargo bay. "Happy landings!"

The men went out single file, clutching their chest packs. Once out, the wind whipped them to one side. Their drag lines pulled taut from static-line tension.

So rapidly did they jump that the last man in each transport was in free-fall before the first chutes deployed.

The first man in the lead plane was Colonel Frederick Davis. He had served his country for over ten years in peacetime and he was never prouder of himself than on this day as he led his men into cinematic greatness.

He didn't notice that his back chute hadn't deployed.

He twisted his head around and saw that, above him, his men were falling, their arms jerking like the legs of beetles that had been turned on their backs.

He realized their chutes weren't yet open. And, with a shock, that his hadn't deployed either.

"Goddamn cheap Japanese equipment!" he snapped.

He yanked the D-ring of his reserve chute.

"Jesus Christ!" The ring had pulled free of the tab. He threw the useless ring away and grabbed at the tab with both hands. He pulled. The tab tore free like cheesecloth, leaving a tiny shred. Cursing, Colonel Davis pinched at that little shred with his fingertips. It was all that stood between him and a hard, hard landing.

Colonel Davis was so absolutely enthralled by that ragged, frayed bit of cloth that time seemed to stand still. The piece of frayed nylon became his whole world. He pulled at it until it was down to three threads. And even though it was hopeless, he pulled at those too.

But time wasn't standing still—not when you're falling at terminal velocity.

Colonel Frederick Davis struck the Yuma Desert so hard he bounced four feet. He was only the first of many.

Remo Williams was the last to leave his plane by a scant second. He felt a tug as the drag line, still attached to the static line, pulled free. It felt weaker than he expected. But he wasn't worried.

He began to worry when he realized that although there were approximately five hundred airmen free-falling in nine lines that stretched for nearly two miles above the desert floor, he wasn't seeing any parachutes. Including his own.

Remo went for his D-ring. It tore free of the tab. Remo threw the tab away and clawed at the folds of his reserve chute. The canvas separated and a billowing eruption of white silk spewed in front of him.

The updraft filled the chute. It turned into a white bell, as perfect as a big silk flower.

Remo vented a gusty sigh of relief. The sigh was short-lived as Remo realized that while the parachute was floating gracefully above him, he continued dropping like a stone.

The shroud lines had pulled free of their anchorage.

Remo looked down and saw a gentle puff of sand. It looked like smoke. Another puff followed it. And another.

And then, as the first concentration of bodies reached the ground, there came a silent spattering of puffs, which repeated until the beige desert floor erupted into a pocked lunar landscape, and Remo realized that he was witnessing cold-blooded, wholesale murder in which he was simply the last to die.

13

The waitress at the Shilo Restaurant and Lounge set two steaming plates on the table.

The Master of Sinanju looked at the boiled brown rice on his plate and his face broke into a pleased smile. His hazel eyes shifted to Sheryl Rose's plate and his mouth wilted in prim disapproval.

Sheryl Rose let the succulent smell of steak fill her nostrils and start her mouth juices flowing. She regarded Chiun's brown rice with muted distaste.

"How can you eat that for breakfast?" she asked.

"How can you eat that at all?" Chiun snapped back.

"I'm a western gal. I was raised on steak and home fries for breakfast."

"It is a wonder you survived your childhood," Chiun sniffed disapprovingly.

"You're right welcome," Sheryl returned tartly. What a pain, she thought. Well, it beat holding up cue cards for the local news airheads.

"There's no one in the production office," Sheryl told Chiun after they had chewed their food in silence for several moments. "No call sheets either. 'Course, if there were, I'm not sure I could read them. But it is powerful odd, you know."

They were seated in a window booth with a spectacular panoramic view of farmland north of Yuma. Beyond, flat desert stretched for miles. It seemed to reach all the way to the Mohawk Mountains.

"I do know," Chiun returned. "There is something wrong with this so-called shooting schedule."

"You're not going to start with that Alexander stuff? I mean, you're not going to write it up that way."

"A true author does not discuss his work before he has written it," Chiun said flatly.

Sheryl sighed as she cut off a wedge of steak. Red

145

juices ran freely, causing Chiun to look away. He noticed, high over the desert floor, three tiny dots. To his magnificent eyes, the dots resolved into bulky aircraft. Tiny figures began to drop from them like jimmies falling off an ice-cream cone.

"They are performing the parachute fall," Chiun said testily. "Why are we not there to observe it?"

Sheryl looked up. "What?"

"There," Chiun said, pointing. "They are doing it."

Sheryl squinched her gray eyes. "I don't see anything."

"Are you blind? They fill the sky."

"All I see are a couple of itty bitty dots."

"There are three of those. They are aircraft."

"If you say so," Sheryl said, returning to her steak. "I can't make out a dang thing."

"There are men falling from those planes."

"I don't see any parachutes."

Chiun's voice was cold. "There are no parachutes. They are falling to their death."

"Oh, go on. That can't be."

"I see them as clearly as I see you," Chiun insisted.

"Probably dummies. It must be a rehearsal run."

"I see their limbs waving in terror," Chiun said.

"Probably the updraft. It's fierce. Can you imagine jumping out of one of those things? Brrr. Gives me chills, thinking about it. Know what I mean?"

"Yes," Chiun said. "I feel such a chill even now." He stood up. "Come, we must investigate this."

"Why?"

"Because while you were devouring the bloodied flesh of some unfortunate cow, many hundreds of men have been falling to their doom."

"Now, listen you—" Sheryl started to say. The brittle look in the Master of Sinanju's eyes stopped her, a piece of red beef suspended on a fork before her face.

"Okay," she said as she signed the bill, "one less steak in my life isn't going to be missed, I guess. Although it was a good one."

They walked out to the parking lot in silence.

"I was unable to reach Remo," Chiun said tightly.

"Your friend? I plumb forgot you were looking for

him. Don't you worry, Sunny Joe probably took him out on the town—what there is of it."

"Was Remo to participate in the parachute scene?"

"Probably. I don't know. If we could scrounge up a call sheet, I could tell you. Why?"

"Because if he did, then he is now dead. And a terrible price will be exacted from those who were responsible."

Sheryl suddenly understood why the tiny Korean's cold demeanor had quelled her will to resist him. She said nothing as she opened the door to her jeep.

Chiun noticed that a chrome plate on the glove compartment said: "Nishitsu Ninja."

"Why is this vehicle called that? Ninja?"

"It's advertised as the Stealth jeep," Sheryl told him as she turned the key in the ignition. "But everyone knows it is because of the sneaky way it will tip on you when you take a corner. Jiro stuck me with this thing until my replacement is shipped."

Chiun nodded. "True ninjas fall over without reason as well. Usually due to rice wine."

"That explains why this beast guzzles gas like she does," Sheryl muttered as she took Route 8 east. "You're really fretting about your friend, aren't you?"

Chiun said nothing.

"Now, look. We'll just go to Luke and see for ourselves. And don't you worry," she added, patting Chiun's bony silk-covered knee, "I'm sure your friend is fine."

Chiun lifted Sheryl's hand from his person and replaced it on the steering wheel.

"We have a destination," Chiun snapped. "I suggest you take us to it."

"You're the boss," Sheryl told Chiun as she sent the jeep toward the city outskirts.

They were surprised when they passed a lone T-62 tank on the way.

"That little dogie must have strayed from the herd," Sheryl remarked. Chiun ignored her. He was looking at the city skyline. A column of smoke suddenly boiled up from the downtown area.

Seconds later, there came a distant boom and the jeep began to slew from side to side.

"My goodness," Sheryl said. "They weren't kidding when they said these Ninjas are prone to falling on their sides. A little piece of thunder and we almost turned turtle."

"That was not thunder," Chiun intoned.

Sheryl peered past Chiun's parchment profile.

"Fire," she decided. "Wonder where it is."

"That was an explosion," Chiun intoned.

Before Sheryl could say another word, two more explosions rocked the city. Sheryl had to pull over, the Nishitsu Ninja began bucking so hard.

"My God, will you look at that?" she said. "They must be shooting in the city."

"No, those were bombs."

"Probably gasoline charges. I saw them rig a few the other day. They look like those plastic pillows with red cough syrup in them. But they are gasoline. Supposed to make a big blast and column of fire. They do amazing things with special effects, as you probably know."

"We must hurry," Chiun urged.

"Okay," Sheryl said, taking off again. "But if I hear another loud noise, I'm pulling over right quick."

At the point on Route 8 where the city stopped and desolation began, the road was blocked by two desert-camouflage T-72's parked hull to hull. Their fudge-ripple turrets were turned sideways so that one pointed toward them and the other down the road to the desert.

"They aren't supposed to be filming way out here," Sheryl muttered as she slowed the Ninja. The tanks did not part for her, so she leaned on the horn.

A Japanese in a Chinese PLA uniform popped the turret hatch and scrambled down to the road. He un-limbered an AK-47 and pointed it at the jeep as he advanced in a classic "marching fire" stance.

"Road crosed!" he barked.

"What?" Sheryl called.

"That cretin is trying to tell you that the road is closed," Chiun said flatly.

"I know that. Now, hush up a minute while I get this straightened out."

Sheryl pushed her head out of the driver's window. "I'm Sheryl," she called. "I work for Jiro Isuzu as unit publicist. We're trying to get out to Luke. Would you mind making way?"

Another Japanese came out of the tank. This one lugged a video camera on his shoulder. He knelt down beside the tank and sighted through the lens.

"Why the heck are they filming us?" Sheryl wondered. "And with a camcorder to boot."

"Road crosed. Go back!" the Japanese with the AK-47 shouted again.

Sheryl muttered, "He probably doesn't speak English. Wait. Maybe the tank driver can help us out."

Sheryl alighted from the jeep and, leaving the driver's door open, started for the Japanese. Her cowboy boots covered exactly seven steps; then the Japanese gave a hiss like a cat and let go with a short burst.

Sheryl jumped nearly a foot. The noise was suddenly all around her. A burst of pops in front and a rattling drumroll behind her. The drumroll worried her the most. Blanks didn't make sounds striking targets, she knew. The paper wadding burned away in flight.

She looked back at her open door. It was riddled with vicious black holes. The glass had shattered.

"Are you insane!" Sheryl screamed at him. Her pretty face worked angrily, but she didn't budge from where she stood. She couldn't because, as impossible as it seemed with a camera taping her, the extra had been firing real bullets.

"Is this a take?" Sheryl stuttered nervously.

The Japanese laughed raucously. "*Hai!*" he said. "We take city."

"No, no, I mean, is this going to be in the film?"

"*Hai.*" He started to line up on her stomach. Sheryl hesitated. Her heart was pounding high in her throat. Her brain fought two conflicting emotions. Disbelief and a palpable fear of that deadly weapon pointing at her.

"Do you mind lowering that thing?" Sheryl said in a voice that sounded stretched too tight.

The Japanese tightened down on the trigger.

He stopped at the sound of a pungent word delivered in a squeaky voice.

Sheryl looked back over her shoulder. "No! Don't shoot him!" she cried.

For the little Korean named Chiun was out of the jeep and striding for the Japanese, his fists clenched like ivory bone, his sweet face now a mask of cold fury.

The AK-47 burped smoke and noise.

The Korean danced to one side. It was an elegant little two-step. He kept coming on the Japanese. Sheryl blinked. Had the gun been loaded with blanks after all? She looked back at her car door. Still riddled. And off to the side of the road, a cluster of puffs marked the impact points of the rounds Chiun had avoided.

The Japanese hunkered down and braced the rifle stock against his hip. Barely ten feet separated him from his intended target.

Sheryl couldn't bear to look. She covered her face and twisted around. A horrible high-pitched scream assaulted her ears and she transferred her hands to them to keep out the sound of the poor Korean gentleman's death screams. They were unearthly. It sounded like he was being torn limb from limb—although no more shots rattled out.

Slowly, Sheryl found the courage to turn around. She was on her knees in the middle of the road. The Japanese with the AK-47 was flat on his back. The one with the video camera was the one who was screaming.

He was attempting to clamber onto the open tank. Chiun had caught him by one ankle. Even though the Japanese was much younger than the Korean and outweighed him by at least fifty pounds, he was howling as if an alligator had snapped at his foot.

It was unbelievable. And then it became absurd.

Chiun pulled the cameraman to the ground. One sandal lashed out. Sheryl could almost feel the gravely crunching sound of the cameraman's skull fragmenting. Then Chiun was atop the tank.

A helmeted head lifted up from the other tank's turret. Chiun pushed it back in and slapped the hatch shut. He hammered on it rapidly and stepped to the forward hull. He stamped on the driver's hatch, then leapt to the second tank. He performed some violent manipulation on that tank's hatches.

Sheryl knew they were violent because metal squealed like mice under the old Oriental's nimble fingers.

Chiun alighted and padded back to her. He stopped, his hands sliding into his voluminous sleeves.

"You may go around these Japanese deceivers without fear for your safety," he intoned.

Sheryl followed Chiun to the jeep and got into the driver's seat, pulling the shattered door closed. The bullet-chewed handle came off in her hand.

Before she could start the engine, reaction set in. She hugged herself and started to worry her lower lip with her teeth.

"My God! What's happening here?" she asked weakly.

"They are taking Yuma," Chiun said. "And they will be punished. First we must see to Remo's fate."

Getting a grip on herself, Sheryl got the jeep going. She drove it over the sand and around the tanks and back onto the road on the other side. As they passed the tanks, she could hear frantic yelling coming from inside the vehicles. It was in Japanese. The tone was universal, however. The tank crews were trapped.

But they were not helpless, as Sheryl realized when she caught a flicker of movement in her rearview mirror.

The turret cannon was elevating. It coughed a blast of dirty smoke and flame.

A geyser of sand erupted beside the road. Sheryl pressed the accelerator to the floor. She no longer questioned what was happening. It was happening and she wanted only to get away from it.

There were Red Chinese tanks blocking the main gate to Luke Air Force Range. But that was not the strange thing. On the flagpole near the guard box, a white flag was flying. It was not the white flag of surrender. In its center was a blood-red ball.

"Call me superstitious," Sheryl said, turning off the engine suddenly. She let the jeep coast to the side of the road. "But I don't think we should go in there."

"A wise decision," Chiun said. "You will stay here."

He got out of the jeep.

"Where the heck do you think you're going?" she called after him.

"I seek my son. I will return."

"You and MacArthur," Sheryl muttered. She clutched the steering wheel anxiously. Her arms trembled. And up in the impossibly blue sky, the first of three C-130 Hercules transport planes were coming in on approach.

The Master of Sinanju drifted to the air-base perimeter fence. It was a wire-link fence. Chiun's fingernails slipped into the holes like so many darning needles. They clicked busily. Links snapped and parted. A tear opened up in the fence like a rip in a screen door.

Chiun slipped through quietly. He moved from low building to shrubbery. He passed many Japanese attired in their ridiculous Chinese military uniforms. Whom did they think they were trying to fool? Chiun wondered. It was so transparent.

He found his way to the flight line, where several tanks were moving in the shelter of a row of hangars.

Chiun saw a Japanese in a captain's uniform lunging about, directing his men into positions.

The first transport rolled to a halt. The second touched the tarmac with a barking of landing wheels. The third was fast behind it.

The pilots took a long time to shut down the engines after the C-130's rolled to a stop, wing tip to wing tip. Before they could emerge, the drop gate of the third plane eased down and Bill Roam, known as Sunny Joe, walked out on wobbly knees.

Oblivious of the men moving on him, he sank to the grass and put his head in his hands, and began making long arduous retching noises.

Two Japanese tried to haul him to his feet.

That was a mistake. Bill Roam got to his feet like a

water buffalo breaking the surface. He decked one Japanese with his first punch. The other took three punches. Two to the stomach and one which turned the man completely around before sprawling him on the grass.

"You bastards!" he screamed. "You cheap mother-loving bastards!" He shouted it to the sky. When his head came down, his eyes saw the helmeted Japanese marching toward him. They were fixing bayonets.

All except the one with the video camera. He scrambled along beside the others, trying to keep them all within camera range. He dropped to one knee as the Japanese, led by First A.D. Moto Honda, advanced on Sunny Joe Roam.

"They're all dead!" Roam said in a grinding voice. "Do you hear me, Honda? Every one of those boys ate sand for his last meal."

Honda's answer was in Japanese. Bill Roam didn't understand it, but the Master of Sinanju did. It was an order to stab Roam to death.

Bill Roam realized this only after the little Oriental appeared in front of him. The Oriental stood resolute in the face of the advancing Japanese. He paused, only to turn his head slightly and whisper a question.

"Those who died. Was Remo among their number?"

"Yeah," Bill Roam croaked. "He was a good kid."

The bald head swiveled back. The scrawny neck stiffened and the long-fingered hands clutched into fists.

"*Aaaieee!*"

The cry split the still air. The Japanese froze, for it was no war cry, no shout of defiance, but a scream of pure anguish. It shook their inflexible robot faces.

Then the Oriental was among them. He slapped bayonets away with curt blows. The bayonets quickly shifted back. Some began to poke at the Oriental's vermilion kimono. They seemed to score several hits, but the Oriental was unfazed.

Then a Japanese screamed. A comrade's bayonet was sticking through the fleshy part of his forearm. Another Japanese lunged at the Korean. Somehow he managed to impale the man who had been behind him.

The Oriental whirled, going deep into the knot of

men. The Japanese lunged, never realizing that they were being manipulated like chess pieces. For they soon became a hurricane of hate, whose object defied the eyes.

Japanese struck Japanese. Honda shouted at them. Others went down. Blood squirted. They were at too close quarters to shoot. But they might as well have, for those who did not fall victim to their comrades found cold hands drifting toward their throats. One man's collar split and his jugular gushed like a fountain. He placed a hand over it and staggered off.

First A.D. Honda saw his men turned into self-mutilating buffoons and realized his honor was at stake.

He raised a pistol to shoot the Korean and aimed carefully. He shut one eye, blinked the other in that millisecond of adjustment, and it turned out to be Honda's final millisecond.

His stiffened arm compressed like a spring. He fell, his gun hand buried in a cauliflower of flesh that had been the flesh and blood of his arm.

"What the hell is going on?" Bill Roam yelled when Chiun reappeared in front of him. "Are they on drugs?"

"I will explain later," Chiun said. "You will take me to the body of my son, Remo."

"Remo! He's your son?"

"I will explain later," Chiun said. "We must hurry. The roads are fast becoming impassable."

Sheryl Rose saw the expressions on the faces of Chiun and Bill Roam when they appeared in her rearview mirror. They filled her with dread.

"Drive," Chiun said when they got in.

"What's happened, Sunny Joe?"

"The drop went bad. They're all dead."

"Including Remo." Chiun's voice was a tight string.

Sheryl checked his austere profile for tears. She saw none. It surprised her.

"Where are we going?" she asked dully. "Where *can* we go?"

"To the place where the bodies fell," Chiun said.

"We'll have to go through town to do that."

"Then we will go through town."

"I'm afraid of what we'll find when we get there."

"I understand your fear. Mine lies out in the desert, but I will go to it bravely, for what else have I on this terrible day but my own courage?"

14

The first indication the outside world had of the situation in Yuma was when Wooda N. Kerr switched channels to watch his favorite program.

Wooda lived in a house trailer in Mesa, Arizona. Mesa was 150 miles northeast of Yuma, but it received the Yuma TV stations. KYMA showed *Tombstone Territory* reruns at ten A.M. and Wooda never failed to watch it, even though he had seen each episode a dozen times.

Today he saw only static on the channel. Wooda grumbled as he fiddled with his rabbit ears. When they didn't help, he went next door to John Edwards' trailer. John got cable.

The door was open and Wooda stuck his head in.

"Hey, John. Can you get Channel Eleven?"

"Let me see, now," John said, reaching for his remote control. He got static too.

"Now, don't that beat all?" Wooda said. "I can't figure it out. TV stations don't broadcast static like that. The least they do is run a test pattern."

"Channel Nine is dead too," John grunted. "That's a Yuma station. Let me check Two."

Channel Two was dead as well. All the local stations were coming in fine. Those from Yuma were off the air.

"What do you think it is?" Wooda wondered, playing with the turquoise stone of his bola tie.

"Cable from Yuma must be on the fritz," John Edwards ventured.

"That don't explain why I can't get it off the air,"

Wooda pointed out. "I'm gonna ask my sister, Mildred. She's down there. This has got my curiosity tweaked."

But when he dialed his sister's phone number, all Wooda Kerr got for his pains was a recorded message saying, "We are sorry but all circuits are busy at this time. Please hang up and try your call later."

Wooda did. The operator told him that the lines to Yuma were down.

Wooda shrugged and ended up watching *The Dating Game*. He was sixty-seven years old, and thought it was the most outlandish nonsense he had ever seen. He became a regular viewer.

By late morning the lack of telephone communication with Yuma was known in Phoenix, the state capital. It was unusual, but hardly important enough to warrant special attention. Yuma was, after all, way down in the desert by the Mexican border. Back before telephones and the automobile, it had been a rough little outpost. The people could get along without their phones for as long as it took to get them fixed.

Telephone crews were dispatched to the city. They did not return. That was not thought unusual either. It was a big desert.

The abrupt cessation of television and radio signals emanating from Yuma went completely unnoticed by the state government. Thousands of people missed their favorite soap operas and game shows, but when they were unable to get through to the Yuma stations to complain, they simply switched channels and forgot about it.

Official Washington became aware of the developing situation slowly. It began when telephone traffic between Luke Air Force Range and the Pentagon stopped. Calls did not go through. On an ordinary day, this might have been shrugged off, except that the Air Force's senior general was anxious to know how the Bartholomew Bronzini filming was going. He ordered radio communication established with the base.

The radio calls went unanswered.

"This is damned strange," he muttered. He put in a call to Davis-Monthan Air Force Base in Tucson.

"We can't raise Luke," he told the base commander. "Send up a couple of planes to check it out."

Ten minutes after the general had hung up, two F-15 Eagle combat jets were streaking over the Santa Rosa Mountains, east of Yuma.

Captain Curtis Steele watched the endless desert crawl under his wings. The other F-15 flew on his left, and in his ear was the tinny voice of his backseat fire-control officer, saying, "What do you suppose is up at Luke? It's spooky, no radio contact at all."

Steele laughed. "Maybe they went Hollywood on us."

"Yeah, probably living it up with some babes right now. But this is one party they're gonna pay for!"

Just then, the cockpit radar beeped and Steele called out, "Look sharp! I have two bogeys at angels twenty-three. Seventy miles and closing."

Steele checked his IFF display—Identify Friend or Foe. A graphic display would tell him if the two aircraft closing on him were American or not.

Steele was not surprised when an F-16 Fighting Falcon graphic appeared on his heads-up display.

"They're ours," he said. Then, in a louder voice he called, "Come in, come in, this is Echo oh-six-niner. Come in, I say again, this is Echo oh-six-niner from Davis-Monthan. Do you read?"

Staticky silence came over his helmet earphones.

"I don't like this," Steele's wingman said flatly.

"Stay in tight," Steele muttered. His eyes sought the IFF display again. Friendly. Definitely friendly.

"So why no answer?" his backseat wondered.

"Oh, damn," the wingman croaked. "They're locking onto us."

"I see it," Steele cried. Radar told him that the F-16's were arming and locking their missiles onto them. He called for a split. He sent his F-15 left. The wingman went right. The two bogeys were not yet visible. But it wouldn't take long. They were approaching one another at over thirteen hundred miles per hour.

Steele radioed the airborne-warfare commander at

Davis. He explained the situation and got a Weapons Hold command. He was not to fire unless fired upon.

And his instrumentation was screaming that he was about to be fired on.

"It's our asses," he growled. "Screw it. Master armament on," he told his backseat officer.

"Master arm on," backseat called back.

The oncoming planes whipped between the separating F-15's so fast they were a blur.

"Did you see them?" Steele radioed his wingman.

"F-16's. Confirm. They're ours."

"Then why the hell did they lock on?" Steele said anxiously, twisting in his cockpit to get a fix on them. "Attention, unidentified F-16's, this is Captain Steele out of Davis-Monthan. Do you copy? Over."

The helmet earphones were eerily silent as Steele sent his bird careening around in a slow 180. The unresponsive planes were also coming back.

"Bogeys are jinking back," the wingman warned.

"I got them."

"They're trying to lock on again."

"Okay, wingman, we have to assume they got a good look at us too. We can't assume these are friendly birds. Repeat. These are not friendly birds."

"Roger. Good luck, Steele."

"Stay sharp."

Steele saw the F-16's closing on him. Thirty miles separated them. Then twenty-five. Steele maneuvered the nose of his jet until the T-for-target symbol on his canopy lined up with a dot projected by the fire-control system.

"Select Fox-1," he called.

"Roger."

Steele kept his bird steady. Twenty miles. Then nineteen. Eighteen. He was within firing range now. He hesitated. These were American birds. What if their radios weren't working? He dismissed that thought instantly. Not both planes. Not at once.

"Seventeen miles," he called tightly. "Fox-1!"

A Sparrow missile *fwooshed* out from under the wing. Steele banked sharply. Sky and earth swapped perspectives. When he came back around, his radar man was screaming excitedly.

"Good hit. Good kill!"

Steele didn't see it until he got the jet level again. The sky was a pristine blue. There was a blot like floating ink. Falling from it, trailing fire and smoke, was a pinwheeling aircraft. As he watched, one wing separated from the fuselage like a broken blade.

"I got one!" Steele shouted exultantly. "Where's your kill?"

There was no answer from his wingman.

"Stockbridge. Do you copy?"

Captain Stockbridge didn't copy. He would never copy anyone again. Steele realized this when two jets formed up and jinked back on him like darts at a target. Both were F-16's. Stockbridge was the one going down.

"They got Stockbridge," Steele said in an arid voice.

"Aw damn," the wingman said hoarsely.

Steele saw the F-15 Eagle auger in as he tried to get a radar tone on the approaching bogeys. It hit the desert floor in a splatter of boiling flame.

"Any parachutes?" he asked his backseat anxiously.

The reply was subdued. "No, no chutes. Sorry."

"Not as sorry as those two are going to be," Steele promised when he finally got a tone signal. "Fox-2!"

A Sparrow rocket cut loose for the approaching attackers. They split, but not before a boil of fire spat from one wing tip.

"He got a missile off," Steele warned. He threw the plane into an evasive turn, and G-forces smashed him against his seat. The blood drained from his head faster than his constricting G-suit could fight it. His vision went gray, then black. He fought to stay conscious.

He pressured the fly-by-wire stick right. His vision went gray again. Then black. He risked joining his wingman as a smoking hole in the desert, but Steele had no choice. He had to lose that missile.

The desert floor spun under the F-15's nose as it fell into a tailspin, a heat-seeking missile fixed on its tailpipe.

Steele recovered. He leveled off hard, skimming the

ground. The Sparrow, not as maneuverable, kept going. It kicked up a cloud of dust when it hit.

"Still with me, guy?" Steele called.

"Barely," the radar man said.

"Where are they? Do you have them on visual?"

"I'm looking, I'm looking. There! I see them. They're banking. Jesus Christ!"

"What?"

"I see markings."

"Identify."

"You're not going to believe this, but they're Zero markings."

"Say again. I don't read you."

"Zeros. You know. Like the Japs used to fly."

Steele's mind raced. He was so focused on his flying that his brain refused to sort out the chatter of his radar man. Did he say they were Zeros? They were F-16's. Steele had seen that as plain as day.

Then the radar man was shouting. "They're diving!"

Captain Curtis Steele couldn't go down. There were mountains on his right. So he climbed.

His F-15 stood on her tail and strained toward the sun.

"Lock him up!" the backseater cried.

"I can't get a tone," Steele said.

"There're two of them. You gotta."

"I can't get a fucking tone," Steele shouted, pounding on his instrument board. "I'm gonna go through them if I can."

Steele held the stick steady. He let them lock on him. He intended to bluff his way through. It would take nerve, but anyone willing to strap on forty thousand pounds of careening machinery and go head-to-head with another jet had that in spades.

The paired F-16's were diving now. Steele focused on the space between their wings. If only they didn't launch too soon. . . .

Then, sickeningly, his afterburner flamed out and Steele felt himself lifted out of the nearly horizontal seat back as the powerless F-15 Eagle began to fall back like a dart thrown up into the air.

"I've lost it! I've lost power!" Steele was shouting. He clawed at the restarter. The engine whined. Nothing. The nose of the jet was tipping earthward again and there was the desert floor spinning like a plate.

"Eject! Eject!" he called, hitting his ejection button.

The canopy popped. Then he felt a gorge-lifting kick in the butt as the ejection-seat charge exploded. Then everything exploded. The F-15 burst like a pressurized can in a microwave, going in an instant from magnificent winged metal bird into so much slicing shrapnel.

A section of wing decapitated Captain Steele before he realized what had happened. His backseater was too slow hitting his ejection button. He went down with the plane.

High above, two F-16 Fighting Falcons with Rising Sun markings streaked away like fugitive arrows.

When Davis-Monthan Air Force Base informed the Pentagon that they had lost contact with their scout planes, the Joint Chiefs of Staff were assembled. Admiral William Blackbird, chairman of the Joint Chiefs, ordered two Marine F/A-18 Hornets to the Yuma Marine Air Station, which had also stopped communicating with the outside world. Then he put in a call to the President of the United States.

He was told by the President's chief of staff that the President was pitching horseshoes in the new White House pit and would he mind waiting for a callback.

The chairman of the Joint Chiefs told the chief of staff that a callback would be just fine. Then he turned to the assembled Joint Chiefs.

"It's ours. That idiot chief of staff must think that if we don't scream emergency, then the Pentagon can wait. So what's the situation on those Hornets?"

The commandant of the Marine Corps held up an annoyed hand. Then he clapped it to an ear while he listened to a voice on the other end of the telephone line. When he lifted his head, his face was pale.

"We've lost contact with the Hornets."

"What happened?"

"The Air Force shot them down."

The silence in the room was palpable.

"Check all bases," Admiral Blackbird ordered. "Find out what's going on."

"We're doing that, Admiral." All around the room, the combined leaders of America's military command structure were doing what they did best: making phone calls.

One by one, they updated the chairman. All other bases and units reported normal situations.

"It seems to be confined to the Yuma area," suggested the chief of Naval Operations.

"This could be a diversion. I want a worldwide status report."

The order was carried out at once. All over the continental United States and Europe, U.S. bases were contacted. KH-11 recon satellites shifted in their orbits.

Telephone and telex activity centering on the Pentagon grew frantic. It threatened to jam the phone lines of official Washington.

As the hours passed, word came back that there were no unusual events anywhere in the world. There was only Yuma.

And out of Yuma, there was only silence.

Remo Williams closed his eyes.

It was not to block out the macabre bouncing of the airmen's bodies as they struck the desert floor. Too many of them had hit like rag dolls for it to hold meaning anymore. The screams were faraway in his ears, masked by the rushing of air as Remo fell in the so-called "dead-spider" free-fall position.

Remo closed his eyes to better focus on his breathing. For in Sinanju breathing was all. It unlocked the reservoirs of potential that lay in every man. Some men, when faced with a crisis, could summon up a portion of that inner power. Great strength, inhuman speed, impossible reflexes—all were within the spectrum of human ability. Remo, because Sinanju training put him at one with the universe, could utilize every aspect of that spectrum in simultaneous harmony.

People had fallen out of airplanes before and survived, Remo knew. Usually they shattered every bone in their bodies. And those were the lucky ones.

Remo intended to survive. He shut his eyes, the better to attune his breathing to the universe. He locked out all sound and sensation and looked within himself.

And somewhere deep in the pit of his stomach, a cold fire began to burn. Remo willed himself into that point. He willed every essence of his being to compress into a pinpoint of icy fire. The wind roaring in his ears cut off as if they had been shuttered. He felt his fingertips go numb. And his toes lose feeling.

The feeling drained from his limbs and rushed, like blood, to his stomach—according to Sinanju teaching, the seat of the human soul.

Remo felt lighter, as light as a snowflake. But even a snowflake fell. Remo dared not strike the desert with the force of a falling snowflake, for in this state, his bones were too fragile to survive. All his mass was concentrated in one point. He weighed no more than a snowflake. His bones were as hollow as a snowball. But, like a snowball, he was bound by the irresistible pull of gravity.

Remo willed his essence tighter. He would never understand the physics of what he was attempting to do, any more than he comprehended the natural laws he bent every time he sent a forefinger through plate steel or saw as clearly as a cat in absolute darkness.

When he felt his mass to be nearly negligible, he allowed his shuttered ears to open. The wind was no longer a roar. Remo smiled. He was no longer dropping like a stone. But he was still dropping. He reached out to feel the wind, his fingers touching the palpable updrafts of heat rising from the desert floor. He was at one with those updrafts. They were his friends. He would ride them to a gentle landing on the ground far below.

Remo opened his eyes.

He saw the sand. It was inches from his face. His smile broke into an open-mouthed shout. He never got any sound out because his mouth was suddenly full of sand, and his neck snapped back with a dry crack.

And in the black heart of the universe, angry red

eyes snapped awake and a cruel mouth opened in howling rage.

Retired Master Sergeant Jim Concannon had been too young for World War II. By the time Vietnam came around, he had a paunch, although during his long Army career he had served in Pleiku and Da Nang.

But for the Korean conflict, Jim Concannon was just right. It was in Korea that then-Private Jim Concannon learned to fight, to survive, and to witness horror without being psychologically incapacitated by it.

But here, in peacetime, out in the Yuma Desert, as Bronzini's technical adviser watched more than five hundred young airmen fall to their death, he stood, his mouth agape, for once in his life paralyzed into inaction.

When the final body, which took an agonizingly long time to land, finally did strike, retired Master Sergeant Jim Concannon pulled the binoculars from his staring eyes and turned to Fourth A.D. Nintendo Toshiba.

Toshiba was smiling. It was a sick, twisted smile. Concannon jumped the Japanese.

Toshiba went down under his pummeling fists. Concannon took him by the throat and tried to squeeze his eyes out of his head. Then one of the crewmen in desert utilities came up from behind and knocked him flat with the butt of his AK-47.

Concannon was dimly aware of his being lugged into a waiting APC and unceremoniously dumped in back. His ribs hurt. As the APC started off, he understood why. He had been thrown onto a stack of boxes.

Concannon played dead while he slowly walked his fingers to the side of a crate. It smelled faintly of lettuce. A lettuce crate. He wormed one hand into the spaces between the rough slats and touched something smooth and nonmetallic. He pulled the object out and opened his eyes a crack.

Jim Concannon saw that he had his hands on a Chinese stick grenade. A Type 67. He suppressed a pleased smile. In Korea, he used to carry a box of grenades during patrols. He was laughed at for lugging all that weight. Until one day, outside of Inchon, when his unit was ambushed by a Red Chinese patrol. As his buddies were mowed down, Jim Concannon wrenched open the box and began pulling pins and tossing grenades in every direction. There was no science to what he did. He just let fly.

When the forest had fallen silent, Jim Concannon got up off his stomach. On all sides, there were Red Chinese corpses—corpses dressed much like the two lines of soldiers sitting in the back of the rolling APC nearly forty years later and half a world away.

Jim Concannon had saved his patrol that day back in 1953. He knew he could not save those who died on this day, but he could avenge them.

One by one he slipped stick grenades from the crate. When he had five, he unscrewed the blade caps at the ends, exposing the pull cords. He yanked the caps, igniting the time-delay fuses. Then he made his move. He rolled suddenly, and hurled the grenades.

There is no place to run in a sealed APC. Not that the Japanese soldiers didn't try. They saw the bouncing sticks and leapt to their feet, bumping helmets and tripping over one another's feet and suddenly-forgotten rifles in a desperate effort to escape.

But there was no escape. One by one, the grenades detonated, and although only three exploded—which was par for the Type 67 stick grenade—they rendered the human cargo of the APC unrecognizable.

15

They came for Arnold Ziffel as he was having his morning coffee.

Arnold Ziffel always knew they would come. Sometimes they were Russian and sometimes they were Cuban. Other times they were black or Asian or even Mexican. The face of the enemy that coveted the Land of the Free continually changed in Arnold Ziffel's mind.

But Arnold Ziffel's resolve would never change, he vowed. That was why he had laid away a three-month food supply in his garage. That was why he kept his AR-15 assault rifle fully loaded at all times. He was not going down without a fight. The bumper sticker attached to the back of his pickup truck summed up Arnold Ziffel's philosophy perfectly: "My wife, yes. My dog, maybe. My gun, never!"

When they came, they didn't want Mrs. Arnold Ziffel. They kicked his dog, Rusty, out the front door and locked him out. They also locked out Arnold Ziffel's AR-15. It was in the back of his pickup.

"What do you want?" Arnold sputtered, rising from his breakfast nook as three soldiers prodded his wife into the room at the point of fixed bayonets.

"Christmas tree!" one of them screeched. "Where is?"

"My tree?" Arnold blurted. "You want my *Christmas* tree?"

"Where tree?"

"For God's sake, Arnold," Mrs. Ziffel said shrilly. "Tell them!"

Arnold Ziffel decided that he could live with handing up his Christmas tree.

"In the next room," he said.

"You show!" the leader demanded. He was Asian. As he pulled Arnold into the den, he recognized their People's Liberation Army uniforms. He was a regular reader of *Soldier of Fortune* magazine. The funny thing was, these folks didn't look Chinese at all.

"Here it is," Arnold said, waving to a stunted Scotch pine growing in a tree box. It was tastefully decorated with alternating red and silver ornaments.

"Stand by tree!" the Chinese soldier said.

"Come on, Helen," Arnold said, taking his wife by the arm.

"What can they want?" Helen Ziffel whispered.

"Shhh." Arnold put his arm around his wife's thin shoulders. He felt her tremble. Suddenly, despite her faded pink housecoat and rat's-nest hair, she seemed more precious to him than his beloved AR-15. He was about to tell her so when the leader shouted something

in a foreign tongue and into the den came other soldiers, lugging camera equipment and lights. They set
up the lights in opposite corners of the den and turned
them on. They hurt Arnold's eyes. Then the camera
was put into position, and Mrs. Ziffel said something
that sent a wave of relief through Arnold's wobbly legs.

"Arnold. These must be the movie people."

"Is that true?" Arnold stammered. "Are you with the
movie they're shooting?"

"Yes, yes," the leader said distractedly. He conferred
with a cameraman. They were holding up a pocket
device and trying to read the meter. It looked exactly
like the light meter that came with Arnold's thirty-five-
millimeter Nishitsu Autofocus.

"Arnold, do you suppose we're going to be in the
movie?" Helen Ziffel wondered.

"I'll ask. Hey, friend, are you going to shoot us?"

The leader turned, his eyes cold black opals. "Yes,
we shoot you soon. Wait, prease."

"Did you hear that?" Arnold told his wife excitedly.
"We're going to be in a Bronzini movie." Arnold Ziffel
had seen all the *Grundy*'s twice, once for the story and
then a second time to count the technical mistakes.

Then the cameraman got behind his camera and the
leader called out to the Ziffels.

"Adorn tree, prease," he said.

"Beg pardon?" Arnold said, blinking.

"Tree. You make rike you adorn with ranterns, okay?"

"I think he wants us to pretend we're putting the
bulbs on, Arnold. That's what he meant by lanterns."

"But the dang things already decorated," Arnold hissed
through a set-toothed smile. He didn't want to have a
fight with his wife in front of thirty million moviegoers.

"Then let's pretend," Helen Ziffel said tightly. "This
is a major movie, for goodness' sake. Try to go along,
for once in your life."

Arnold and Helen got on either side of their Christmas tree and each removed a bulb. Helen took a silver
one and Arnold took a red one.

"How's this?" Arnold asked, and he fumbled the tiny
hook back onto the tree.

The leader barked something unintelligible and the ornament exploded in Arnold's surprised face. His wife screamed. The tree shivered manically, ornaments popping like flashbulbs, limbs snapping like brush.

Arnold Ziffel saw the raw ruin that had been his upraised hand and felt the sledgehammer blows of automatic-weapons fire punctuate his trembling body. He joined his wife on the floor. The new light fixture he had bought for the den shattered within its Santa Claus wrapping under the impact of his 195-pound weight. His surviving hand fell onto his wife's cheek, and even though he couldn't feel it, Arnold knew she was dead.

The gunfire stopped.

Arnold Ziffel lifted his face shakily and tried to see into the blinding lights. Just before he died, he wondered why, if this were just a movie, the bullets had been real. And why, if, as he had suddenly suspected, they had finally come for him, were they filming it?

Mayor Basil Cloves wanted to know if this was in the script when the uniformed Japanese barged into his office and dragged him out of his executive chair.

He was still asking it five minutes later when they forced his head into the V of the curb in front of city hall and rolled a tank up onto the sidewalk. The left front track stopped just inches from his head.

Third A.D. Harachi Seiko demanded, "One rast time, I ask for your surrender. Do you agree?"

Cloves hesitated. "Is this in the script?" he asked again. Seiko barked an order in Japanese. The tank inched closer. Cloves felt the coldness of the curb against his face. A kneeling Japanese kept his face pressed to the gritty street. Another one squatted harpy-like on his legs. A third pinioned his arms behind his back.

"Tell me what you want me to do!" Cloves said in an agitated voice. "If the script calls for it, I'll surrender."

"Choice is yours," Seiko said flatly. "You surrender and terr citizens to ray down arms. Or you die."

Basil Cloves cringed from the spittle spraying from the Japanese's screaming mouth. Through the triangular frame of the arm of the soldier who had his head, he could see a video camera aimed at his own face. Maybe he should play the brave public servant.

Behind the video camera a man was walking down the street, looking dazed and crying in a voice choked with disbelief, "But this is America. This is America!"

He was quickly surrounded and bayoneted in the stomach.

It occurred to Mayor Basil Cloves that perhaps this wasn't a movie after all. That the explosions he kept hearing were not special effects. That the sporadic gunfire was not harmless.

Basil Cloves in that moment realized what he had done. And he made his decision.

"I'll never surrender," he said quietly.

The next sound he heard was a guttural order, then the clanking of the tank. The man holding his head down turned his face to the dirt-caked track, which gleamed at its wear points. The track inched forward.

"You change mind?" Third A.D. Seiko demanded.

"Never!" Mayor Cloves spat. He knew they could not run him down. Not with four men holding him down. They'd be run over too.

Yet the track continued gnashing toward him.

The man at his head suddenly released his hair. He stepped back. Cloves lifted his head. But that was all he could lift. The others kept his arms and legs down.

Then the track bit into the mayor of Yuma's nose. He screamed, but the sound was swallowed by the shattering of his teeth and the pulverizing of his facial bones.

Mayor Basil Cloves never heard the pulpy crack that caused yellowish brain curd to erupt from the fissures of his broken skull.

Third A.D. Harachi Seiko ordered the tank to back up so the cameraman could come in for a close-up of the mayor's head. Then the tank rolled forward again. It went back and forth until the mayor's head was nothing more than a meaty stain.

Linda Best was only dimly aware that there was a film being shot in Yuma. It was the day before Christmas vacation and that meant there was a lot of homework to collect and tests to give to her third-grade class in the Ronald Reagan Elementary School.

So when the Asian soldier entered the class as she was passing out a grammar test, the last thing that Linda Best thought of was a movie.

She saw the AK-47 in the Asian soldier's hands and all she could think of was the incident in California, where a maniac in fatigues and carrying an automatic weapon had killed or maimed nearly thirty children.

She cried "No!" and flung the papers in his face. The man flinched. Linda Best leapt at the man in the desert camouflage fatigues before he could recover. Her hands clawed for the gun. She never felt the sharp edge of the bayonet as it sliced one grasping hand. The other got the barrel. Linda pulled. The Asian man fought back. He was small. Linda was not. They struggled as the children began ducking under the desks.

"Give me that thing!" she sobbed rackingly.

The man grunted inarticulately. Somewhere, through a rushing in her ears, Linda heard commotion elsewhere in the corridors of the school. A popping like firecrackers. She was barely aware of it. All her thoughts, all her strength, were focused on the sweating face that grimaced only inches in front of her.

Linda Best knew she couldn't hope to overpower him by sheer strength. Surprise had carried her this far. Out of the corner of her eyes she saw some of the children crawl out the open door. Good children, she thought. Run, run. Get help.

Then she felt the strength begin to leave one arm. No, not now, not yet. She moaned silently. Lord give me strength. And she saw why. The blood had practically painted her bare forearm. She had been unwittingly clutching a bayonet.

Linda released the rifle. The Japanese scrambled to bring the weapon to bear. In that instant, Linda Best kicked him in the crotch. The Japanese doubled over. His weapon fell into Linda's waiting arms.

Linda Best had never held a rifle in her life. She had never fired a shot. She had never struck a blow in anger. She never wanted to.

But on that day in December, with the children scrambling between her legs to safety, she found the strength to place the muzzle of the unfamiliar weapon to the face of the man who had had the temerity to enter her classroom with murderous intent, and gave him the contents of its clip in one pull of the trigger.

"Everyone, hurry," Linda called, looking away from the result of her courage. "Follow me!"

The children came, some of them. Others huddled and cried. Swiftly, gently, Linda Best went among them, prying fingers from desk legs. She pushed them to the safety of the door, admonishing them not to look at the man who lay with agitated limbs across the doorway.

She carried the last two in her arms. They were crying for their mothers.

It was too much to hope that in their panic the children would all reach the fire exits. Linda stumbled out into the corridor hoping for best, fearing the worst.

She did not expect the sight that awaited her.

The corridor swarmed with students. And among them were armed soldiers, men with hard foreign faces and merciless weapons. A fellow teacher bumped into Linda. It was Miss Head, who had the fifth grade.

"What is it? What's happening?" Linda asked breathlessly.

"We don't know," Miss Head hissed. "They want us to assemble outside."

"But why? Who are they?"

"The assistant principal thinks they're with the movie. But look at how they're behaving. I think it's real."

"I know it is," Linda said, holding up her hand. It was stiffening. Miss Head saw the already-browning blood and put her hand in front of her mouth.

Then they were both prodded toward the front doors by insistent bayonets. There, the children were being forced to sit on the grass, their hands clasped behind their heads like POW's in a war movie. It would have been cute had it not been so grotesque.

Rough hands segregated Linda and her colleague from the milling children. They were made to stand with a growing knot of teachers.

Linda found herself shoved next to the principal, Mr. Mulroy. "Can this be for real?" she asked.

"They're serious. Rothman and Skindarian are dead."

"Oh, no!"

"No talking!" a voice barked.

When the last of the children were forced onto the ground, the soldiers turned to the teachers. One wearing captain's bars directed the others. The faculty was forced to stand in a line as a camera was set up.

"Look, they're filming this," Miss Head whispered. "Maybe it is a movie, after all."

That happy thought lived only as long as it took for several soldiers to drag the blood-spattered corpses of three fallen teachers out into the sunlight.

No one believed it was only a move after that.

The Japanese captain waited tensely for the cameraman to signal him. He nodded back. Then the captain called, "Rorring. Fire!"

The camera hummed. And AK-47's slapped to uniformed shoulders. The gunfire came in single shots, execution-style.

The entire teaching staff of the Ronald Reagan Elementary School were executed without benefit of blindfolds or final words. The captain went among the dead and delivered a vicious kick to each body. Those who groaned had a bayonet plunged into their throats.

The children watched this in silence.

All over Yuma, the schools were cleared and the staffs put to death. Every food outlet was placed under armed guard. The gun shops were quarantined. All roads were closed and the Amtrak rail beds were dynamited.

Three hours into the Battle of Yuma, the electricity went out. The Yuma reservoir was placed under occupation control and water supplies shut off. Telephone lines to the outside world were severed. All television and radio stations were seized and taken off the air.

The police station was surrounded by T-62 tanks, which opened up with their .125-millimeter smoothbore cannon until the one-story stucco building was a shattered tumble. Individual police units were hunted down and crushed. The National Guard headquarters was seized and its weapons stores confiscated.

By noon, the tanks and the bodies had convinced the majority of the population that this was no film. Those with firearms took to the streets. For two more hours, pockets of resistance, snipers and roving groups of citizens, fought back with hunting rifles and handguns.

Then, at 2:06 in the afternoon, tanks blocking the runway of Yuma International Airport rolled aside to allow a squadron of five propeller-driven planes to take off. They lined up and crossed the sky under the high cirrus clouds. Simultaneously, each plane emitted a puff of white vapor. Then another puff.

Across the sky, in fluffy dot-matrix-style letters, the skywriting planes spelled out a message: RESISTANCE WILL END OR YOUR CHILDREN WILL DIE!

All over the city, sporadic gunfire began to die down. Not all citizens threw down their weapons at first. A few—those without families—kept on fighting. Those who weren't hunted down by Japanese troops were quelled by Yuma citizens with children at risk.

By six P.M. the city was quiet. The chill of afternoon deepened into a still cold. Fires burned at scattered locations, sending smoke into the air. Tanks prowled the streets with impunity. The sun fell behind the mountains, casting long, forlorn purple shadows on the surrounding sea of sand. It was magic hour.

Yuma, Arizona, had fallen to the Nishitsu Corporation.

16

The closer she got to the Yuma city limits, the more afraid Sheryl Rose became. Yuma was her home. She had been born in Yuma, gone to school there, and after graduation from nearby Arizona Western College, got a job at a local television station. A scary day was when she got the cue cards out of order.

Sheryl fiddled with the radio. Stations as far away as Phoenix came in clearly. But none of the hometown stations were on the air.

If Sheryl hadn't been in broadcasting, it might not have hit her as hard. But the dead air was like a knife in her stomach.

"They got the radio stations," she sobbed. "How could this happen? This is America."

"And Rome was Rome," said Chiun gravely. "It, too, fell when it became old. Where is the Greece of days gone by? The Egyptians no longer rule their part of the world. Do not think because your nation has existed without knowing the tread of an invading army, that it could never happen. It has. Now we must deal with what has taken place, not deny it."

Bill Roam spoke up for the first time since they had left Luke.

"You're acting like Yuma has fallen to the Nazis," he said. "It's only a movie company. Sure, they've gone crazy, but they can't hold an American city indefinitely. And they sure can't widen their area of operations. They barely have the manpower to hold this city. When the shock wears off, the people will grab their guns and beat them off. You watch. You'll see."

No one responded to that. They came to the roadblock. The two T-62 tanks were still in place. But now they were quiet. As the Ninja passed them, the sound of its engine caused the trapped Japanese crews to begin pounding and shouting for attention.

"What happened to them?" Bill Roam wanted to know, looking back in bewilderment.

"He did," Sheryl said, jerking a thumb at Chiun.

"You must know some right powerful medicine, chief," Roam said.

"Yes," Chiun said. "Very powerful."

"Well, I know a few tricks myself," Roam said, his eyes on the desert. "Maybe I'll get to use them before this is done. I helped three planeloads of airmen step into eternity out there. Only blood will redeem that."

Chiun's eyes were on the desert too. He said nothing.

They followed Route 8 through the city. Abandoned

cars burned, releasing smudgy smoke that hung in the air like the visible stench of defeat. They stopped at a roadside pay phone at Chiun's insistence, but he returned complaining that it was broken.

Every pay phone they encountered was out of order.

"Face it," Roam told him. "They've cut us off from the outside world."

"Oh, my goodness," Sheryl said in a small shocked voice. "Look!"

Off the road, there was a school. A desert-camouflage armored personnel carrier stood parked in front like some absurd ice-cream truck. Uniformed soldiers stood guard over the grounds, where rows of children squatted, their hands folded behind their heads. Other soldiers dragged adult bodies back into the building.

"Jesus!" Bill Roam muttered. "This can't be happening."

"Stop the car," said Chiun.

"Are you crazy?" Sheryl cried. "They look like they'd shoot us as soon as look at us."

"I cannot allow those children to be threatened."

Sheryl grabbed Chiun's sleeve. "Look," she pleaded. "Think this through. There are more of them than there are of us."

Chiun looked into Bill Roam's weather-beaten face.

"I'm up for it," Roam said quietly.

They both looked to Sheryl.

"All right," she said reluctantly. "But I don't think I'm going to be much help. My knees are shaking so hard I can barely keep my feet on the brake."

"Just keep the engine running, little lady," Bill Roam said as the jeep pulled over to the side of the road a ways beyond the schoolgrounds. "The chief here and I will do the rest."

"Why do you call me that?" Chiun asked.

"Because you look like a chief. Ready? Let's go."

The two men left the car in silence. They worked their way toward the building. Chiun seemed to drift like so much silent smoke. Bill Roam walked low, so his tall lanky frame was not so obvious. Sheryl thought he

moved like a stealthy Indian brave; then she remembered that Sunny Joe Roam *was* an Indian.

She watched anxiously through her rear window.

The Master of Sinanju took a position behind a cactus
that afforded a commanding view of the school, front
and rear. It was as tall as a man and shaped like a
barrel. He touched one of the long needles and found it
quite sharp. With one fingernail he razored the needles
off, collecting them in his hand like so much straw.

Chiun peered around the side of the cactus and looked
for Sunny Joe Roam. He frowned. There was so sign of
him. Could he have been captured already? Even for a
white, that would have been inordinately clumsy.

Taking care not to be seen, Chiun moved to the
other side of the cactus. He spotted Sunny Joe Roam
sneaking up on a Japanese guard loitering near the back
of the school, out of sight of the others. The Japanese
was half-turned from Sunny Joe Roam. As Chiun
watched, the soldier pulled a cigarette pack from his
uniform blouse pocket and shook out a cigarette. He
struck a match. The wind blew it out.

Moving on cat feet, Sunny Joe quickened his approach. Chiun, knowing the reason why, felt a tingle of
admiration for the Indian. He realized that the guard
would have to turn out of the wind to light his cigarette. And Sunny Joe was walking into the wind.

Chiun lifted a handful of needles, preparing to throw
them.

He never had to. The Japanese turned; Sunny Joe
shifted to one side and froze beside a lantana shrub.

The guard was looking directly at the bush as he lit
the stubborn cigarette. The bush shook slightly from a
desert breeze. The Japanese seemed not to notice.

Chiun's parchment face relaxed in mild surprise. He
had never seen a white move so stealthily. Not since
Remo. He lowered the needles and watched.

The guard reached for his fly, turned to the schoolhouse wall, and Sunny Joe came out from behind the
bush like a ghost, one fist up.

Chiun turned away. Roam would not need his help.

He directed his attention to the guards surrounding the hostage children. Chiun shook his arms free of his sleeves and prepared to hurl the twin handfuls into the air. Above his head, he heard the drone of planes flying in unison. The wind was strong, but steady. He could compensate for it.

The Master of Sinanju brought his hands up in an underarm throw. The needles left his splayed fingers like splinters of pure light.

The first fusillade went the furthest. The needles arced high. Dropping their points as if programmed by a computer, they began to fall. The other needles reached the apex of their flight almost at the same time.

The Master of Sinanju jumped out from behind the sheltering cactus. If he was seen now, it would not matter. Arms pumping, he ran toward the children.

Then Sunny Joe came out from behind the schoolhouse. He carried an AK-47. Chiun hoped he had restraint enough not to use it.

The needles fell in two focused groups. They struck the soldiers wherever they stood, but none fell within the circle of guards to hit the children.

Seeing needles seemingly sprouting from their arms and shoulders, the guards had a perfectly sensible reaction. They gave the Japanese equivalent of "Ouch!" and looked up. They also raised their weapons defensively.

They were still looking up when the Master of Sinanju began to explode their internal organs within their bodies.

Chiun's bony fists found abdomens and backs. He struck only once at each man, but his splindly arms struck like steam-driven pistons. No soldier made a sound after he fell. And all of them fell.

Instantly Chiun was in the midst of the children.

"Make haste!" he scolded. "On your feet, little ones. You must flee. Return to your families. Go!"

The children reacted slowly. Not so the Japanese in the APC. They boiled out of the back like cockroaches from a lighted oven.

Bill Roam picked them off as they came with cool single shots from his AK-47. The first two out went down without firing a shot. Others ducked behind the machine and tried to return fire from under the eight-wheeled undercarriage.

Roam dropped to his stomach and lined up. He hit a tire, corrected his aim, and erased the face of a Japanese who was sighting down the barrel of his rifle. Roam's next shot took out the front tire. The APC listed suddenly, and the driver started the engine in an effort to escape. He didn't get far. There was still one sharpshooter under the chassis. The good rear tires ran over him, splintering his rib cage with a sickeningly loud sound. The Japanese must have been packing grenades, because his body exploded when the tires ran over it.

The APC jumped four feet into the air, then fell back, blowing the remaining tires.

Bill Roam peppered it with single shots, taking his time to aim, but giving the occupants of the APC no time to organize a response.

By that time, prodded by the Master of Sinanju, the students had all taken shelter inside the school building. Chiun shut the door after the last one.

He hurried to Bill Roam's position.

"Cease your firing," he told Roam. "The children are safe. I will deal with these vermin now."

"Mind if I join the festivities?" Roam said, standing up.

"Only if you do two things for me."

"What's that?" Roam wondered.

"Leave the weapon and do not get yourself killed."

"You got 'em both," Roam said, letting his AK-47 fall onto the grass. "It was about out of bullets anyhow."

They moved on the APC from two directions. Chiun took the back. Roam went for the driver. He slipped up under the driver's angle of vision and took the door handle. He yanked it open so fast the driver, huddled under the steering wheel, only realized he was in trouble when an unexpected breeze touched his face. He opened his eyes. He saw Bill Roam's fist. Then he saw nothing.

In the rear, three Japanese were crouched, their rifles aimed at the open doors. Smoke came up through the damaged floor, but no shrapnel had penetrated the APC's hard steel flooring.

The Master of Sinanju appeared framed in the opening like some wrathful spirit. One clawlike hand swept out, batting aside a rifle muzzle before its owner could pull the trigger. Another was sucked from its owner's clutch so fast that skin came off his fingers.

Chiun's fingernails found both men's throats at once. They sank in and then slipped out in a flash. Blood followed them out, in bright arterial streams. He hurled the dying soldiers from the vehicle with careless yanks.

One soldier remained. He fired a burst that would have gone through the old Korean's head had it not been for the unfortunate fact that between the time the trigger was pulled and the first bullet emerged from the muzzle, the rifle inexplicably swapped ends.

Instead, the bullets destroyed the soldier's intestinal tract. He looked down at his stomach. It was a ruin of camouflage cloth, now suitable only for blending in with hospital wastes. He noticed that he was holding his rifle the wrong way. How had that happened?

Then the old Korean set his palm against the butt end of the stock and pushed. Too late, the soldier realized that his bayonet was affixed to the muzzle. His eyes rolled up into his head. He was still clutching his weapon when he collapsed to the floor.

Chiun emerged from the APC with hard visage. A hulking shadow came around the side. Chiun whirled suddenly, taken by surprise. It was Bill Roam.

"You are very silent on your feet for a white," he said with a hint of respect in his dry voice.

"I'm an injun, remember?" Roam laughed. "And I told you I knew some powerful medicine."

"Your tribe. By what name does it go?"

"You never heard of them," Roam said evasively. "So what are we going to do with the children? They sure won't fit into our little jeep. Or this thing either," he added, smacking the APC's flank with his meaty hand.

"Perhaps they are safer here," Chiun said slowly, as he saw Sheryl drive up. She honked her horn repeatedly.

"Uh-oh, I don't like the sound of that," Roam said ominously.

Sheryl leaned her head out the jeep's window, calling, "Look!" She pointed at the sky.

There, five airplanes were finishing writing a message in puffs of white vapor: RESISTANCE WILL END OR YOUR CHILDREN WILL DIE!

Roam grunted deep in his throat. "Empty threat now."

"No," Chiun replied. "For if they have this school, they have the others."

"Damn! What are we going to do?"

"I know the Japanese mind," Chiun said levelly. "They ruled my homeland for many bitter years. They will instigate reprisals for what we have done."

"We gotta get those kids to safety. How about we make a dash for the reservation? The Japs might not have bothered with my people. The kids would be as safe there as anywhere."

"No," Chiun said. "There is a better way. We will send them back to their own homes."

"I get it. It's harder to bring down one pigeon than a flock of them, right?"

"Exactly. Come."

Moving rapidly, they emptied the school. The children were sent off in groups, older ones paired with the younger. It took most of the afternoon, but by the time they were done, every child had escaped into the city.

"Some of them might not make it," Sheryl said as she watched the last of them go.

"Some of them will not," Chiun said flatly.

"Then why send them? Wasn't there a better way?"

"The only other way was the desert. None of them would have survived the desert. Come."

They got into the jeep in silence.

Sheryl put the key into the ignition. "Look. If it's as bad as we think, we won't get through the city unchallenged. Not in broad daylight. My house isn't far from here. What do you say?"

"The little gal makes sense," Roam said.

"Agreed," Chiun said. "For if we are to deal with this situation, I must devise a plan."

"Deal?" Sheryl said as she spun the car around and

ran in toward the city. "I vote we just wait until the Marines or the Rangers or whatever land."

"That is the problem with you people," Chiun sniffed. He was watching the puffy skywriting spread and thin.

"What people?" Sheryl wanted to know as she took an off ramp.

"Americans," Chiun returned. "You are such creatures of your technology. Do you remember the time those whales were trapped in an ice hole?"

"Sure thing. It was in all the papers. What about it?"

"The Eskimo wanted to begin cutting a channel to the sea to release them," Chiun went on, "but the Americans refused to allow this. They said that when their ice-crushing ships arrived, they would do the job faster."

"And they came."

"After many delays in which the animals suffered. The ships could not break the ice fast enough. Finally the Americans relented and the Eskimo were allowed to begin cutting a channel by hand."

"As I recall, between them they got the job done."

"One animal died. Had the Americans not insisted on waiting for their mighty technology, no animals would have died, and the others would not have suffered."

"Am I missing something here? What does that have to do with our situation?"

"Americans always act helpless while waiting for their technology to arrive. It does not always arrive in time, nor does it always work when it does."

"What he's saying, Sheryl," Bill Roam cut in, "is that we can't afford to wait for the Marines."

"But they're coming, aren't they? I mean, the U.S. government isn't exactly going to sit on their duffs while Yuma is terrorized."

"You don't know the military," Roam said tightly. "The first thing they're going to be looking at is their posteriors."

"That's crazy talk, Sunny Joe," Sheryl retorted. "This is America, not some banana republic where anyone can just waltz in and take over."

"Got news for you, kid. They already have."

"Oh." Sheryl sent the jeep down Arizona Avenue and took a right onto Twenty-fourth Street. The roads were deserted. Crude signs hung from lampposts: CURFEW IN EFFECT. VIOLATORS WILL BE SHOT. "We're gonna be awful conspicuous," she muttered.

As they drove past Kennedy Memorial Park, they saw the bodies twisting in the trees.

"Hell!" Roam exploded. "Don't look now, but they hung the City Council."

A T-62 tank suddenly lunged from the park like a sluggish spider from its lair. Sheryl hit the brakes. The Ninja slewed wildly. She pulled hard on the wheel and sent the machine in a tight circle.

Too tight, as it turned out. The Nishitsu Ninja heeled like a sloop in a stiff crosswind. It went over on its side and it slid until friction brought it to a halt.

Chiun flung the door open and crawled out. Bill Roam unfolded his long lanky frame after him. Together they pulled Sheryl from the interior.

The T-62 clanked to a halt.

Swiftly the overturned vehicle was surrounded by tight-faced Japanese.

"You surrender!" one spat fiercely.

"Dammit, they got us!" Sheryl said woozily. "All right, we—"

"No!" Chiun said coldly. "We will never surrender."

The Japanese stepped closer.

"For God's sake," Sheryl hissed, "they'll shoot us."

"You surrender, woman!" the Japanese repeated.

Before Sheryl could say anything, Chiun snapped, "None of us will surrender. We demand to be taken to your leader."

The Japanese hesitated. Their rifle muzzles quivered nervously. Finally the squad leader relaxed slightly.

"Okay, we take you," he said.

"Do as they say," Chiun whispered. "The Japanese despise those who surrender. Trust me."

"Look, chief," Bill Roam protested, "I can't go along with this. We may not be prisoners exactly, but we sure as hell ain't free either. I've got to get to my people."

"You are no good to them dead," Chiun warned.

Roam's big fists were clenched tightly. His sun-squint eyes switched between the encircling Japanese.

"My people depend on me," he said quietly.

"I understand your concern. Do as I say, and you may live to see them again."

"And if they're dead?"

"Then I will help you avenge them," Chiun promised, his steely eyes on the Japanese.

"I'm going to count on that," Roam said as the Japanese yanked them apart and searched them for weapons. Roam endured it stoically, his arms raised. Sheryl's face turned a bright red as two soldiers ran their hands up and down her tight dungarees. Chiun slapped the first Japanese who dared to lift the hem of his kimono. The second one lost the use of his hands. None of the others made a move toward him after that.

They were marched at gunpoint down the center of the deserted street. The sun was setting. The T-62 muttered behind them.

"What do you think is going to happen to us?" Roam asked out of the side of his mouth.

"I will meet the man who has killed my son."

"And what are you going to do when you meet him?" Sheryl asked nervously.

"I do not know," Chiun admitted.

Sheryl and Sunny Joe both looked at the impassive face of the Master of Sinanju. It was fixed, as if preserved by a veneer of beeswax. His old eyelids squeezed into walnut slits.

The Nishitsu corporate jet circled Yuma International Airport while tanks were withdrawn from the runway.

Jiro Isuzu watched it touch down. He stood at attention in his PLA uniform, his ancestral samurai sword at his hip. Behind him, a black Lincoln Continental limousine waited like a hearse. As the jet rolled to a whining halt, an honor guard of his men rushed to form two lines between him and the aircraft.

The ramp dropped and down the stairs came Nemuro Nishitsu. He wore a dark business suit. His white shirt-front seemed radiant in the late-evening chill. It was unseasonably cold in Yuma, and Jiro Isuzu was shaken by the difficulty with which his mentor negotiated the steps.

Nemuro Nishitsu walked down the steps on uncertain feet. But he walked alone and unassisted, a cane draped over one hand. He seemed close to falling.

When he reached the ground, he walked stiffly to his second in command. Jiro Isuzu bowed low, saying, "Greetings, Nishitsu san san," he used the most respectful form of address possible.

Nishitsu returned the bow.

"You have brought great honor to the emperor's memory, Jiro kun," Nemuro Nishitsu said quietly. His eyes shone. Isuzu thought he would weep with joy, but Nishitsu did not weep. Instead, he asked a question.

"Has there been any communication from the American government?"

"No, sir. As I told you by radio, we have shot down several reconnaissance planes. There have been none since afternoon."

Nemuro Nishitsu looked up. He wore a Western-style porkpie hat and had to crane to see beyond the brim. His chin quivered with the effort.

"They will use their satellites to look down upon us," he quavered. "And they will fail on this night."

Jiro nodded, looking up at the high cirrus clouds.

"It is cold, sir. Will you come now? I have an entire city to lay at your feet."

Nishitsu nodded, and allowed Isuzu to open the limousine's rear door. Jiro took Nishitsu by the elbow and guided him into the roomy interior. Isuzu hopped in.

The driver pulled out of the airport. The honor guard broke up and returned to their tanks. Within moments, the runway was blocked again.

In the speeding limousine, Nemuro Nishitsu asked the question Jiro Isuzu expected.

"Your captured television stations, will they transmit?"

"Our engineers have familiarized themselves with the transmitting equipment. We can broadcast your demands at any moment you choose."

"I wish to broadcast no demands at this time," Nishitsu said dismissively.

Jiro Isuzu frowned. Before he could comment, Nemuro Nishitsu put to him the question he dreaded.

"Where are you holding Bronzini?"

Isuzu hesitated. He lowered his eyes in shame.

Nishitsu's voice was disapproving. "I understood you pacified the city and all who dwell in it."

"Bronzini escaped in a tank during action at Luke Air Force Range. He disappeared into a sandstorm. Our captured F-16's have been unable to spot him."

Nemuro Nishitsu's wizened visage darkened.

"We need Bronzini," he said firmly.

"But he has served his purpose."

"We need him. Find him. Find Bronzini." Nishitsu pounded the floor with his cane. His eyes squeezed into black slits of venom. His voice was cold as the desert night.

Isuzu swallowed uncomfortably. "At once, sir," said Jiro Isuzu as he picked up the cellular phone, saying, *"Moshi moshi."* He wondered why his superior wanted the American actor, who was no longer necessary now that Yuma had been conquered. But he dared not question him. For Jiro Isuzu was only *midoru*—middle management.

When the mobile operator answered in Japanese, Jiro Isuzu asked to be put through to Imperial Command Headquarters at the Shilo Inn.

Admiral William Blackbird, chairman of the Joint Chiefs of Staff, leapt to his feet as the President of the United States entered the Situation Room in the White House basement.

"Mr. President, sir," he said, executing a snappy salute.

The President did not return it. The remaining members of the Joint Chiefs pointedly stood with their hands dangling at their sides. And Admiral Blackbird knew he had stepped in it, tactical-wise.

"How was your game, sir?" he asked brightly.

"I lost," the President said sourly in his homogenized

Connecticut/Texas/Maine accent. "Let's have the straight skinny on this emergency thing." He wore a white windbreaker over a red sweater vest.

"Yes, sir. In a phrase: We've lost Yuma, Arizona. These satellite photographs have just been received from NORAD."

The President leaned over the stack of photographs. They were still wet from their chemical bath.

One particularly grisly set of photos showed scores of bodies lying in sand.

"You're looking at the bodies of airmen from Luke Air Force Range," the admiral said. "We believe they were pushed from aircraft. They're all dead."

"This one looks like he's walking away," the President said, tapping a photo showing an apparently upright man.

"Probably an optical illusion. Nobody walks away from a fall like that. Maybe he struck feetfirst and *rigor mortis* did the rest."

Other photos showed ordinary city streets, deserted of people and moving traffic. Except for the tanks and armored personnel carriers.

"Whose tanks are these?" the President demanded.

The Secretary of Defense, who had entered with the President, spoke up a beat before the chairman could frame his answer.

"They're Soviet," he said confidently.

Because that was the answer he was going to give, Admiral Blackbird contradicted the Secretary of Defense.

"Not necessarily," he said. "They could easily be Chinese. The main Chinese battle tank is a knockoff of the Soviet T-62. These are T-62's."

"Yes, they are T-62's," the Secretary of Defense insisted just as firmly. "Soviet T-62's."

"None of these photos show markings," Admiral Blackbird countered. "Without markings, we can only make an educated guess."

"And mine," the secretary said pointedly, "is that they are Soviet machines."

"In other words," the President interrupted, "neither of you can give me a straight answer."

"It's not that simple," the Secretary of Defense said.

Deciding that he was about to be outflanked, Admiral Blackbird quickly added, "I concur with the secretary." The sour expression that crossed the President's face told the admiral that he had made another tactical mistake. It also told him that the secretary had taken the President in horseshoes. No wonder the old man was ticked off.

The President sighed. "Is there any indication of this thing spreading?"

"No, sir. They—whoever they are—have Yuma. They appear to be consolidating their position. But we can't be sure that the city isn't merely a staging area."

"By gosh, how many soldiers can there be?"

"We estimate no more than a brigade."

"Is that as big as it sounds?"

"Normally a brigade could be isolated and easily neutralized, Mr. President. Not in this case. If you'll take a look at this map, you'll understand."

The President followed the others to a wall map of Arizona. The admiral poked Yuma with a fat finger.

"As you can see," he rumbled, "Yuma is completely isolated. It's entirely surrounded by desert and mountains. The Mexican border is only twenty-five miles south, and the border with California a mere stone's throw west. It's entirely self-sufficient for its electric and water needs. It's surrounded by three military installations, MCAS Yuma, the Yuma Proving Grounds, and Luke Air Force Range. The invader apparently overran Luke and the Marine Air Station by force. Using aircraft captured during those operations, they bombed the Army proving grounds here to the north. It was a brilliant tactical and strategic move. In one stroke, they acquired a staggering air defense capability they could never have hoped to bring into our borders. F/A-18 Hornets, AV-8B Harriers, and Cobra attack helicopters. As we've already discovered, when we send our planes in, they shoot them down. At the moment, we're stalemated."

"Are you telling me that we can't retake our own city?" the President demanded.

"It's not that we can't, it's that we don't yet know who our enemy is. The dogfight suggests highly trained Russian pilots, but the Chinese can't be ruled out."

"Why don't we put feelers out to both governments. You know, kinda take their temperature?"

"We can't do that, Mr. President. It would show weakness and indecision."

"And what are we showing here? So far, I haven't heard a concrete suggestion out of anyone in this room."

"There's a reason for that, Mr. President. They have two of our air bases, and all the communications equipment that goes with them."

"My God," said the Secretary of Defense as he realized the importance of the admiral's words.

"Don't tell me they've captured nuclear weapons," the President demanded.

"Worse than that," the admiral replied. "We have to assume they're listening in on our message traffic. If we go to Defcon One—which I do recommend—they'll know it. Normal contingency for a situation such as this would be to mobilize the Eighty-second Airborne out of Fort Bragg, but we'd have no element of surprise. We can't make a move without their seeing it coming. Whoever these people are, they are tactically brilliant. They pinpointed the most isolated, vulnerable, yet defendable city in the nation. In one bold stroke they have coopted our entire military communications network and all our ground assets in the war zone."

"War zone . . ." the President muttered. "How?"

"This is where it gets sticky, Mr. President. We've had no inkling of any military activity that could be read as a precusor to a strike of this brilliance. We are assuming that the tanks came across the Mexican border."

"Wouldn't we have detected them?"

"Er, it may be that we let them in."

"Explain," the President said tightly.

"Customs allowed a tank column to legally enter this country only two days ago. They were to be used in the making of a film. Simultaneously, permission was given to film scenes at MCAS Yuma and Luke. We believe that's how the bases were penetrated."

"The Pentagon allowed this?"

"We thought it would be good for the image of the service branches involved," the admiral said defensively.

"I don't understand."

"It was a Bartholomew Bronzini film. I think it's *Grundy IV*."

"No," piped up the commandant of the Marines Corps, "it's not a *Grundy* at all. It involves another character. A new one."

Everyone looked at him as if to say, "Thanks loads for the non sequitur." All except the President, who was looking at the floor in stunned silence.

"Sir?" asked Admiral Blackbird.

The President looked up from his thoughts. "Go to Defcon One. Continue to monitor the situation. I'll get back to you."

"Where will you be?" the admiral asked, surprised at the President's sudden forcefulness.

"I'll be in the john," said the President as he slammed the Situation Room door behind him.

The admiral looked at the Secretary of Defense and asked a low question.

"How bad did you take him?"

"Bad enough," the secretary said morosely, "that I'm going to make a point of losing every match for the remainder of the President's first term."

The President of the United States did not go to the bathroom. He went directly to the Lincoln Bedroom and to the top drawer of a nightstand, which he pulled open to reveal a red telephone with a smooth blank area where a dial would normally be. He lifted the receiver.

The sound of ringing penetrated his ear. After only one ring, a lemony voice asked, "Yes, Mr. President?"

"Is your man still in Yuma?"

"Actually, both of them are."

"Have you had any contact in the last few hours?"

"No," Smith admitted. "This is a routine assignment. Check-ins are not necessary. Is there a problem?"

"We've lost all communication with Yuma. There are tanks in the streets."

"It *is* a war movie," Smith pointed out.

"Well, it's turned real. A Marine air station and an Air Force range are in unfriendly hands. They already shot down two recon patrols."

"Oh, my God," said Harold W. Smith.

"This *is* a Japanese production, isn't it?"

"Yes, you know it is. The Nishitsu Group is behind it."

"The Japanese are supposed to be our allies. Is there any chance that this is actually a Soviet or Chinese operation? Could Nishitsu be a dummy corporation or something?"

"If so," Smith returned, "then the situation is graver than Yuma. There are literally hundreds of Nishitsu plants in the country. But I do not believe that theory makes sense. Nishitsu is too big. They're definitely Japanese."

"How about Japanese Red Army connections? They're among the most vicious terrorists in the world."

"Doubtful."

"Smith, use your computers," the President rapped out. "Dig into Nishitsu's background. Find out everything you can about them. I need answers."

"Specifically, Mr. President?"

"Specifically, why they would invade the U.S. I need something I can take to the Japanese ambassador. Maybe we can sort this out quietly."

"Mr. President," Smith said sternly, "if what you tell me is true, we have an American city under occupation. I do not think this is something that can be negotiated away. It calls for a swift response."

"That's why I came to you, but you can't reach your people."

"If Remo and Chiun are in the area, you can be assured that they will not stand idly by while an American city is overrun."

"You're using the wrong tense, Smith. Yuma *has* been overrun. It's fallen to the Japanese or whoever these people are. And where are your people?"

Smith had no answer to that.

The President continued. "If I unleashed our military, the civilian casualties would be enormous. No, I can't have that. Quiet diplomacy, Smith. This must be solved with quiet diplomacy. Get back to me as soon as you can."

The President hung up. Miles away, Dr. Harold W. Smith hunched over his computer terminal. As his fingers flew over the keys, he wondered what could have happened to Remo and Chiun.

17

It was bad enough, thought Bartholomew Bronzini, that he had been shot at by a crazed movie crew. It was bad enough that he had been chased out into the desert with his tail between his legs. Running from a fight was not Bartholomew Bronzini's style, in real life or on the screen.

But as night fell over the desert and the cold got worse, he started sneezing over and over.

"Perfect," he said, trying to keep the T-62 tank pointed at Yuma. "Just when it couldn't get worse, I've caught a freaking cold."

Bronzini had run the tank blindly through the desert until he knew he was in the clear. The sandstorm had long since died down. There was no water. Just mountains and low rippling desert sand as far as the eye could see. He had to go around the mountains frequently in order to stay on course for Yuma. The detours cost him all sense of direction.

Bronzini was no longer sure that he was still headed toward Yuma.

He came across the bodies quite unexpectedly. First there was a man lying in his way. Bronzini stopped the tank and leapt out of the driver's pit. He went to the body, which lay on its stomach, clad in desert utilities. An unused parachute pack was strapped to the body.

Bronzini rolled the body over. One look at the face confirmed that it was a body. The man's eyes were wide open. His face was undamaged, but the expression on it was one of stark horror. The mask of the face had hardened with the mouth open in a frozen scream.

Bronzini wondered what had killed the man. There wasn't a mark on his body. Had Bronzini had the nerve to squeeze the body at any point, he would have felt the gravelly grit of pulverized bone under the skin instead of a skeleton structure.

Finding nothing, he got back into the tank and pushed on. Bronzini ran the tank around a sandhill, hoping for fewer sandhills beyond it. He got what he wanted.

Before him lay a sea of sand. And like motionless corks on the undulating waves were hundreds of bodies. Bronzini jockeyed the tank between them gingerly. It was a sight of unearthly stillness. Every body wore a parachute pack. They looked as if they had simply dropped dead as they walked through the sand.

It took a while for the enormity of it all to sink in. Bronzini might not have figured it out except that beside one of the bodies was a smoke canister stuck in the sand. It had been used.

"The fucking parachute drop," he said. His voice was etched with disbelief. He looked up into the sky. It all made sense then. The drop had been sabotaged.

Bronzini hunkered down in his seat and pulled the hatch closed. It was harder to pilot the tank using the periscope, but it was preferable. He didn't see as many staring dead.

Bartholomew Bronzini immediately picked up the tracks of heavy vehicles. He lined up on the tracks and followed them, figuring they would lead him to Yuma.

Along the way, he came upon an APC that lay, still smoking, in the sand. There was a horrible stench coming from it. He popped the hatch and circled the APC. The back was blown open, uniformed bodies hanging out the door like they had been expelled from a dragon's mouth. One of the bodies looked familiar. It wore a bush hat. The man who had worn that hat in life had been his military adviser through all three *Grundy* films. Jim Concannon.

"What is this shit?" Bronzini howled.

Bronzini didn't stop. He pointed the muttering T-62 toward Yuma and kept on going, pushing the tank as hard as he dared. He started to wonder if going to Yuma was such a smart idea after all. He tried not to think of what had happened back at MCAS Yuma. It made no sense. It was only a movie. But now that he knew the parachute drop had gone bad, all hope that the Marine unit had simply gone berserk evaporated. He felt cold inside. And he couldn't stop sneezing.

Bronzini drove all night long, fighting to keep awake. The coyotes helped. When the sun broke over the mountains, he popped the hatch.

He was astonished to see a man walking ahead of him in the clear dawn light. The man was striding through the desert at a steady, monotonous pace. Bronzini ran the tank up alongside the walking man.

"Yo!" he called over, struggling to keep the tank on course.

The man didn't respond. He simply walked in a direct line. Bronzini took in the profile of his face. The man's features looked vaguely familiar, but he couldn't place them. Bronzini saw that his face was red from a combination of sunburn and wind abrasion.

"Hey, I'm talking to you!" Bronzini shouted.

No reaction. Bronzini noticed the robotlike swing of his arms, the masklike impassivity of his face. It was devoid of expression, like something chopped out of rock. He wore desert utilities like those of the dead paratroopers, but his hung in rags, leaving the arms bare and exposing the white of a T-shirt.

"Is it something I said?" Bronzini joked, not expecting a response. He was not disappointed. He tried again in a joking voice, "I don't suppose you can direct me to Yuma. I'm late for first call."

Nothing.

Finally, in frustration, Bronzini put his fingers into his mouth and gave an attention-demanding whistle.

This time the man did react. His head swiveled like a jewelry display in a rotating pedestal. The metronomic swing of arms and legs continued without varying. But

the eyes that looked back at Bartholomew Bronzini
frightened him. They were as unwinking as a serpent's.
Set deep in hollow sockets, they seemed to burn with a
fanatical light against dry, wasted flesh. The guy's face
looked dead. There was no other word for it.

"Why don't I go bother someone else?" Bronzini said
suddenly.

The head swiveled back and the man kept walking.

Bronzini stopped the tank. He watched the man walk,
like an automaton, along the APC tracks.

It was only then that Bartholomew Bronzini noticed a
curious thing. It caused him to turn the tank north and
stomp the gas pedal down as hard as his combat boots
could press.

The man was striding through sand so loose that the
wind blew it off the prominences in hissing sprays. It
was not hard-packed stuff at all.

Yet the man left no footprints behind him.

Nemuro Nishitsu looked up from the reports on his
desk. The nameplate on the desk read "Mayor Basil
Cloves." He had not bothered to change it. He did not
expect to occupy this office for very long.

Jiro Isuzu bowed in greeting.

"A man insists upon meeting with you, Nishitsu san
san," he said in a respectful tone.

Nishitsu's old brow wrinkled distastefully.

"Insists?"

"He is a Korean, very old. He claims to represent the
American government. And he asks to hear your terms."

Nemuro Nishitsu put aside his reports. "How do you
know he is Korean?" he demanded. "How did he get
here?"

"I do not know the answer to your second question,
but to the first, I can only say that he claims to be the
Master of Sinanju."

Nishitsu raised a tired eyebrow.

"Sinanju? Here? In America? Is it possible?"

"I thought the line had died out."

Nishitsu shook his tremorous old head. "During the
occupation of Korea," he said, "I heard stories of how

our forces dared not enter one fishing village, called Sinanju. This village was respected, not for tradition's sake, but out of fear of reprisals. I will see him."

Nemuro Nishitsu waited pensively for Jiro Isuzu to return. He came back accompanied by a cold-eyed Korean in a vermilion kimono.

"I am Chiun, Reigning Master of Sinanju," the Korean said in excellent Japanese. His face lacked warmth. It also lacked respect.

Nishitsu frowned. "How did you come to be in this, of all cities?" he asked, also in Japanese.

"Think not that your evil scheme was hatched in total secrecy," Chiun said craftily.

Nemuro Nishitsu accepted this in silence. Then he said, "My aide, Jiro, informs me that you are with the Americans. How is it that the House of Sinanju has come to this?"

"I serve America," Chiun said haughtily. "Their gold is greater than that of any modern nation. The rest does not concern you. I am here to hear your terms."

Nemuro Nishitsu regarded the old Korean at length. His thin lips compressed into a bloodless line.

When he spoke, his words surprised Jiro Isuzu as much as they did the Master of Sinanju.

"I offer no terms."

"Are you mad?" Chiun spat. "You cannot hope to hold this city against the might of the Americans forever."

"Not forever, perhaps, but long enough."

"I do not understand. What is your purpose here?"

"It is about *kao*. It is about face."

"You and I understand face. But Americans do not."

"Some do. You will see. You will understand in time. Everyone will understand."

Chiun's face puckered.

"What is to prevent me from extinguishing your life, here and now, Japanese?" he queried levelly.

Jiro Isuzu went for his sword. He was surprised that the Master of Sinanju simply stood there as he placed the tip of the blade before the old Korean's chest.

Chiun's eyes went to Nemuro Nishitsu.

"Do you value this *bakayaro*?" he asked quietly.

"He is my right arm," Nishitsu said. "Please do not kill him."

Jiro Isuzu could not believe what he was hearing. Did he not have the upper hand?

Nemuro Nishitsu's next words told him that despite all appearances, he did not.

"Jiro kun," Nishitsu whispered, "put that away. This man is an emissary. He must be treated with respect."

"But he threatened you," Isuzu protested.

"And he has the means to carry out that threat. But he will not, for he understands that if he spills my blood, there is nothing to prevent my soldiers from putting to the sword every man, woman, and child in this city. Now, put your sword away."

"Tradition demands I quench this sword in blood now that I have drawn it," Isuzu said stubbornly.

"If you wish to commit *seppuku*," Nishitsu told him coldly, "then it is your choice. Either way, you are dead. But do me the courtesy of not ensuring my death along with yours, and with it, the ruin of all we have achieved together."

Jiro Isuzu's face was stung. He lowered his eyes as the sword whispered back into its sheath. His chin quivered uncontrollably.

"Know, Japanese," Chiun said forcefully, "that if the lives of innocents were not in peril, I would rend your very heart and lay it steaming at your worthless feet."

"You may take my words back to your American masters," Nemuro Nishitsu said pointedly. "I will see that you are given safe passage to the desert."

"I have two others with me, a man and a woman. The man is of a tribe that dwells in the desert. It is there that I wish to go."

"Tribe?" Nishitsu said. His eyes sought Jiro.

"Indians," Jiro supplied. "They do not matter. Our tanks surround their land. They are known to be a peaceful tribe. None have ventured out, nor will they. Indians do not love the whites, their oppressors."

"Then go," Nishitsu told Chiun.

"One other matter," Chiun said quickly. "I demand

to ransom the children. They are innocents. Whatever you intend by this outrage, they are not a part of this."

"They keep the adults passive. Fewer of my men die this way, and I am able to spare more Americans."

"Then the youngest of them," Chiun suggested. "The ones under eight years. Surely they are not necessary to your plans."

"The youngest ones are the most precious to their mothers and fathers," Nemuro Nishitsu said slowly. "But I might offer you, say, the students of one school if you will do something for me in return."

Curiosity wrinkled Chiun's wise face. "Yes?"

"I seek Bartholomew Bronzini. If you can deliver him to me, alive and in good condition, I will surrender to you the school of your choice."

Chiun frowned. "Bronzini is not your ally in this?"

"He is a pawn."

"I will consider your offer," said Chiun. And without bowing, he turned and left the mayor's office.

Jiro Isuzu followed him with hate-filled eyes. Then he turned to Nemuro Nishitsu.

"I do not understand. Why do you not offer terms?"

"You will see, Jiro kun. Is the television station ready?"

"Yes."

"Then begin broadcasting."

"This will enrage their military."

"Better. It will humiliate them. They are impotent and soon the entire world will know it. Go now!"

The Master of Sinanju was silent all during the ride to the reservation, his eyes fixed on some imaginary point beyond the sand-scored windshield.

Neither Bill Roam nor Sheryl Rose tried to converse with him after Sheryl offered what she thought was a comforting suggestion.

"You know, Remo might not be dead. I read about a fellow who survived a skyjumping accident. It happens."

"He is dead," Chiun had said sadly. "I do not sense his mind. In the past, in times of great urgency, I have been able to touch him with my thoughts. I cannot now. Therefore he is no more."

Bill Roam was driving. They were in Sheryl's Nishitsu Ninja, which Chiun had restored to its wheels with what had seemed to be an effortless expenditure of strength. So stunned were they by the events of the day that neither Bill Roam nor Sheryl remarked on Chiun's many feats.

A single road led to the reservation. It was fenced off, but the gates were open. Beside it was a weather-beaten wooden sign. The legend was half-obliterated by desert sun and wind-driven sand. The top line was nearly unreadable, except for the letter S at the beginning of an indecipherable word. The bottom line said: RESERVATION.

"I could not read the name of your tribe," Chiun said as they passed through the fence.

"You wouldn't know the name," Bill Roam replied dully. His eyes searched the road ahead as a line of cracked adobe buildings came into view.

"I did not suggest that I would," Chiun said flatly. "I asked the name."

"Some people call us Sunny Joes. That's where I get my nickname. I'm sort of the tribal guardian. It's a hereditary title, being a Sunny Joe. My father was one."

"Your tribe, they are mighty warriors?"

"Hell, no," Roam scoffed. "We're farmers. Even back before the white man came."

Chiun's brow wrinkled in puzzlement.

Bill Roam let out a relieved sigh as signs of life began to show in the doorways of the buildings they passed. He pulled up in front of one and got out.

"Hey, Donno, everything okay here?"

"Sure thing, Sunny Joe," a fat old man in blue jeans and a faded cowboy shirt replied. He clutched a bottle of Jim Beam. "What's doing?"

"There's trouble in the city. Spread the word. Nobody goes off the reservation unless I say so. And I want everyone in the meetinghouse inside of ten minutes. You hustle now, Donno."

"You got it, Sunny Joe," said the fat old man. He slipped the bottle into a back pocket and disappeared down the sidewalk, which was raised off the dusty street like an old-fashioned western boardwalk.

Bill Roam parked in front of the meetinghouse, a long wooden building that resembled an old-fashioned one-room schoolhouse right down to the rows of folding chairs inside. Roam went among the chairs, clapping them shut in his big hands. He stacked them against the walls with intent fury.

"Hope you don't mind squatting on the floor," he said after he cleared it. "It's clean."

"It is the preferred way in my village too," Chiun said. He gathered his skirts up and settled to the floor. Sheryl joined him. They watched as the reservation Indians drifted in, their faces sun-seamed and stoic. Most were older than Sunny Joe Roam. There were no children and very few women of any age.

Sheryl leaned over to Chiun. "Will you look at them! I've never been here before. But darned if they don't look sort of Asian about the eyes."

"Don't you read books?" Bill Roam said. "Every one of us sorry redskins came across the Aleutian Islands from Asia."

"I have never heard that," Chiun said.

"How could you, chief? You're one of the ones who got left behind. But it's a fact. If the anthropologists can be believed."

The last tribesmen slipped in and took their places on the floor in stony silence.

"That's everyone," the fat old man named Donno called out as he closed the door.

"You forgetting the chief?" Roam asked.

"Not me, Sunny Joe. He took off for Las Vegas with the money he got for leasing the reservation to that Bronzini fella. Said he was gonna double it or get drunk."

"Probably both," Roam muttered.

"What kind of leader deserts his people in their hour of need?" Chiun said querulously.

"A savvy one," Roam remarked dryly. He stood up, raising his hands, palms open. "These are my friends," he announced. "I bring them here because they seek refuge. The man is called Chiun. The girl is Sheryl. They are here because there is trouble in the city."

"What kind of trouble, Sunny Joe?" a wizened old man asked.

"An army has come from across the seas. They have captured the city."

The tribespeople turned to one another. They buzzed in conversation. As it settled down, an old woman with iron-gray pigtails asked, "Are we in danger, Sunny Joe?"

"Not now. But when the government sends in troops, we could be in the middle of a powerful lot of fighting."

"What can we do? We aren't fighters."

"I am the Sunny Joe of this tribe," Bill Roam rumbled. "I will protect you. Don't anyone worry. When the bad times came, my father, the Sunny Joe before me, kept us fed. During the hard days of the last century, his father watched over his people. Before the whites came, your forebears lived in peace going back all the way to the days of the first Sunny Joe, Ko Jong Oh. This will not change while I walk the ground of our ancestors."

Chiun had been listening to this with growing interest on his parchment face. His head snapped around suddenly.

"What name did you speak?" he insisted.

Roam looked over. "Ko Jong Oh. He was the first Sunny Joe."

"What is the name of this tribe?" Chiun demanded. "I must know."

"We are the Sun On Jos. Why?"

"I am known as the Master of Sinanju. The place I come from is called Sinanju. Does that name mean anything to you?"

"No," said Sunny Joe Roam. "Should it?"

"We have a legend among my people," said Chiun slowly, "of the sons of a Master of Sinanju, my ancestor, whose wife bore him two sons. One was named Kojing." Chiun paused. In a firm voice he added, "The other went by the name Kojong."

"Ko Jong Oh was the progenitor of the Sun On Jos," Roam said slowly. "Coincidence."

"It is tradition that the son of the Master of Sinanju be trained to follow in his father's footsteps," Chiun said, his voice rising so that everyone heard him clearly. "For Masters of Sinanju were great warriors. But only one Master of Sinanju could exist in a generation. The mother of Kojing and Kojong knew this. And she knew that if the father of the boys learned she had borne him twins, one would be put to death to prevent a dangerous rivalry when they became men. But the mother of the two youths could not bring herself to do this. She concealed Kojong from his own father. And when it became time to train Kojing, the mother artfully switched babies every other day, so that both Kojing and Kojong were trained in what we call the art of Sinanju."

Chiun's hazel eyes swept the faces in the room. The eyes that looked back were so like those of his own village, far away on the West Korea Bay. The men and the old men. They had unfamiliar faces, but each was touched by something Chiun recognized.

Chiun resumed his story, his voice deepening.

"The father, who was called Nonja, never knew this, for he was old when he sired the twins. His eyes were failing. Thus, the artifice went unsuspected. And one day, Master Nonja died. He went into the Void never knowing that he left behind two heirs, not one. On that day, Kojing and Kojong appeared together in the village for the first time, and the truth was revealed for all to see. No one knew what to do, and for the first time in history, there were two Masters of Sinanju."

Chiun took in a deep breath that expanded his frail chest.

"It was Kojong who provided the solution," he continued. "He announced that he was leaving the village to find a place in the outer world. He swore never to pass along the secrets of the sun source, but to pass along the spirit of Sinanju in case there would ever come a time that Sinanju would need it."

Chiun looked at Sunny Joe Roam.

Bill Roam spoke up slowly.

"We have a legend too," he said. "Of Ko Jong Oh, who came from across the western sea. From the east.

He was the first Sunny Joe, for he bore the spirit of Son
On Jo. He taught the Indians the ways of peace, how to
farm and not hunt the buffalo for meat. He showed the
Indians another way, and in gratitude, they, our ancestors, took on the tribal name of Sun On Jo. Each
generation, his eldest son would replace him as the
guardian of the tribe. Only these sons, which we call
Sunny Joes, were allowed to fight. And then only to
protect the tribe. For the Sun On Jos believed that if
they used their magic powers to kill, it would bring
down upon the entire tribe the wrath of the Great
Spirit Magician, Sun On Jo—He Who Breathes the
Sun."

Chiun nodded. "Your words ring true. Kojong understood if he plied the art of Sinanju, the art of the
assassin, he would be in competition with the true
Master of Sinanju, and would have to be sought out and
destroyed, for nothing must interfere with the work of
the Master of Sinanju. Not even competition from blood."

"You think we're kin?" Roam asked slowly.

"Do you doubt it?"

Bill Roam paused before answering.

"When I was young," he said at last, "I believed in it
all. A lot has happened to me since then. I'm not sure
what I believe now. There are a lot of legends in the
world, full of great warriors, civilizers, culture heroes.
Just because your legend and mine have a few syllables
in common, I don't see that that's any reason to get all
worked up about it. Especially now."

"What happened to you to crush your faith, you who
are to your people what I am to mine?" Chiun inquired.

Before Bill Roam could answer, a racket outside the
meetinghouse caused the assembled Sun On Jos to
jump to the windows.

"Sounds like a tank," Sheryl breathed.

Bill Roam pushed his way to the door.

Outside, the Master of Sinanju joined him. They
watched a sand-powdered tank rattle up the road,
spinning a slow worm of dust in its wake. Its engine
sputtered and missed like a recalcitrant lawn mower.

"Think we've been double-crossed, chief?" Roam asked Chiun.

"We are dealing with the Japanese," Chiun replied. "For them not to display treachery would be surprising, not the opposite."

The tank suddenly stopped. Its engine died out.

The driver's hatch popped up, and Bill Roam turned and shouted at the faces huddled in the doorway.

"Everyone, back inside! I'll handle this!"

Turning to Chiun, he said, "If I don't make it, I'm counting on you to protect my people. Savvy?"

Chiun looked up curiously. "You believe?"

"No. But you do. And I'm going to count on that."

"Done," said Chiun. His smile was tight.

A head poked up from the open hatch and a flat voice called out, "Sunny Joe! That you? Man, am I glad to see a friendly face."

The voice belonged to Bartholomew Bronzini.

18

On the morning of December 24, Radio Free Yuma went on the air.

Radio Free Yuma was a lawyer named Lester Cole with a ham radio set in his den. He put out a call to all stations listening on his band. A dentist in Poway, California, acknowledged his QSL.

"We've been invaded," Lester Cole said tightly. "Get word to Washington. We're cut off. It's the Japanese. They've pulled another Pearl Harbor on Yuma."

The Poway dentist thanked Lester for his entertaining story and signed off with a curt "Out."

Lawyer Cole—as he was known to friend and foe alike—had better luck with his second call. He happened to get an Associated Press stringer in Flagstaff. The stringer listened to his story without interruption.

At the end, Lawyer Cole told the stringer, "You can check this out. We have no phones, no TV, no radio."

"I'll get back to you. Out."

The AP stringer confirmed that Yuma was incommu-
nicado. He put in a series of calls to the state capital.
No one in Phoenix could explain the problem. The
stringer didn't repeat Lawyer Cole's wild invasion story.
Instead, he returned to his ham set and tried to raise
Cole.

There was no answer.

Clarence Giss didn't look at it as betraying his country.

Yuma was under curfew. He dared not set foot outside his house because they were shooting anyone caught
out-of-doors. Giss lived alone. The way he saw it,
America hadn't done much for him. His social-security
disability check wasn't even enough to stock his refrigerator properly. Giss had been on disability since a bad
acid trip in 1970 made it impossible for him to hold a
steady job. As he had explained it to his caseworker,
"My foot flips out right regularly. I can't work."

So when the Japanese rolled in and shut down Yuma,
Clarence Giss just settled back to wait. Who knew,
maybe things would improve. They couldn't get any
worse on only $365 a month.

He stopped thinking that when the APC rolled down
the streets blaring a warning in Japanese.

"A man is broadcasting his radio," the amplified voice
thundered. "This man wirr surrender himserf or one
house on every street wirr be set on fire."

Clarence Giss didn't want to lose his house. He also
knew that the man who owned the only ham set in the
neighborhood had once beat him good on a vandalism
charge. He also had a feeling the Japanese didn't intend
to let anyone out before they set their fires.

But most of all, Clarence Giss was out of beer.

He stripped off his sweaty undershirt and attached it to
a mop handle with a rubber band. Giss waved his make-
shift white flag out a window and waited for a response.

Presently an APC pulled up and two Japanese came
to his door. They pounded on it with their rifle butts.

"I know who's doing the broadcasting," he told them
through the door.

"Terr us name."

"Sure thing, but I want something in return."

"What do you want?"

"A beer."

"Terr us name and we wirr bring you *biru*," he was told.

"His name's Lester Cole. He's a lawyer. Lives six or seven houses down, this side of the street."

The soldiers humped down the street at top speed. Clarence could hear them break in Lawyer Cole's door all the way up the street. There came a pause. Then a shot. Two. Two more. Then silence.

Clarence Giss was shaking when the soldiers returned to his door. He opened it a crack. One soldier shoved a can of Buckhorn through the crack.

"Here," he said, "*biru*."

"Much obliged," Clarence said hoarsely. "Maybe we can do business again sometime." The soldiers went away and he returned to his living room, where he popped the pull-tab. Clarence Giss took a short swig and started crying uncontrollably.

The beer was warm.

When the AP stringer finally gave up on reaching Lester Cole, he thought long and hard. He decided that the transmission was not a hoax. He called his boss.

"I know it sounds insane," he said after he finished relating his story, "but there was something in the guy's voice. And I haven't been able to raise him since."

"Did you say Yuma?"

"Yeah. My atlas puts it near the border."

"Something came over the wire about a funny TV transmission from Yuma," the AP desk man said slowly. "Sounded like filler-story material. Hold up. It's on my desk here somewhere. Here it is. Get this. Station KYMA went off the air yesterday, along with two other Yuma stations. Now KYMA is back, showing what looks like war footage. Executions. Hangings. Bizarre snuff-film kinda stuff. It's been going on all day. People have been watching it, thinking it's some kind of grisly movie, but there's no plot. It's just atrocities."

"What do you think?"

"I think I'd better boot this upstairs. Back to you later."

The networks had the story of the weird TV transmission by noon, Pacific standard time. They broke into regular programming with footage videotaped off network affiliates in Phoenix. An entire nation watched in shock the sight of foreign troops occupying an American city. That it was a city hardly anyone outside of Arizona had heard of, or could place on a map, didn't matter. Most Americans couldn't find Rhode Island if it were outlined in red. They watched as fellow Americans were hunted through the streets and bayoneted to death. Footage of the Ziffel family gunned down as they were trimming their Christmas tree was seen in all fifty states. The capture of MCAS Yuma and Luke Air Force Range was shown in all its grisly spectacle.

Among the viewers was the President of the United States. His face looked like dried white clay even though everyone else in the White House Situation Room was sweating. The Joint Chiefs of Staff were clustered behind him.

"This is the worst thing that could happen, Mr. President," Admiral Blackbird said angrily. "Now the whole world will know."

"What could they want?" the President said half to himself. "What do they hope to gain from this?"

"If the world sees this," the admiral continued, "then we'll look weak. If we look weak, then some aggressor nation could see this as an opportune time to strike. For all we know, this could be a diversionary action."

"I disagree," said the Secretary of Defense. "Every reconnaissance flight, every surveillance satellite shows the world situation to be quiescent. The Russians are on standdown. The Chinese are minding their own business. And our supposed allies, the Japanese Self-Defense Forces, are not mobilized."

"I've spoken with the Japanese ambassador," the President said, turning from the screen to face the Joint

Chiefs. "He assures me that his government has nothing to do with this."

"We can't exactly take an assurance like that on faith," Admiral Blackbird sputtered. "Remember Pearl Harbor."

"Right now I'm thinking of the Alamo. We've got an American city held hostage. They're slaughtering people indiscriminately. But why? Why broadcast it?"

Admiral Blackbird drew himself up stiffly. "Mr. President, we could debate the whys until the next century, but we've got to knock out those transmissions at their source. They're practically commercials for American military impotence. The loss of prestige will be incalculable."

"Am I hearing you right?" the President snapped. "Are you talking about prestige when we're helpless witnesses to a slaughter?"

"You've got to understand the geopolitical reality of deterrence," the admiral insisted. "If we lose face in front of our competitors on the world stage, we might as well fall on our swords. They'll come after us like pit bulls. We must neutralize the situation."

"How? We've already been over the military options. There's no way we can mount a full-scale assault without huge civilian casualties."

"This is going to be hard for you to understand, but please try," said the admiral. "During the Vietnamese action, we regularly faced operational dilemmas such as Yuma. Sometimes we were forced to resort to extreme measures to prevent certain villages from being overrun by enemy forces. Regrettable as it was from the human-factor standpoint, we had to destroy certain villages in order to save them."

The President of the United States took an involuntary step backward.

"Are you suggesting that I order an air strike on an American city?" he asked coldly.

"I see no other alternative. Better we show the world that we're not going to flinch from the tough decisions when it comes to protecting our borders. Do this and I guarantee there'll never be another Yuma."

The President's mouth came open. The words on the

tip of his tongue never came out because, behind him, the endlessly repeating images of slaughter and death were replaced by the benign face of an old Japanese man. He began speaking in a quavering voice.

"My humble name is unimportant, but I am pleased to call myself Regent of Yuma," he said.

Every man in the Situation Room watched him in silence. The old man was seated at a desk. The white flag of Japan was spread out on the wall behind him. The red rising sun precisely circled his old head like a bloody halo. He resumed speaking.

"In my country we have a saying, 'Edo no kataki wo Nagasaki de utsu.' It means 'Take revenge at an unexpected place.' I have done this in the name of Showa, known to you as Emperor Hirohito. He was my emperor, whom I served with honor, and whom you humbled. Although he is with his ancestors, I now exalt him with this mighty deed."

"Nagasaki?" said the Secretary of Defense. "Didn't we nuke that city once?"

"If the American President is watching me," the old man continued, "I bring you greetings. I regret the loss of life, but it is necessary. I fear it will, and must, continue until the American government has surrendered itself to me. Sayonara."

The picture went black. Then another film clip came on the screen. It showed a man being held down while a tank ran over his head. At the bottom of the screen a legend flashed. It read, "The Execution of the Mayor of Yuma by New Imperial Army Forces."

"He's mad!" the President said. "Does he think we'll really surrender?"

"I don't know what that old rice-gobbler thinks," Admiral Blackbird growled, "but I implore you to consider my advice before the Russians or Chinese decide to take advantage of this."

"Hold on," the President said, leaping for the door.

"Where are you going?" the Secretary of Defense demanded.

"To the john," the President flung back. "I've been drinking coffee for nearly twenty-four hours straight. If

I don't relieve my bladder, we're all going to be pushing mops."

The President did go to the john this time. When he was finished, he slipped into the Lincoln Bedroom and got on the red telephone to Dr. Harold W. Smith.

"Smith. Anything?"

"No word from my people."

"How do you interpret that?" the President asked anxiously.

"Knowing them," Smith said tonelessly, "if they haven't intervened in the Yuma Emergency by now, I must conclude that they are either dead or incapacitated."

"The chairman of the Join Chiefs is pressuring me to take out Yuma," the President said after a pause.

"I wish I could offer you some hope," said Smith, "but there is something to the admiral's argument. As a last resort, of course."

The President was silent for a long time.

Smith broke in reluctantly.

"Mr. President, I saw the recent transmission. That man who called himself Regent of Yuma is the man I've been trying to locate for you, Nemuro Nishitsu, head of the Nishitsu Group."

"How could a conglomerate mount an invasion?"

"If you are asking me how in operational terms," Smith replied, "the answer to that is that they have the resources of a small country. In fact, it would not be far from the truth to categorize Nishitsu as a country without borders. Thanks to its many offices and factories, it has a presence in virtually every developed nation. I have been looking into the company's background. There is a disturbing pattern. Nemuro Nishitsu founded the firm shortly after World War II. At first, it was an electronics firm. It began expanding during the days of the transistor revolution. They made cheap radios, things of that sort. By the early seventies they had subsidiaries manufacturing cars, computers, VCR's and other high-ticket items. More recently they have branched out into global communications and military equipment. You might remember the attempt by one of their subsidiaries to buy out an American ceramics company last

year. You yourself stopped it when it was brought to
your attention that this company manufactured critical
nuclear-weapons components."

"I remember. There was no way I could allow that to
happen."

"Unfortunately, this is also the company you permit-
ted to manufacture the Japanese version of the F-16."

"Oh, my God," the President gasped. "That explains
how they were able to outfight us in our own fighters.
Their pilots had trained in the Japanese version."

"Regrettable, but true."

"What about Nishitsu himself?"

"He was, by all accounts, a fanatic follower of the
emperor during the war. He has become something of a
recluse in recent years, with a history of psychiatric and
medical problems dating from the time he was extracted from the Burma jungle. These were thought to
have been temporary. Once he had been reassimilated
in Japanese society, he was considered perfectly normal."

"Does he have a wife, a family? Someone we could
contact. Maybe he could be talked out of this."

"No family. They died when the atomic bomb fell on
Nagasaki. If you're looking for a motive for his actions,
you might not go any further than that."

"I see," the President said distantly. "Then there is
nothing you can do for me."

"I am sorry, Mr. President."

"Of course. Now, if you'll excuse me, I have to make
one of the most difficult decisions of my presidency."

The President woodenly hung up the red telephone.
He turned on his heel and walked in his tennis shoes to
the Situation Room. He felt his gorge rise just thinking
about the decision he faced. But he was the nation's
commander in chief. He would not shirk his responsi-
bilities to America, or to the people of Yuma.

19

Bartholomew Bronzini was adamant.

"Absolutely, positively, no fucking way!" he bellowed.

Then he screamed and fell to his knees. He clawed at the dirt outside the meetinghouse on the Sun On Jo reservation. His eyes were wide with pain but he couldn't see anything except a kind of visual white noise.

"Arrgghh!" he cried.

A stern voice intruded upon his agony. It was the voice of the tiny Oriental, Chiun.

"Since you do not appear to understand the enormity of your position, Greekling, then I will repeat it," Chiun was saying. "The Japanese leader has offered the lives of the children of any school I choose in return for you. This tragedy is your doing. If you have any honor, you will agree to be handed over to this man."

"I didn't know," Bronzini squeezed out through set teeth. "I had no idea this was gonna happen."

"Responsibility has nothing to do with intent. Your innocence is obvious. Otherwise you would not be fleeing from this army. Still, you will do as I say."

"Please, Mr. Bronzini, they're only children." It was a girl's voice. That publicity girl, Sheryl. "Everyone thinks of you as a hero. I know that's only in movies, but none of this would have happened if it wasn't for you."

"All right, all right," Bronzini groaned. The pain went away. Not slowly, the way pain sometimes recedes. But abruptly, as if it hadn't ever existed in the first place.

Bronzini stood up. He checked his left wrist, the focal point of his pain. There was no mark or cut. He looked at the long fingernails of the tiny Korean who called himself Chiun as they disappeared into his sleeves.

"I want you to know I didn't say yes because of the pain," he said stubbornly.

"Whatever you tell your conscience is your business, Greekling," Chiun sniffed.

"I just had to get used to the idea," he insisted. "And why do you call me Greek? I'm Italian."

"Today you might possibly be Italian. Before, you were a Greek."

"Before what?"

"He means in another life," Sheryl said. "Don't ask me why, but he thinks you were Alexander the Great in a previous life."

Bronzini looked his skepticism. "I've had worse things said about me," he said dryly. "Most people think I crawl out of the La Brea Tar Pits once a year to make a movie."

"Do you have a cold?" Sheryl suddenly asked, "Your voice sounds real nasaly."

"How can you tell?" Chiun sniffed.

"I resent that!" Bronzini said. "Okay, never mind. Let's just get this over with."

Chiun turned to Bill Roam, who was standing with his arms folded. "The woman stays with you," he told the big Indian. "If we do not return, I ask you a favor."

"Sure. What?"

"When this is over, if I have not returned, go into the desert and recover the body of my son. See that he receives a proper burial."

"Done."

"Then you will avenge us both."

"If I can."

"You can. I have seen the greatness in you."

And without another word, the Master of Sinanju pushed Bartholomew Bronzini to the waiting tank.

"You will drive," he said.

"What happens if they just kill us?" Bronzini wondered.

"Then we will die," said Chiun. "But we will cost them dearly."

"I'm with you on that," Bronzini agreed as he eased into the driver's cockpit. Chiun climbed onto the turret like a nimble monkey. He ignored the open hatch and assumed a lotus position beside it.

Bronzini looked back and remarked, "You're gonna fall off."

"See to your driving, Greekling," Chiun said sternly. "I will attend to my balance."

Bronzini started the tank. The engine made wounded mechanical sounds, but eventually the machine turned on one track toward the reservation gate.

"What do you think they'll do to me?" he wondered aloud.

"I do not know," Chiun replied. "But the one named Nishitsu desires to see you very much."

"Maybe he's got some kind of Japanese Oscar for me," Bronzini grunted. "I hear I'm a sure bet for best supporting idiot in a movie gone amok."

"If so, be certain to shake his hand," Chiun said.

"I meant it as a joke," Bronzini said. He sneezed before Chiun could reply.

"You *do* have a cold," Chiun said.

"I have a cold," Bronzini said sourly.

"Yes," Chiun said, a faraway light in his eyes. "When you meet this man, be certain to shake his hand. Do not forget. For it is not too late for you to atone for what you, in your ignorance, have brought to pass."

Bartholomew Bronzini thought he was prepared for the sight of Occupied Yuma. He was wrong.

The tanks blocked the road at the city limits. They parted as he approached. The Japanese kept a respectful distance. Their eyes sought Chiun. The Master of Sinanju kept his hazel eyes on the road, disdaining to meet their challenging glances.

As they entered the city, Bronzini saw the guards at every food store and gun shop. Here And there, bodies lay in brown-black patches of dried blood. A man hung from a lamppost. Another was on his stomach, hands bound behind his back, his head tilted up grotesquely, both eyes impaled on the needles of a cactus.

They were given safe passage to city hall, where a Japanese flag flapped in the wind. The sight turned Bronzini's stomach.

As he dismounted, Chiun floated to his side.

"Well, this is it," Bronzini said. "The denouement. Or is it the climax? I get them mixed up."

"Wipe your nose," Chiun said as they walked to the front door. Two Japanese guards flanked the entrance, standing at attention. "It is dripping," Chiun added.

"Oh," Bronzini said, pulling at his Roman nose with a thumb and forefinger.

"Do not forget what I told you. The Japanese will deal with you less harshly if you show respect."

"I'll try not to sneeze all over their uniforms."

Nemuro Nishitsu received the news with pleasure.

"Bronzini san is here," Jiro Isuzu reported stiffly. "The Korean has brought him."

Nemuro Nishitsu reached for his cane. He pushed himself from his chair and with difficulty stepped out from behind the desk. He had gone without sleep for more than twenty-four hours. It felt like a week.

The Master of Sinanju floated into the office first.

"I have brought the one you seek," he said loudly. "And I demand that you fulfill your part of our agreement."

"Yes, yes, of course," Nishitsu said, looking past Chiun.

Bronzini stepped into the room then. His hangdog face was devoid of expression. He ignored Isuzu.

"So you're Nishitsu," he said quietly.

"I am he," Nishitsu said. He bowed slightly.

"I got one question for you. Why me?"

"You were perfect. And I have seen every one of your movies several times over."

"I knew I should have let Schwarzenegger have this one," Bronzini said with ill-disguised distaste.

"I wonder . . ." Nishitsu said, his eyes twinkling. "Please to honor an old man with your autograph?"

"Blow it out your bazooka, sushi breath."

Bronzini suddenly felt a sharp pain. He looked and saw his elbow pinched between tiny fingernails.

"It will go easier on you if you abide by this man's wishes," Chiun said pointedly.

"Who's it for?" Bronzini grudgingly asked.

Nishitsu gave him a cellophane-dry smile and said, "For me."

"That figures. Sure. Why not?"

Bronzini accepted a pen and paper, and using the palm of one hand for a hard surface, dashed off an autograph. He handed it to Nemuro Nishitsu.

"Do not forget to congratulate this brilliant military leader on his great accomplishment," Chiun prodded.

"What's that? Oh, yeah." Bronzini put out a big hand. "Brilliant casting."

Jiro Isuzu suddenly rushed forward. Chiun tripped him with a sandaled toe.

"He will not harm him. I give you both my word," Chiun said.

"I would be honored to shake Bronzini san's hand," Nishitsu said after the surprise left his face. He offered a quivering hand. Both men shook hands warily.

"You were a perfect Trojan horse," Nemuro Nishitsu said smilingly.

"That explains the nagging hollow feeling," Bronzini grunted. "Now what?" he laughed self-consciously. "The last time I was a prisoner of war, I got star billing, six million dollars up front, and points against the gross."

Nemuro Nishitsu's face flickered doubtfully.

"They're not laughing," Bronzini told Chiun out of the side of his mouth.

"That is because you are not funny. And this is not a movie. Try to hold that thought in your infantile mind."

"You will be taken to a safe place," Nishitsu said. He pounded the floor twice with his cane. Two soldiers came and took Bronzini by the arms.

"Forrow," Jiro Isuzu barked.

"Whatever happened to 'prease to,' Jiro baby?" Bronzini asked as he was escorted away.

"What will you do with that one?" Chiun asked when he was alone with Nemuro Nishitsu.

"This is my concern. I will have the children released into your custody."

"I will need a vehicle," Chiun said. "One large enough to bring them to the Indian reservation."

"As you wish. Now, leave me, I have much to do."

"I am again prepared to hear your terms," Chiun offered.

"I have no terms at this time. Now, please be gone."

Chiun looked at the fragile old Japanese as he limped back to his desk. His mouth thinned. Without another word, he was gone in a swirl of kimono skirts.

They threw Bartholomew Bronzini into the back of an armored personnel carrier and clanged the door shut. He sat in darkness, and felt a cold dread that had nothing to do with personal peril.

The ride was long. Bartholomew Bronzini wondered if they had left the city behind.

Finally the APC stopped. The door opened. The light hurt his eyes. When he emerged too slowly for the guards' liking, Bronzini was pulled from the machine.

Bronzini blinked until his eyes adjusted to the light. The sun was going down, casting lavender shadows.

"Come," a guard barked.

Bronzini allowed himself to be led toward a group of buildings. A sign over one of the them said "Yuma Territorial Prison Museum." It was a gift shop. Bronzini looked around. The other buildings were rude stone prisons with Spanish-style wrought-iron doors. Prison cells.

A sign said "Tickets $1.40 per person. Under seventeen admitted free."

"What am I, a trophy?" he grunted. "I'll bet people would pay a whole five bucks to see the sucker of the century."

Bronzini was shoved through a gate and down a narrow stone corridor past empty cell doors in silence. He smiled bravely. "Just my luck. My first time playing to a live audience and they're all stiffs."

As he was marched to the end, the smile vanished from his Sicilian face. A number of Japanese were erecting a structure of rude wood beside an old guard tower. The structure wasn't completed, but even in its unfinished state, Bronzini recognized it as a gallows.

The cold dread settled into the pit of his stomach.

They flung Bartholomew Bronzini into one of the cells and padlocked the door after him. He went to the criss-cross bars, and found he had a perfect view of the scaffolding. They were raising the L-shaped crosspiece that would support the noose.

"Jesus H. Christ!" Bartholomew Bronzini said in a sick voice. "I think this was in the fucking script."

As Christmas Eve approached, opening presents was forgotten. Carols went unsung. Church services were canceled for lack of attendance.

The nation was glued to their TV sets. Regular programming had been suspended. For the first time in memory, *It's a Wonderful Life* wasn't playing somewhere. Instead, network anchors reported the latest in the "Yuma Emergency."

The news consisted of videotape of the early hours of the takeover. Although they had been played and replayed a hundred times over, these scenes were the only news the networks had. The White House had announced and postponed a presidential address to the nation several times. Official Washington, for once, was not leaking. The situation was too grave.

Then, in the middle of a live transmission showing carolers singing "White Christmas" as they were executed by automatic-weapons fire, the face of Nemuro Nishitsu, the self-proclaimed Regent of Yuma, reappeared.

"My greetings to the American people and their leadership," he said. "In times of conflict it is sometimes necessary to resort to regrettable action in order to accomplish ends. So it is on this, the day before one of your most precious holidays. Tomorrow will be the beginning of the third day of the occupation of Yuma. Your leadership has made no move to unseat my forces. In truth, they cannot. But they dare not admit this. I will force them to admit this. If the American leadership is not impotent, I challenge them to prove it. Tomorrow morning, as a demonstration of my contempt for them, I will hang your greatest hero, Bartholomew Bronzini, by the neck until he is dead. The time of his execution has been set for seven o'clock. This necessary action will be televised on this station. Until then, I remain the unchallenged Regent of Yuma."

*   *   *

Nemuro Nishitsu signaled the cameraman that he was done. The red light under the lens went out.

Jiro Isuzu waited until the cameraman was out of earshot before he approached the desk.

"I do not understand," he said anxiously. "You have as much as dared them to take action against us."

"No, I have *goaded* them into taking action. If they fail to do so, they will lose face before the world."

"I do not think they will fail to act."

"I agree, Jiro kun. For the insult is calculated to incite the American people into demanding action."

"I will order the perimeter forces back into the city," Isuzu said quickly. "We can hold out longer if we concentrate them."

Nemuro Nishitsu shook his head. His slit eyes sought the desktop absently.

"No," he said. "They will not come by land. They know, just as I do, that the crossing through the desert would not go unchallenged."

"Then what?"

"They will send no troops. It is too late for that. In less than twelve hours their greatest hero will be hanged, his last moments of agony to be seen on their television. No assault force could hope to act in time to prevent that. Instead, they will send a plane."

"And we will shoot it down!" Isuzu cried. "I will alert our air defense forces."

"No," Nishitsu said coldly. "I forbid it! For this is the fruition of my plan. A city so isolated that once captured it cannot be retaken. The American military, if they have any stomach, must resort to the unthinkable to wipe this stain of shame from their land."

"You cannot mean . . ."

"Think of the irony, Jiro kun. America, the mightiest nuclear power in the world, invulnerable to invasion, immune to attack, forced to obliterate one of their own cities with one of their own weapons. In one stroke, the shame of Hiroshima and Nagasaki will be as if it never transpired. With the dropping of one bomb, Nippon is avenged. Think of how proud our emperor will be."

Jiro Isuzu stood stunned. His mouth opened like a gulping fish. He could not force from it the words he wanted to speak.

Nemuro Nishitsu smiled tightly. Then his face quirked up in surprise. He sneezed. His hands fumbled around the desk for a box of Kleenex.

In the White House Situation Room, the President shut off the television. He turned to face the stony array of faces that was his Secretary of Defense and his Joint Chiefs of Staff. Everyone knew what was on the President's mind, but no one ventured to speak before the commander in chief did.

"We can't let this happen," he croaked at last. He reached for a glass of water, gulped it down greedily, and then cleared the frog from his throat. "I want a bomber ready to go, but not until I give the word. There may still be a way out of this dilemma."

The Joint Chiefs rushed to their telephones.

At Castle Air Force Base, in Atwater, California, a B-52 bomber from the 93rd bombardment wing was designated for the Yuma mission. A single nuclear bomb was cocked and placed in her bomb bay. The pilots took their seats and went through a cockpit check. They had not yet been given their orders, but they had a sickening inkling of what those orders might be.

In the Yuma Desert, a man continued walking with an inhumanly measured gait. His eyes, like burning coals, were fixed on the horizon beyond which lay the blacked-out city of Yuma, Arizona. His regular, mechanical strides made no imprint in the endless sands.

20

On Christmas Eve the sun set slowly on Yuma. It disappeared behind the Chocolate Mountains, leaving the still light of its passing. It was magic hour.

At precisely 5:55, a man appeared on the crest of a hill overlooking the city. He paused, the rags on his emaciated body a memory of desert utilities, his white T-shirt as brown as brick dust, and his black chinos a powdery beige.

No one noticed the man as he stood, immobile as a presentiment, his empty hands hanging from his thick wrists like dead nerveless things. But everyone heard him.

In a voice like thunder he spoke, and even though there were over fifty thousand people living in the city sprawled under his burnt-coal gaze, each pair of ears heard his words clearly.

"*I am created Shiva, the Destroyer; Death, the shatterer of worlds. Who is this dog meat who challenges me?*"

Nemuro Nishitsu heard those words and sat up in alarm. He had been dozing in his chair. He reached for his cane and climbed stiffly to his feet. Quickly he sat down again. His legs felt weak.

"Jiro kun," he called in a dry, raspy voice. "Jiro!"

Jiro Isuzu came running. His face was stark with bewilderment. "You heard it too?" he demanded.

"Find out who that was," Nishitsu said. "But first, help me to the couch. I do not feel well."

"What is wrong?" Isuzu asked anxiously as he wrapped Nishitsu's arm around his shoulder. He levered the old Japanese from the leather chair, surprised at his lightness, frightened by his frailty.

"It is nothing," Nishitsu rasped as he allowed himself to be half-led, half-carried to a couch. "A cold, perhaps. It will pass."

"I will summon a doctor. Even a cold at your age is not to be taken lightly."

"Yes, a doctor. But first, locate the source of that voice. For it fills me with dread."

"At once, sir," Jiro Isuzu said, and sped off.

Ninth A.D. Minobe Kawasaki scanned the darkening horizon with his Nishitsu binoculars. The voice had come from the south, he felt certain. He sat up in the turret seat of the T-62 tank. Word had just reached him from Imperial Command Headquarters—formerly the mayor's office—to capture the author of those unearthly words that had boomed over the city. Kawasaki thought they must have come from the lungs of some god or demon.

His gaze ran along the line of a near hill. The preternatural blue of the sky was shading into indigo. Already there was the faint suggestion of stars.

He gave out a cry when the lenses came in contact with a magnified pair of eyes that burned him with their awful gaze. Those eyes made him think of dead planets spinning in a cold void.

Unsteadily he recovered the glasses and sought out the figure again. The face that held those eyes was not that of a god, he saw. They were set in skull-like hollows on an emaciated face. The throat was blue, as if painted. It was not paint, however. The color was too organic for paint. The neck was horribly bruised, as if broken. The skin of the face and bare arms was sunburned a lobster red.

Then, to Kawasaki's horror, the eyes seemed to fix upon him and the figure started down the hill in a jerky, stumbling, yet purposeful stride.

"Driver!" he called. "The one we seek is coming this way."

The T-62 leapt into action. Kawasaki primed the turret-mounted .50-caliber machine gun. He was afraid, even though the figure he rushed to intercept held no weapons in his hands.

Kawasaki lashed his driver up and down the streets. The figure had disappeared after it reached the base of the hill, making it difficult to determine which road he would take into the city. Kawasaki was forced to guess.

He guessed correctly, he learned as the tank turned a corner onto a residential street. It stopped at the edge of the desert. And walking up that street like a corpse come back to life, was the dead-eyed man.

He came steadily, fearlessly, like a machine.

Kawasaki's orders were to bring the man in alive. He began to regret them. His voice lifted. "I carr upon you to surrender to Imperial Occupation Force."

The man made no reply. His empty hands swung at his sides lifelessly. Kawasaki turned the snout of his machine gun at the man's thin chest. He could almost count the ribs outlined by the snug T-shirt fabric.

The man didn't flinch. He advanced purposefully, his dusty feet utterly soundless as they trod the asphalt.

On a hunch, Kawasaki reached into the turret hatch for the turret control lever. He goosed it until the smoothbore cannon lined up with the man's chest.

Annoyed that the powerful cannon maw did not hinder the dead-eyed man's advance, Kawasaki dropped the machine-gun muzzle and sent a short burst into the man's path.

A section of pavement erupted. The man walked over it unconcernedly.

"I do not have to take you arive," Kawasaki called. It was a lie, but he didn't know what else to say. If he was forced to kill, how could he explain bringing back an unarmed corpse?

Kawasaki put a second burst over the oncoming man's head. It proved unpersuasive. He came on as if utterly unafraid of death.

Or, Minobe Kawasaki suddenly thought, as if he were already dead.

"Driver!" he ordered in Japanese. "Approach that man. Slowly!"

The tank started forward. The smoothbore muzzle was bearing down on the man's chest like the finger of doom. If both man and tank continued along their stubborn paths, the maw would ram the man, knocking him down. That was Kawasaki's intention.

The distance between them shrank. It was several yards. Then three. Then six feet. Then two. One.

Just when a collision seemed unavoidable, the man's right hand came up as if jerked by a string. That was as much as Minobe Kawasaki saw, for he was suddenly knocked off his perch. He struck the hull of the tank and slipped over the side. He missed being drawn into the big rollers only by inches. Kawasaki realized his narrow escape only later. The sound, a horrendously flat crack of a noise, beat upon his eardrums. He clapped his hands to his ears, thinking it had been an explosion.

Minobe Kawasaki felt it was safe to open his eyes only after the ringing in his ears ceased. He looked up fearfully. He was relieved to find he still had all his body parts. Then he saw the tank. It had come to a dead stop. The driver's helmeted head was turned around in his seat to look back at the turret.

Minobe Kawasaki's eyes went wide with incredulity.

The turret of the tank was no longer sitting on its ring mount. The top flange of the great steel mount had that bright graininess of sheared metal.

The turret lay on the pavement a good dozen feet behind the tank. And beyond it, walking with a mechanical assurance, was the man with coals for eyes and thunder for a voice.

Minobe Kawasaki ran to the decapitated tank. He grabbed the radio from his driver and began speaking in a high, excited voice.

Jiro Isuzu almost dismissed the first report as the excesses of a victory-drunk salaryman-turned-soldier. But then more reports started coming in, all loud, all excited, all tinged with the unmistakable oil of fear.

The New Japanese Imperial Forces had lost five tanks in short-lived encounters with a single opponent every vanquished unit insisted upon referring to as "it."

"Be more specific," Isuzu barked at the first unit to call the opponent that. "Is 'it' a war machine?"

"It," the arid reply insisted, "is a man with death in his eyes and steel in his arms."

And that was actually the most coherent description

of the several that followed. Isuzu ordered more tanks into the area of the last sighting of "it." He waited. Some of the tank commanders reported back, some could not be raised. The surviving tank commanders told stories of defeat and shame. One, after completing his report, dropped the microphone and gave out a tremendous grunt that was mixed with a ripping-of-cloth sound.

Isuzu understood that the man had sat down at the scene of his defeat and opened his stomach with his own bayonet. *Seppuku.*

Every report agreed on one impossibility. The opponent was a lone unarmed man. And he was walking remorselessly, unstoppably in the direction of city hall, as if guided by radar.

Jiro Isuzu ordered his forces to pull back to city hall. Then he rushed to the office where Nemuro Nishitsu lay on the couch. His eyes were closed.

Gently Jiro Isuzu touched his leader's shoulder. Black slit eyes opened feebly. Nemuro Nishitsu opened his mouth to speak, but only a dry rattle came out. Jiro touched his forehead. Hot. A fever.

Jiro Isuzu put an ear close to Nishitsu's mouth. He felt the warm breath and, mixed with that hot moistness, came faint words.

"Do your duty," Nemuro Nishitsu said. "Banzai!"

Then Nemuro Nishitsu turned his face to the back of the couch and closed his eyes. He slept.

Jiro Isuzu got to his feet. It would be up to him now. He went out to issue more orders. He wondered when the bombers would come.

The Master of Sinanju stared at the bleak horizon like an idol draped in scarlet cloth. The wind whipped his kimono skirts around his spindly legs.

Bill Roam came up behind him, clearing his throat noisily. Chiun did not acknowledge his approach.

"The women have tucked in the children," he said, taking his place at Chiun's side. He looked in the direction Chiun's wise old eyes stared. There were flashes of light beyond the low horizon.

"There is fighting in the city," Chiun intoned.

"That sure ain't heat lightning," Roam agreed. "You know, I feel right sorrowful about Bronzini."

"Every man pays a price for his actions in time," Chiun said dismissively. "Some pay for their failures, some for their successes. Bronzini's successes brought this down on all of us. I have lost my son because of him, and with him goes the hope of my village."

"I know what you mean. I'm the last Sunny Joe."

Chiun turned, sympathy smoothing his wrinkled features.

"Your wife bore you no sons?"

"She did. He died. A long time ago. I never remarried."

Chiun nodded. "I know that pain," he said simply. He turned back to the display of red and blue lights that lit the sky. They were too far away from the city for the sounds of conflict to reach their ears.

"When I'm gone," Sunny Joe Roam said, "there'll be no one to protect the tribe. What's left of it."

Chiun nodded. "And when I am gone, there will be no one to feed the children of my village. It is that fear that has made every Master of Sinanju reach beyond his limitations, for it is one thing to give up one's own life, another to surrender those who depend upon you."

"Amen, brother."

"Know, Sunny Joe Roam, that I do not hold you responsible for anything that has transpired in the last two days. But I intend to make those who brought this pain down upon me to suffer for their evil. I cannot, as long as they hold innocent young lives hostage. For all children, not just those of our blood, are precious to Sinanju. Is this so among the Sun On Jos?"

"I think that's one of the universal ones," Roam said.

"Not to the Japanese. When they took my country, no one, from those who sat on the Dragon Throne to even the babes suckling at their mothers' breasts, were safe from the bayonets."

"This can't go on much longer. The Marines ought to be landing soon. Washington isn't going to ignore this."

"And then how many lives will be lost?" Chiun said,

looking back toward the flashes of light that shook the sky. After a pause, his dry lips parted.

"Your son. What was his—"

"Sunny Joe! Sunny Joe! Come quick!"

Roam spun around. Sheryl Rose was in the doorway of an adobe house, her face a mask of horror.

"What is it?" Roam called.

"They're going to hang Bronzini! It just came over the TV."

"Come on," Roam said harshly.

Chiun followed him into the house. Sheryl led them to the TV, talking nervously. "I don't know why I turned on the TV. Reflex, I guess. But Channel Eleven is on the air again. Look."

The TV screen showed a scene out of Dante's *Inferno*. A group of policemen were marched, blindfolded, their hands tied behind their backs, into a room festooned with Christmas decorations. A red-and-white banner with the words "Peace on Earth Good Will Toward Men" hung mockingly above their heads.

"Oh, dear God," Sheryl choked out. "That's the studio commissary. I used to work for this station."

Off camera, a high-speed whine started up and then casually, with ruthless efficiency, a Japanese in desert camouflage stepped up to the blindfolded police and, holding their heads steady with one hand, one by one drove the bit of a drill into their temples.

Sheryl turned away, making sick noises in her throat.

"Why are they doing this?" Bill Roam asked, clenching his fists. No one had an answer.

"They . . . they announced that they were hanging Bronzini at dawn," Sheryl choked out. "This harmless-looking little Japanese man said it. He claimed it would prove America was too weak to stop them."

"Can this station be seen in other cities?" Chiun demanded coldly.

"They get it in Phoenix. Why?"

"The Japanese can be a cruel people, but they are not stupid," Chiun said thoughtfully. "They must know that this will force the American armies to strike."

"That's what I've been saying all along," Sheryl said.

"We hold out long enough, and Washington will put a stop to this."

"It is as if they wish this to happen," Chiun said softly. "But why?" His hazel eyes narrowed. He turned to Sunny Joe. "Do you have a copy of the script?"

Roam looked startled. "The script? Sure. Why?"

"Because I wish to read it," Chiun said firmly.

Roam went out the door. He returned with the script.

"At a time like this?" Sheryl asked, dumbfounded.

"I should have thought of this before," Chiun said, accepting the script.

"I think this is the final draft," Bill Roam said. "They kept revising it on us. Sort of makes you wonder why, now, doesn't it?"

"How does it end?" Chiun asked as he leafed through it.

"Don't ask me. I didn't get that far. There was too much to do, what with all those Jap extras not speaking English or knowing how to die on cue."

"I never got a script," Sheryl said. Her face was pale, but the color was slowly returning. She kept her eyes averted from the flickering TV screen.

Chiun read in silence. His parchment features lost their animation. Only his eyes moved as they skimmed the pages.

He looked up with grave features when he was finished. "I understand now," he said, clapping the script shut. "We cannot wait. We must go into the city. Now."

"What is it?" Bill Roam demanded.

"I will explain on the way."

"I'm coming too," Sheryl said.

"No offense, Sheryl," Bill Roam rumbled, "but no squaws this time out. This is men's work."

"I've got just as much right to fight those bastards as you do," Sheryl shouted. "It's my city, Sunny Joe. Not yours. You're a damn reservation Indian. And Chiun isn't even American. But those are my family and friends they're butchering. I have to do my part."

Bill Roam looked to Chiun. "The little lady has a powerful point, I guess."

"Then come," Chiun said. "We must act swiftly."

*   *   *

The Christmas-morning sun broke over the eastern seaboard like a slow radiant kiss. As the planet revolved, the twilight zone between day and night crossed the continental United States like a shadow in retreat.

The last place to see the sun rise was California. And at Castle Air Force Base, the word came down the Air Force chain of command to cart-start the B-52 bomber chosen to carry out Operation Hellhole.

Captain Wayne Rogers, USAF, received his orders in a sealed envelope. Face ashen, he turned to his copilot.

"Well, this looks like it."

The big B-52 bomber rolled out of its revetment and onto the flight line. Rogers eased the throttle forward, and the big lumbering bird surged ahead, gathering airspeed for takeoff.

They rolled past a line of K-135 aerial tankers. They would not be needed for midair refueling. Not on this mission. Even though he hadn't opened his sealed orders, Captain Rogers knew his target.

The bomber lifted off and swung in a 180-degree right turn. Not toward the Pacific and some foreign target, but inland. Into the continental United States. When he had leveled the ship off at cruising altitude, Captain Rogers nodded to his copilot. The other man tore the envelope open.

"It's Yuma," he croaked.

"Holy Christ!" Captain Wayne Rogers said.

He tried to concentrate on his instruments. The hundreds of red and green lights were like a high-tech Christmas tree. From time to time they blurred and he wondered if his sight was going. Then he realized he had been crying unawares.

"Merry Christmas, Yuma," he muttered bitterly. "Wait'll you see what Santa's bringing you *this* year."

21

Bartholomew Bronzini watched the sun rise on the final day of his life.

The red light came in through the ornate bars of his cell in the main cellblock at Yuma Territorial Prison. It transformed the now-completed scaffolding into a smoldering silhouette. The cameras had long ago been put in place; they were using a three-camera setup.

"Like they were filming a cheap sitcom," he spat.

Bronzini had not slept all night. Who could sleep when he was worth an estimated one billion dollars, had a face that hung in millions of dorms and dens, and was about to be hanged by the neck for the crime of agreeing to star in a Japanese movie?

Besides, all night long, sounds of fighting had come from the city. Bronzini wondered if the Rangers had landed. But he saw no parachute drop, heard no planes overhead. Maybe the citizens had found their balls.

Hope had begun to rise in his heart, hope of rescue, but as the night wore on, it was dashed time and again as the fighting died down, began anew, and nothing happened at the Yuma Territorial Prison except that his guards continued fussing with the camera setup. They rushed back and forth nervously, which Bronzini attributed to being up all night without sleep.

With the dawn, Bartholomew Bronzini, America's number-one screen superstar, knew exactly how prisoners felt on death row.

He decided they wouldn't take him without a fight. Bronzini withdrew from the door and hunkered on one side of the cell. His fist compressed into bloodless mallets of bone. He waited.

The sounds of commotion stabbed at his heart. He set himself. Sounds of running, yelling, and frantic activity swept through the prison-turned-museum. APC

motors started up. A tank growled to life, and its tracks
clanked on asphalt.

"Ready when you are, you sake guzzlers," Bronzini
growled under his breath. "You're going to need more
than a tank to get me up on that stage."

To his surprise, the sounds faded in the distance. An
eerie silence fell over the Yuma Territorial Prison. It
was broken only by the distant percussive stutter of
automatic-weapons fire and intermittent explosions.

Bronzini came up out of his crouch. In the courtyard,
cameras stood unattended. His guards were gone.

Bronzini wasted no time. He attacked the cell door.
The wrought iron was held in place by two horizontal
crosspieces attached to hinges. Since the former hellhole
of Arizona had been turned into a tourist attraction, the
cell doors had been maintained with an eye toward
appearance, not practicality. Bronzini knelt beside one
crosspiece and tried to force it. The screws were embedded in three-foot-thick stone walls. He felt some
give, but not much. The top crosspiece felt solid.

Bronzini looked around the cell. There were only a
bed and a plain wooden dresser for furniture, but in the
center of the stone floor a fat steel restraining ring was
bolted to a metal plate. Bronzini went to this. He
squatted over it, taking a position not much different
from one he used to lift heavy weights.

Bronzini began pulling slowly, then with greater force.
The veins in his reddening neck bulged. He groaned.
The ring refused to budge, but he was Bartholomew
Bronzini, the man with the greatest muscles in Holly-
wood. He grunted and groaned with the strain. Sweat
soaked the back of his black leather combat suit.

Bronzini's animallike groans grew into a crescendo,
and were joined by another groan—the inhuman cry of
metal stressed to the breaking point.

The plate gave. Bronzini fell on his ass. But he had
the ring. He jumped up and attacked the door with it.

It took very little time. One hinge cracked. Another
one came free. The door hung by the padlock. Bronzini
shoved it aside impatiently.

He stepped out into the stone courtyard and made

his way past the rows of open-air cells until he came to the parking lot. He moved cautiously, although he expected to encounter no opposition.

There was a pickup parked in front of the museum gift shop. Bronzini got in and hot-wired the engine and soon had the pickup squealing up Prison Hill Road.

Bronzini drove recklessly, not exactly sure where he was going or what he was going to do once he got there. The roads were deserted, but as he pulled into the city, there were people standing in their yards, looking anxious and confused. Bronzini pulled up to one of them.

"Yo! What's going down?" he barked.

"The Japanese have pulled back into town," an older man said excitedly. "There's heavy fighting, but no one knows who they're mixing it up with."

"Rangers?"

"Your guess is as good as anyone's. We're all wondering what to do."

"Why don't you fight? It's your city."

"With what?" the man demanded. "They took all our guns."

"So? This is Arizona. The wild west. Take 'em back."

The man peered closer. "Say, now, aren't you that actor fella? Bronzini."

"I'm not exactly proud of it right now, but yeah."

"Didn't recognize you without your headband."

Bronzini cracked a pained grin. "This wasn't supposed to be a *Grundy* movie. Know where I can find some guns?"

"Why?"

"Back where I come from, if you make a mess, you clean it up."

"Now, that's right smart reasoning. They're supposed to have weapons cached at the Shilo Inn," Bronzini was told. "Maybe you could sort of spread 'em around."

"If I do, will you and your friends fight?"

"Shucks, Bart. I seen every one of your movies. I'd fight with you any day."

"Tell your friends, I'll be back."

Bronzini took off. He floored the pickup until he got to the Shilo Inn. As he pulled into the parking lot, he spotted uniformed Japanese troops in the lobby. Bronzini wheeled the pickup into a parking space, and there, leaning between two cars, was his Harley. He slipped over to it and kicked the starter.

The Harley gave a full-throated roar that brought a smile to Bronzini's sleepy-eyed face. He backed it up and sent it rocketing toward the lobby entrance.

Attracted by the noise, two Japanese came out shouting. The Japanese had AK-47's. But Bronzini had the element of surprise. He went through them like a hurricane. They threw themselves to the ground. The bike hit the curb and vaulted through the glass doors. It wasn't special-effects candy-glass, however. Bronzini sustained a gash that opened up one cheek, and a shard embedded itself in his right thigh.

Undeterred, Bronzini danced off the careening bike and landed on the plush lobby seats. He yanked the triangle of glass from his thigh and used it to slash open the jugular of the Japanese who jumped from behind the front desk.

Bronzini pried the AK-47 from the guard's fingers. He pulled off the bayonet and sheathed it down his boot. Then he stepped outside and sprayed the two guards while they were picking themselves off the ground.

That accomplished, Bronzini raced through the first-floor rooms. He found the guns behind a door marked with the Red Christmas Productions symbol—a Christmas tree silhouetted against a mushroom cloud. This was the film's in-town production office. Bronzini carried the rifles out to the pickup under both arms. He filled up the bed with rifles and crated hand grenades and then lifted his Harley into the back by main strength.

Before he drove off, he tore one of the sleeves off his combat suit and used it to dress his leg wound. There was some cloth left over and Bronzini tied it over his forehead to keep the sweat out of his eyes.

"What the fuck," he said as he climbed behind the wheel. "Maybe we'll retitle this *Grundy's Last Stand.*"

Bronzini returned to the knot of men. It had doubled in size. He distributed the guns from the back of the pickup. While the men checked their weapons, he raised his voice.

"Yo! Listen up, everybody. There's more guns back at the hotel. Form teams and go get them. After that, it's up to you. It's your city."

Bronzini mounted the Harley and started her up.

"Hey, where are you going?" a man asked.

"It's your city, but it's my problem," he said, shoving stick grenades into his belt. "I got a score to settle."

And with that, Bartholomew Bronzini roared off, his ponytail dancing after him like a fugitive spirit.

Jiro Isuzu no longer had to rely on radio reports confirming that his crack units were being decimated. He had only to look out the window where the tanks formed a bristling line of cannon muzzles.

As he watched, one smoothbore coughed a shell. The recoil made the tank roll back. The shell reduced an already-shattered storefront to further ruin.

"It" walked in under the shell, which overshot him by no more than a hand span. Now that he had penetrated the outer perimeter, by all accounts destroying men and tanks with his bare hands, the burning-eyed man had come to Isuzu's last line of defense.

Isuzu shoved open the window. "Crush him!" he shouted. "Crush him in the name of the emperor. *Banzai!*"

The tanks started up. It was a calculated risk, breaking the last bulwark that separated him from that creature that walked like a man, but they had no choice.

Isuzu was alone. Nemuro Nishitsu lay unconscious on the couch. He was crying out in his fevered sleep. Isuzu tried to block out the words. "Death comes," Nemuro Nishitsu warned over and over. "Death that leaves no footprints in the sand."

Nishitsu was obviously delirious. Isuzu turned his attention to the conflict.

The once-supreme New Japanese Imperial Army had been reduced to a small band of defenders. All night long the battle had raged. Tanks, men, and heavy guns against a lone man who walked unarmed and unafraid.

They would surround him and he would render the tanks helpless with his bare hands, breaking the tracks and snapping off gun barrels with openhanded blows.

He had progressed to city hall, remorseless, unstoppable. At first it was reported that he moved with impunity, as if the mere soldiers who got in his way were insignificant fleas to be swatted and thrown aside. But as more tank units were thrown up against him, the unknown man had shaken off his zombielike demeanor as if coming out of a trance. He moved with increasing grace and speed, until, as one frightened assistant director cried over a walkie-talkie, "We cannot halt his advance. He dances out of the way of our bullets. He crushes everything under his feet. We must pull back."

The weird picture that had been conjured up over scores of frantic radio reports was of a mad dance of death and destruction. And Isuzu was forced to withdraw his units into a smaller and smaller circle around city hall until those tanks that had not fled in blind panic remained. With growing dread he awaited the approach of the unstoppable one.

Finally Jiro Isuzu got a clear look at "it." The sight froze the breath in his lungs. "It" looked like death walking. No, like death dancing.

It was beautiful, yet ghastly. A squad of fresh Japanese troops rushed up to confront the aggressor. He spun like a dervish from the bullet tracks of their chattering rifles. He weaved around them, limbs flung with abandon, feet leaping, turning, kicking. One stiff index finger entered many skulls, creating dead Japanese.

A soldier charged him with fixed bayonet. Suddenly the soldier was flailing, impaled on his own bayonet, which the creature held up like a triumphant banner.

It was a dance of death, yes, but only Japanese died.

The tanks fared no better. Two circled him. A foot flashed left. A hand, open and stiff of finger, knifed right. Tracks whipped free and the tanks careened helplessly into the smoking ruins of the street.

Foot by foot, the thing advanced. Stick grenades flung toward it. The creature caught each one with unerring reflexes and hurled them back in the faces of those who threw them. Some exploded; others did not. Isuzu cursed the unreliable Chinese-made weapons. It had been easier to buy them on the Hong Kong black market than to make Nishitsu versions. A mistake. The entire operation had been a mistake, he now knew.

Jiro Isuzu was prepared for death. His loyalty to Nemuro Nishitsu required it. His feelings for Nippon demanded it. Death, he could face. Defeat, he could not.

Jiro Isuzu took up an assault rifle and knelt before the open window. He attempted to sight on the oncoming fury. He emptied one clip. The only reaction was that the fire-eyed creature turned its gruesome sunburned visage, inhuman in the cold ferocity of its baleful gaze, toward him. The gash of a crack-lipped mouth broke into a cunning grin. The grin seemed to say, "When I am done with these puny ones, you will be next."

Jiro Isuzu gave it up. "Who are you?" he cried, lowering the weapon. "What do you want?"

And a voice like thunder answered him with one word. The word was: *"You."*

"Why? What have I done to you, demon?"

"You have roused me from my ancient slumber. I cannot sleep again until I crush your bones into powder, Japanese."

Jiro Isuzu slammed the window closed. He shrank from the glass. He couldn't bear to look at the carnage anymore. His only hope lay in escape.

Without a glance toward his mentor and superior, now shaking with chills and fever, Jiro Isuzu ran to the back room. He stopped with his hand on the doorknob.

For over his head he heard a dreaded sound. A heavy bomber. And he knew that all was lost.

Woodenly he returned to the office and squatted on the rug. He unsheathed the sword that had belonged to his samurai ancestors. He tore the front of his shirt to expose his belly. There was no time for introspection, regrets or ceremony. He placed the point of the sword against his side and steeled himself to deliver the quick sideways ripping slash that would spill his bowels onto his lap. He prayed that he would die before atomic retribution obliterated him. Better to die by one's own hand than at the hands of the hated enemy.

Outside the window, the sounds of conflict died with the trailing scream of a Japanese warrior. And then a voice that cried, *"I am coming for you, Japanese."*

And Jiro Isuzu broke down sobbing. For his arms trembled so much he could not wield the sword properly. He fumbled a stick grenade from his waistband and pulled the cap with this teeth.

He waited. The grenade sat inert in his hand. A dud. And outside the office walls Isuzu heard the front door shatter under the approach of a demon in human form.

"You are too late," Jiro Isuzu spoke softly when the demon entered the room. "For in another instant we will both be obliterated in nuclear fire."

"A man may die a thousand times in one instant," the demon mocked.

"What name do you go by, demon?"

"I?" The creature advanced. Through the cords of its face, it was possible to make out the hint of an Occidental man. It looked almost familiar, as if Jiro had seen it during the early stages of the operation, before the fighting began. It was not Bronzini. Nor the one known as Sunny Joe. And then the demon spoke its name and Jiro Isuzu was no longer troubled by the face it wore, but by the spirit it represented.

"I am created Shiva, the Destroyer; Death, the shatterer of worlds."

The dance of the dead, Isuzu thought with a shock of recognition. Shiva. The Eastern god who danced the cycles of creation and destruction.

Jiro Isuzu knew not what he had done to rouse a god of the Hindus, but he had. He lowered his head and spoke words he thought would never pass his lips.

"I surrender," said Jiro Isuzu as a palpably cold shadow fell over him.

22

Bill "Sunny Joe" Roam was astonished by the lack of roadblocks leading into Yuma. No tanks prowled the streets, although cannon fire continued without respite somewhere in the heart of the city.

"Something's happened," he said as they cut up and down the streets of Yuma. "Hey, those are Americans over there, and they're armed."

Suddenly the knot of Americans broke into a run. They were firing as they ran between houses. Out from behind a white stucco home, a lone Japanese skulked. He was spotted, and ducked back into the trellis-bordered courtyard. He got as far as an onyx spa, when a crossfire chopped him up like so much celery.

"We have no time for this," Chiun said quickly. "We must reach the television station."

"Look," Sheryl broke in, "even if by some miracle we get there alive, it's probably got a passel of guards."

"I will deal with the guards," Chiun said unconcernedly.

"Then what?" Sheryl said, looking around at the fires. "Suppose I go on the air. What do I say? We were filming a movie and it got out of hand?"

"If you do not go on the air, the bombs will fall."

"I can't believe our government would bomb one of its own cities. It's too farfetched."

"Believe it," Bill Roam said, taking a corner on two wheels. He fought to keep the Ninja on the road. "Worse things happen in wartime."

"I still can't accept that this. It was only a movie."

"Helen of Troy was only a woman," Chiun told her. "Yet many died because of her, and an entire city fell."

"Are we getting closer?" Roam asked. They passed a disabled tank. Here and there bodies hung from the lightpost. They were Japanese bodies.

"Yes. The next right. That's South Pacific. Just follow it until I tell you to stop."

They took the corner at high speed. This time the Ninja didn't go up on two wheels, but it did fishtail wildly.

"I don't know why they went to all this trouble," Roam growled.

"What do you mean?" Chiun asked.

"They'd have killed more Americans by selling these rolling hunks of junk at cost."

"Concentrate on your driving. On our survival depends the fate of this city, and all who dwell in it."

"I think we're past that point," Sheryl said in a sick voice. "Listen."

"Pay no attention." Chiun told Roam. "Drive faster."

"What?" Roam asked. Then he heard it.

Far in the distance came the low sound of jet engines. It was a deeper, throatier roar than that of a commercial passenger jet.

"You don't suppose that's—" Roam began.

"Drive," Chiun admonished.

Roam floored the jeep. He took a sharp left and almost caused Bartholomew Bronzini, coming in the opposite direction, to wipe out.

"Bart!" Bill Roam called out as Bartholomew Bronzini extracted himself from the tangle that had been a Harley-Davidson motorcycle. "We could use a hand."

"Ignore him," Chiun snapped.

"No, wait," Sheryl said quickly. "Don't you see? Everyone knows Bronzini. If we put him on the air, he'd be believed."

"You are right," Chiun admitted.

"Bart!" Roam shouted. "No time to explain. Hop in."

Bronzini leapt into the back of the jeep, his AK-47 in hand. "Where are we going?" he demanded, looking about wildly.

"To the TV station," Sheryl explained. "They're going to bomb the city."

"Those fucking Japs," Bronzini spat.

"No, the Americans. That was the plan all along. We may be able to stop it if we can get you on the air."

"Go go go!" Bronzini shouted as the drone of the approaching B-52 filled the crystalline morning sky.

Television station KYMA was only lightly defended. Bronzini went in the front door spraying bullets. When the clip ran empty, he used his bayonet.

The Japanese, although trained soldiers, were demoralized by the sight of the greatest warrior in cinema history coming at them in full cry. It was too much for them. They dropped their weapons and ran.

None of them escaped. The Master of Sinanju met them at the exit door. His fingernails flashed in the orange light. He stepped over the bodies he made.

Sheryl led them to the main studio.

"I was just a cue-card girl," she said, "but I've seen this done a thousand times." She took one of the cameras in hand. "Sunny Joe, check the monitors. See if this is going out."

Roam hurried into the booth and ran his dark eyes along the screens while Sheryl dollied the camera in to frame Bartholomew Bronzini, sweaty and bloodied.

"My left side is my best," Bronzini quipped.

"I got Bart on one of the screens," Roam called out.

"Okay, we're on the air."

Bronzini faced the camera squarely. In his husky flat voice he spoke. "This is Bartholomew Bronzini. First of all, I want to apologize to the American people for—"

"There is no time for that," Chiun snapped harshly. "Tell them the danger is over."

"Everybody wants to be a fucking director," Bronzini growled. He continued in his stage voice: "I'm broadcasting from station KYMA in Yuma, Arizona. The emergency is over. The Japanese are falling back. I'm calling on the American government to send in the Rangers, the Marines, hell, send the Cub Scouts too. We got the Japs on the run. Repeat, the emergency is over."

The drone of the bomber grew in intensity.

"Are you sure this thing is hooked up?" Bronzini asked fearfully.

"Keep talking!" Sheryl shouted.

"I am not speaking under duress," Bronzini continued. "The emergency is over. We need troops to finish mopping up down here, but the citizens of Yuma are fighting back. The city is in American hands. It's over. Just don't do anything rash, okay?"

The bomber sound made the walls tremble and the trio looked up as if clear sky and not a soundproofed ceiling stood between them and the sight of one of the mightiest bombers in the U.S. Air Force.

"What do you think?" Bronzini said. "Maybe we should do a duck and cover, like when I was a kid."

No one laughed. But no one ducked either.

When it seemed as if the bomber drone could get no louder, it did.

"I don't think it worked," Sheryl said, biting her lips.

"They say if you're on ground zero," Bill Roam said in a faraway voice, "you don't feel a thing."

The sound swelled and then began to recede.

"It's going away," Sheryl said, her words more prayer than hope.

"Don't get your hopes up," Bronzini said. "It takes a long time for one of those mothers to fall."

An anxious minute crawled past. After five minutes, Bronzini let out a pent-up breath. "I think we did it," he said, in disbelief.

Bill Roam stepped out of the control booth.

"What do you think, chief?" The question was addressed to the Master of Sinanju.

In the distance, the sound of tank cannon resumed with renewed ferocity.

"I think our job is not yet done. Come!"

They followed the Master of Sinanju out of the studio, their knees shaking in nervous reaction.

Jiro Isuzu walked backward, his eyes locked with those of the demon who called itself Shiva. He felt like a mouse withering under the cold glare of a viper.

Shiva came closer, his stark stripped-of-flesh shadow falling across the unconscious form of Nemuro Nishitsu. And so great was Isuzu's panic that he did something that mere hours ago would have been unthinkable.

"There!" he cried out. "He is the one you want. It was his plan. His. Not mine. I am only a soldier."

Shiva stopped. His head swiveled, displaying the corded side of his blue-bruised throat.

Reaching down, Shiva touched the twitching brow of Nemuro Nishitsu, his emaciated visage unreadable.

"This one suffers under the vengeance of one who is known to me," said the demon called Shiva. "I leave him to his death. I will be the instrument of yours."

And Shiva came.

There was no place to run for Jiro Isuzu. His back was to the flag-covered wall. Throwing his arms in front of his face, he went through the window.

Jiro Isuzu landed on a pile of dead Japanese. He rolled to his feet, and kept going. He did not look behind him. Isuzu knew that the demon called Shiva would pursue him with that same relentless, remorseless, unhurried gait that said, *"Run, puny mortal, but you cannot escape me, for I am Shiva. I will never tire. I will never give up until I crush your bones to powder."*

Jiro Isuzu stumbled down First Street, past the ruined tanks, past the inert bodies of his New Imperial Japanese Army, knowing he could never outrun Shiva on foot. A Nishitsu Ninja jeep caught his eye and he veered for it. The keys were still in the ignition. The Japanese driver was slumped across the wheel, a deep hole in his forehead exactly the circumference of a man's index finger. Isuzu pushed the body aside.

To his relief, the jeep responded. Isuzu laid rubber for six blocks. He allowed himself the luxury of a glance in the rearview mirror. At the far end of the street, Shiva emerged from city hall like something seeping from hell. Isuzu pressed the accelerator to the floor and turned his attention back to the road.

He saw the intersection coming up too late. He made an instant decision to go to the left. The Ninja, taking the corner at high speed, went up on two wheels. So desperate was Jiro to make that turn that he leaned into the turn. The added weight was enough to throw the jeep completely off balance.

The Nishitsu Ninja went over on its side and skidded

like a toboggan. It struck a mailbox and cracked a fire hydrant. It stopped, wheels spinning madly.

Jiro Isuzu climbed from the jeep and, limping, kept on going. This time he did look back.

Up ahead, he heard the unmistakable grumble and clatter of tanks. He forced his pained legs to go faster.

The Master of Sinanju stepped out of station KYMA onto the street. With him were Bartholomew Bronzini, Bill Roam, and Sheryl Rose. They had no sooner reached the sidewalk than a pair of T-62 tanks clanked around the corner. They were running backward, their turret cannon swiveling as if tracking a pursuing enemy.

Bartholomew Bronzini broke into a wolfish grin when he saw them. Pulling a stick grenade from his belt, he bounded for the nearest tank.

"Where the hell are you going?" Bill Roam called after him.

Bronzini hurled his answer back. "Are you kidding me? I'm the star of this thing, remember?"

Bronzini took a running jump and landed on the rear hull. He scrambled up the turret on all fours and, throwing himself on his stomach, pulled the cap off the grenade. He dropped it in and slid off like a cat from a hot stove.

The open hatch vomited a brief flash of fire. It was followed by a mushroom of black smoke. The T-62 veered out of control, still running backward, and staved in the front of a drugstore.

Bronzini turned and executed a hammy bow.

"And now," he said, "for my next trick."

Then Jiro Isuzu huffed around the corner, practically dragging one leg.

Turning, Bronzini spotted him.

"Well, well, well, if it isn't my old pal Jiro," he said pleasantly, pulling another grenade. He let fly.

"Bronzini," Bill Roam cried, "don't be an idiot! This is no movie." Roam started forward. Chiun held him back.

"No," he said. "Let him be. If he is fated to die this

time, at least it will not be the ignominious death of Alexander."

Jiro Isuzu didn't see the grenade land at his feet. He was too intent on watching the corner around which he had just come. One of his boots encounterd the grenade, knocking it away. It did not explode.

"Fuck!" Bronzini said. He reached for another one.

Then around the corner lurched a silent remorseless apparition.

"Remo!" Sheryl gasped, pointing excitedly. "Look, it's Remo. He's alive."

But the Master of Sinanju, seeing the blue discoloration on Remo's throat, said, "No, not Remo. He wears the wasted flesh of Remo, and walks in his bruised bones. But it is not Remo."

"Don't be ridiculous," Sheryl snapped. "Of course it's Remo. Let me go to him."

"He's right," Bill Roam said, holding her back. "Remo couldn't have survived that fall." He raised his voice. "Bart! Get back! Don't get near him!"

"Jiro's a pussy, I can take him," Bronzini laughed.

"I don't mean Jiro," Roam called back.

The distraction was momentary, but it gave Jiro Isuzu time to catch up with the lone surviving tank. He grabbed hold of a stanchion, and the tank pulled him along. His boots dragged liked deadweight. He felt dead. Once he caught his breath, Jiro Isuzu climbed onto the hull and clambered up the turret. He slid down the hatch with an evident lack of agility.

"Hold up, Jiro, baby," Bronzini shouted, oblivious of the inexorable figure that bore down on the tank. "This is our big scene together."

Bronzini pulled the fuse cord of a stick grenade and tossed it down. He jumped off the tank.

Nothing happened. He picked himself off the ground and searched his belt for another grenade. The expression on his face told the others he was out of grenades. He dug a bayonet from his boot, sticking it between his teeth, and went after the tank with a kind of wild joy in his drooping eyes.

Bronzini disappeared into the tank just as the turret

finished swiveling in the direction of the emaciated man. The smoothbore cannon dropped its elevation to point at Shiva's chest.

A harsh order barked out in Jiro's voice. The tank stopped, its cannon just inches from Shiva's face. Two sun-reddened hands reached up to take the cannon muzzle.

From inside the turret came a rapid tattoo of sounds: fist blows, cries, piglike grunting, and the unmistakable meaty ripping of a knife rending flesh.

And Bartholomew Bronzini's voice, saying, "Eat this!" over and over again.

Shiva's hands compressed, and the smoothbore muzzle, in the grip of a power that was in tune with the universe, could not resist. It was only metal. The metal shrieked.

Then Jiro's voice gasped a one-word command.

Chiun realized what was about to happen. He pulled Sheryl and Bill Roam back into the station and threw them to the floor.

The explosion was deafening. It blew out windows for five blocks in every direction. In the aftermath, the air rang like an invisible bell. And then the T-62's turret, blown twenty feet into the air by the force of the smoothbore blowback, came back down.

It pulverized what remained of the tank, like an anvil falling on an egg crate.

Then there was silence except for the crackle and spit of flames.

Chiun rose from the floor of the TV station, bits of glass falling from his kimono like tinkling bells. He stepped out into the smoky street, his parchment features tight with concern.

The tank was an unrecognizable wreck.

But standing there, watching the tank burn, was a figure of terrible aspect. The flames illuminated his stark face with a hellish light. As Chiun watched, he stepped onto the smoldering T-62 and bent at the waist. His hands, apparently oblivious of the heated metal, pulled and tore until they unearthed something that resembled a blackened pomegranate. Except that it showed discolored teeth in a frozen grimace.

Shiva the Destroyer lifted the head from the wreckage. A blackened, smoking body came with it. Silently, mercilessly, Shiva began to rend the body limb from limb. He stripped the skin from the bones. It slid off easily, for it had been cooked. He broke the bones into short sections and methodically crushed each section in his hands. All the while, he was pulverizing the bones of the rib cage and spinal column as he danced on the fleshy bag of Jiro Isuzu's torso. His crushing feet beat like terrible drums in his dance of death.

Finally he took up the head and held it to his face.

"I consign you to the Hell of Hells, Japanese!" Shiva roared, and pulped the head with a nervous compression of hands. Steaming brain matter bubbled from nose, mouth, ears, and skull fissures. Fingers worked, grinding and cracking bone.

"So perish the enemies of Sinanju!" Chiun said loudly.

Shiva dropped the remains in the pile of charcoal-black meat and pulverized bone that was the mortal remains of Jiro Isuzu. And then the head swiveled around like a radar dish. Twin eyes lit by scarlet flames fixed upon the Master of Sinanju.

And Chiun, his facial hair trembling, stepped up to meet Shiva the Destroyer.

A cold voice emanated from the barely recognizable mouth that had once belonged to Remo Williams.

"I have claimed my vengeance," Shiva said.

Chiun bowed. "If you are done, I demand that you return my son to me."

"Have a care how you address me, Korean. Your son exists only through my sufferance. He would not have survived his fall."

"And I am grateful for that. I did not feel Remo's mind. I thought him dead."

"Death will never claim my chosen avatar."

"All men come to the end of their days in time," Chiun said stubbornly. "Even, perhaps, gods as well."

"Know, Master of Sinanju, that this fleshy envelope exists only for the day I claim him. You have made him the perfect vessel for me, but my hour has not yet

come. Soon. Perhaps very soon. But it will come, and one day I will claim him forever. And leave you weeping."

"As you wish, Supreme Lord," said the Master of Sinanju. "But until the appointed hour, he is mine, and I demand his return."

The voice of Shiva was silent a long time. At last it spoke. *"Seek not to thwart my will, Master of Sinanju."*

Chiun bowed. "I am but a speck on the wheel of inexorable destiny," he said.

"Well-spoken. I now give you back your dead night tiger. Keep him strong for me."

And the red light in Shiva's dark eyes dwindled. The harsh lines of the face relaxed. The eyes closed. And Remo collapsed like a slowly deflating balloon.

Chiun caught him up in his arms and laid him on the ground.

Bill Roam approached respectfully. Sheryl, hand over her mouth, trailed behind.

"Is . . . he dead?" Roam asked.

Chiun hesitated before speaking. His hand lay over Remo's heart. He felt the beat of it, sluggish but regular.

"Yes," Chiun said. "He is gone."

Sheryl sat down on the ground, oblivious of the oil and broken glass, and buried her face in her hands. Her shoulders shook uncontrollably but no sound came forth.

"If you want," Bill Roam said gently, "we can bury him on Sun On Jo land. I don't accept your legend as being the same as mine, but I made you a promise."

"No," Chiun said solemnly, lifting Remo into his arms. "I have decided that you are correct, Sunny Joe Roam. Merely because our legends have sounds in common does not make us brothers. I will take Remo home with me. Lead me to the place where the airplanes come and go. I will await transportation for my dead son there."

Bill Roam nodded. His bleak eyes went to the ruined tank, still smoking and sputtering.

"Bronzini's gone too. No one could survive that blast."

"He achieved in death what he only pretended to be in life," Chiun said distantly.

"Yeah, he died a hero, all right. Too bad no one thought to film it. He would have liked that."

Then the sky was suddenly full of C-130 transport planes. Tiny specks began jumping from them. The specks blossomed into white buds. They stretched in lines across the sky like dandelion seeds strung along filaments of spider silk.

"Looks like the Rangers are landing," Bill Roam said, looking up.

The Master of Sinanju did not look up. "They are too late," he said solemnly. "They are always too late."

23

A week passed. A week in which a stunned nation attempted to pick up the pieces. Yuma was declared a federal disaster area and money and men were rushed into the city before the last of the dead had been laid to rest. A congressional inquiry was launched, but when its report was delivered to the President's desk nine months later, nowhere in its 16,000 pages was mention that on Christmas Day the President of the United States had given the order to drop an atomic bomb on an American City.

That black page was never entered into the U.S. history books. And so only a handful of people ever knew that Yuma had been saved by a television broadcast by the late, great Bartholomew Bronzini.

Because of that omission, the controversy over Bronzini's true role on the Battle of Yuma was never satisfactorily resolved.

Slowly the nation went back to normal. A new year and a new decade were marked on January 1, and although the celebrations were subdued, nowhere was the holiday celebrated with deeper feeling than in Yuma, Arizona, where many Americans had learned for the first time what it truly meant to be free.

*   *   *

On the first day of the new year, Remo Williams opened his eyes. He stared up at the blank white ceiling of a private hospital room in Folcroft Sanitarium. His mind was a blank too.

At first the doctor thought the opening of his eyes was a mere involuntary reflex. The patient had been in a coma for a full seven days. He tested the pupils with a penlight. The reaction he got prompted him to call Dr. Harold W. Smith.

Smith entered the hospital-white room and dismissed the doctor quietly. After he had withdrawn, Smith drew up to Remo's bedside, noticing that the bluish tinge of his throat had largely faded. Remo's brown eyes followed him with only vague comprehension.

"Smitty," Remo croaked.

"What do you remember?" Smith asked flatly.

"Falling. Parachute didn't work. Tried to equalize my mass so I could float to the ground. It was starting to work. Then I made a big mistake."

"What was that?"

"I opened my eyes. Up to that moment, I was doing great. Then the desert jumped me. That's the last thing I remember."

"You were fortunate to survive. Your neck was sprained. I don't know how you escaped breaking it."

"Simple. I landed on my face. Where's Chiun?"

"I called him. He'll be here soon. Remo, there are a number of things you should know."

Remo pushed himself up with both hands. He grunted with the effort. "What's that?"

Before Smith could answer, the Master of Sinanju swept into the room. He wore a simple blue kimono.

Remo cracked a weak smile. "Hey, Little Father, a funny thing happened to me on the way to the movies."

Chiun's austere face softened momentarily. Then, as he spotted an aquamarine box beneath a tabletop Christmas tree, it hardened.

"How long has he been awake?" Chiun demanded of Smith.

"Only a few moments."

"And he has not seen fit to open the present I so carefully prepared for him," Chiun said, annoyed.

"Present?" Remo asked doubtfully.

"Yes, graceless one," Chiun said, going to the tree. He picked up the aquamarine box and presented it to Remo, who accepted it in both hands.

"Feels light," he said, hefting it.

"It contains a present beyond worth," Chiun assured him.

"Really?" Remo said, trying to sit straight. "Is it Christmas yet? Can I open it now?"

"Christmas was last week," Smith told him.

"I've been out a week! Boy, I must have really taken a fall."

"Perhaps it is your white laziness that has reasserted itself once more," Chiun suggested coolly.

"I'm glad to see the spirit of the season hasn't completely overwhelmed your compassionate understanding of your fellow human beings," Remo remarked dryly.

"While you have been a lazy slugabed," Chiun went on, "I have been explaining to your emperor that even though you failed, it should not be held against you. True, I am now forced once again to accompany you on your assignments, but—"

"Failed?" Remo asked.

"Bronzini is dead," Smith said quietly.

"What happened?" Remo asked, shocked.

"It's a long story," Smith said. "When you're better, I'll brief you on the details. Suffice it to say Bronzini is a national hero."

"He *is*?"

"He saved the city."

"He *did*?"

"But no one can ever know," Smith cautioned.

"Well, they won't get it from me. And to tell you the truth, I didn't really like the guy."

"You must not have gotten to know him very well."

"Actually, I only met him in passing," Remo admitted. "He struck me as an egotistical jerk."

"That may be," Smith admitted. "He was a complex man." Smith turned to Chiun. "That reminds me. The autopsy on Nemuro Nishitsu has been made public. It seems that he died of an upper respiratory failure brought on by a common cold. I thought you said you eliminated him."

"Who's Nemuro Nishitsu?" Remo asked. He was ignored.

"I have told you how this Bartholomew Bronzini was the reincarnation of Alexander the Great?" Chiun asked.

"He *what*!" Remo exploded.

"I cannot say I can yet bring myself to accept that premise," Smith said.

"It is true. And one of my ancestors dispatched him."

"As I recall, Alexander died of malaria."

"True. That is how history records it. But the true fate of Alexander lies in the pages of historical records found only in the Book of Sinanju. The truth is as follows . . ."

"Do I have to listen to this?" Remo said sourly. "I'm a sick man."

Chiun's face puckered in annoyance. "This is a wonderfully instructive story," he sniffed.

"That's what you said the last thirty times you told it to me," Remo groaned, folding his arms.

"I was referring to Smith in this case," Chiun returned. "Thirty repetitions, and you still do not appreciate the beauty of this legend."

"The beauty of malaria has always been lost on me," Remo grumbled.

"Now," Chiun continued, addressing Smith, "in the days of Alexander, Masters of Sinanju were in service to India, owing to a minor dispute with our preferred client, the Persian Empire."

Remo broke in. "Translation: India offered more money."

"I do not recall that being recorded in the Book of Sinanju," Chiun said vaguely.

"It's in the appendix."

"And if you are not silent while I finish this story, I will take out yours," Chiun continued in a more reasonable tone. "While the Master of that time served India, that sick Greekling descended upon Persia and destroyed that wonderful empire. The Master of Sinanju heard this news with great displeasure."

"Translation: he was thinking of switching sides again."

"And he approached a sultan of India," Chiun went on, pretending to ignore Remo's outburst even as he added it to the long list of injuries Remo had visited him over the years, "whose lands were threatened by this mad Greekling with the name of Alexander. And this sultan offered the Master much gold to eliminate Alexander. And so the Master chose an emissary and sent him to Alexander with a message. This messenger laid the scroll of the Master before Alexander, saying to him that it would reveal to Alexander his ultimate destiny. But the Greekling flew into a rage when he looked upon the scroll, and slew this messenger himself. It seemed that the Master's message was in Korean, which Alexander could not read." Chiun paused.

"Then what happened?" Smith asked, genuinely interested.

"Sinanju lived happily ever after," Remo inserted.

"For once Remo is correct," Chiun said, casting a baleful glance in his pupil's direction. "Sinanju did live happily ever after, for the messenger that the Master had chosen was sick in the early stages of malaria. By the time he reached Alexander, he was very ill and Alexander's cruel murder was actually a mercy to him. Unfortunately the Greekling also contracted malaria, and so he died, with none being the wiser."

"I see. And what did the scroll actually say?"

"Two things." Chiun beamed. " 'You have malaria,' and an ancient Korean expression that in modern English translates roughly as 'Gotcha.' "

"Remarkable," said Smith.

"It's twice as remarkable when you stop and consider it has absolutely nothing to do with the guy who caught cold and died," Remo groused.

"I was coming to that," Chiun hissed. In a softer voice he resumed his story. "When I encountered this Bronzini—"

"Hold the phone," Remo interrupted. "You met

Bronzini? You were in Yuma? How'd you pull that off—kidnap Smith's wife?"

"I was there as a correspondent for *Star File* magazine, I will have you know," Chiun said loftily.

"Never heard of it."

"Of course not. They pay a dollar a word. Obviously it is beyond your penny-a-word reading tastes."

"I stand corrected."

Chiun went on. "And when I saw that the former Greekling, Bronzini, had a cold, knowing how frail this Nishitsu was, I resolved to surrender Bronzini to the evil Japanese aggressor."

"Japanese aggressor?" Remo said. "The movie people?"

"No, the invasion army," Chiun told him.

"He's joking, isn't he?" Remo asked. Smith didn't reply.

Chiun kept talking. "I knew that if I dispatched Nishitsu, his forces would kill the children. But if he died of natural causes, it would demoralize his occupation forces. No reprisals would have been undertaken."

Remo's mouth formed the silent words "Occupation forces?"

"And so it would have come to pass if the plane bearing the nuclear weapons had not appeared."

Smith nodded. "It was fortunate that Bronzini had escaped his prison, for only one of his reputation could have convinced the military not to nuke Yuma."

"Nuke!" Remo exploded. "The Japanese tried to nuke Yuma?"

"No, the Americans," Chiun said.

"You're pulling my leg," Remo insisted. He turned to Smith. "He *is* pulling my leg, isn't he?"

"It's a long story," Smith sighed. "But every word of it is true. Chiun was instrumental in averting a catastrophe. The President is very grateful to him."

"We will discuss this at another time," Chiun said loftily. "Perhaps when we resume contract negotiations."

Smith winced at the reminder. "If you'll excuse me, I have work to do."

Chiun bowed formally. "Please convey my regards to your illustrious cousin Milburn."

"I will if we ever get back on speaking terms again. He was very unhappy that you submitted your story in poem form. He insists that you were given explicit instructions not to do so."

"The man is a philistine not to recognize great literature when it is offered to him at a mere dollar a word," Chiun said sharply.

"I won't tell him that part. He returned your manuscript, and I've promised to rewrite the story myself."

"I will not have my name attached to your drivelous writings, Smith. Put some other name on it. Perhaps Remo will be pleased to lend his name to your work. But be certain that the check is in my name."

"We'll discuss it another time," Smith said, closing the door after him.

"I get the feeling I missed a lot," Remo said after he and Chiun were alone. "You were in Yuma?"

"That is the past now. I wish you to forget it. You are in Folcroft now, where you are safe."

"I gathered that much. Too bad. I wanted to say good-bye to Sheryl. I never really got to know her."

"Forget her," Chiun said quickly. "Why don't you open your Christmas present?"

"You know, I don't have any presents for you."

"It is nothing," Chiun said with a dismissive wave. "When you are yourself again, I am certain you will shower me with the gifts I so richly deserve. Although I am certain none will be as fine as that I have made for you," he added pointedly.

"Handmade, huh? Nice to see you're getting into the Christmas spirit," Remo said as he pulled at the silver ribbon, "even if it is a week late."

Remo stopped suddenly. "I met a guy on the set named Sunny Joe. Did he make it?"

"Alas, no," Chiun said. "You will not see him again."

"Too bad. He seemed like a nice guy."

"I would not know. I never met him."

Remo looked up suspiciously. "Then how do you know he died?"

"He was a friend of Bronzini's. All of Bronzini's friends were put to the sword by the Japanese."

"Damn."

Remo tore the wrapping free and fumbled at the lid of a simple cardboard box. The expression of sadness on his face gave way to pleasurable expectation. When he lifted the lid, the expression fell like a piano.

"It's empty!" Remo blurted.

"How white," Chiun spat. "How deeply you wound me with your base ingratitude."

"I'm not ungrateful," Remo said. "I'm just . . . uh . . ."

"Disappointed?" Chiun suggested.

"Yeah. Kinda. Yeah, I *am* disappointed. There's nothing in this thing."

"Look again."

Puzzled, Remo held the box up to the light. He turned the box so that every corner was illuminated.

"It's still empty," he complained.

"You are so dense."

Remo dropped the box into his lap. He folded his arms.

"Okay, I've been asleep for a week. I'm a little slow. So tell me."

"I offer you a thing of beauty and you tear it to pieces."

"The box was the present?" Remo said wonderingly.

"It is no mere box," Chiun corrected. "I chose it from countless others, rejecting many as flawed or unworthy to hold the gift I offer you."

"It looks like an ordinary cardboard box," Remo said sullenly.

"The wrapping paper was aquamarine. I chose aquamarine because I knew it was your favorite color."

"It is?"

"One of them. Perhaps not the most favorite."

"Well, I do kinda like aquamarine—after red, blue, yellow, green, and magenta. Maybe mud-brown too."

"The ribbon was silver. I chose it because it harmonized with the aquamarine paper I so painstakingly selected. When I had the box and the paper and the ribbon, I set them on the floor and meditated over them for an entire afternoon. Only after I had prepared myself mentally did I wrap the paper over the box and tie it with the magnificent bow which you plucked apart with your childish fingers with no thought given to the effort put into tying it."

"Sorry. Obviously I lost my head. Must have been delirious."

Chiun's hard countenance softened slightly.

"It might be that I can restore this present beyond measure, for in truth it is but a symbol of something greater."

"What's that?"

"A father's love. For I am the only father you have ever known."

"Oh," said Remo. And he understood. "How can I top this?" he asked, holding up the simple aquamarine box, which no longer seemed empty at all.

"You already have," Chiun told him warmly. "For I have you, who are the true treasure of Sinanju."

Chiun beamed. Remo smiled back. Their smiles met and seemed to fill the room.

"This is the best Christmas I never had," Remo said. And he meant it.